FEAR ON THE PHANTOM SPECIAL

By Edward Marston

a&b

FEAR ON THE
PHANTOM SPECIAL

EDWARD MARSTON

Allison & Busby Limited
11 Wardour Mews
London W1F 8AN
allisonandbusby.com

First published in Great Britain by Allison & Busby in 2019.
This paperback edition published by Allison & Busby in 2020.

Copyright © 2019 by EDWARD MARSTON

A CIP catalogue record for this book is available from
the British Library.

10 9 8 7 6 5 4 3 2 1

ISBN 978-0-7490-2423-9

CHAPTER ONE

Hallowe'en, 1861

It was dark as they clambered aboard the train, laughing and joking as if they didn't have a care in the world. Hampers filled with food and champagne were loaded into the carriages. It was to be a riotous party on a very special night and they intended to enjoy it to the full. In the gloomy interior of the train, there was a mood of exhilaration. The moment that the gentle puffing of the engine disappeared, however, it changed abruptly. They were jolted by the sudden explosion of noise and movement. Pleasantly drunk when they'd arrived, they were instantly sobered. The ride on the Phantom Special was no longer the prelude to a midnight picnic in a haunted wood. It was a source of real fear. It was as if they realised for the first time the risk that they were taking. A couple of the women screamed involuntarily, and one demanded to be let off the train. But it was too late now. Their fate was sealed.

Everyone suddenly felt the cold and shivered. They were

cowed, rueful and quietly terrified. The one exception was Alexander Piper, the handsome young man responsible for hiring the train and filling it with his friends. Tall, lean and commanding, he jumped to his feet and tried to raise the spirits of those in his compartment.

'Cheer up, everyone!' he shouted, arm aloft. 'There's nothing to be afraid of. We've set off on a great adventure. It's something to relish. There's safety in numbers, remember. We're not in any danger.'

Most of them were rallied by his bravado and shook off their doubts and anxieties, but one or two remained in the grip of a deep unease. They were going to a place notorious for a series of supernatural events and they needed more than a few brave words from Piper. All they could do was to grit their teeth and pray that they'd come through the excursion unscathed.

Gathering speed all the time, the train clanked, rattled and swayed on through the darkness. The flickering lamps inside the carriages gave little reassurance. Having departed from Kendal, they had less than ten miles to go to Windermere where horse-drawn transport would take them on to their destination. That, at least, had been the plan. But there were passengers who were already thinking of ending their journey at the railway station and waiting there until the train took the entire party back to their point of departure.

'I knew this would happen,' said Piper, scornfully. 'You're losing your nerve. There's no need. Ignore all that nonsense about weird events and mysterious deaths at Hallowe'en. None of it is true. They're just tales devised to frighten credulous, weak-minded people. You'll meet no witches. You'll see no black magic. There are no grotesque creatures waiting to devour you alive. We're having a midnight party to show our defiance of Hallowe'en myths. Eat, drink and be merry, my friends.'

He carried on in the same vein for minutes, putting heart into them while not entirely banishing their fears. Then something unexpected occurred.

Squealing and shaking, the train slowed down.

'What's going on?' asked Piper. 'We can't be there yet.'

Unsettled by the sudden loss of speed, the passengers in his compartment were even more upset when one of the lamps went out, deepening the gloom until they could hardly see the people sitting opposite them. It caused fevered speculation. Piper was unable to reassure them this time. They were about to stop and he didn't know why. When the train finally shuddered to a halt, Piper opened the door and looked out.

'Why the hell have you pulled up here?' he shouted.

But the only sound he could hear was the hissing of steam. It was pitch-dark outside, so he had no idea where they were. He was seething with anger.

'I'll sort this out,' he said and jumped down beside the track. 'The rest of you can wait there.'

Men in other compartments had also opened doors to see what was going on. A few of them joined Piper as he strode towards the locomotive. Standing beside it was the burly figure of the driver.

'I'm Alex Piper,' he yelled, 'and I hired this train to get us to Windermere. Don't you understand that we have a timetable to keep to? It's imperative that we reach our destination before midnight.'

'It's no use bellowing at me, sir,' said the driver.

'I'll do more than bellow if you don't do as you're told. Drive us on, man! That's an order.'

The driver shrugged. 'We can't go anywhere as long as *that's* in our way.'

He pointed a finger at the track ahead of them. Piper pushed him aside and walked past the locomotive. What he saw brought him to a dead halt. Fifty yards or more ahead of them, a fire was blocking the line. Red flames were climbing up into the air. The sound of mocking laughter was carried on the wind. It frightened the other passengers who'd alighted, but it only served to increase Piper's fury.

'Leave this to me,' he called out, using an arm to wave everyone back. 'Nobody is going to stop my excursion.'

And he went sprinting off along the track while the others watched in trepidation. More people had now climbed out of the train and rushed to join the audience beside the locomotive. They were absolutely horrified. To their eyes, the blaze seemed momentarily to take on human shape. Piper ran on regardless, as if ready to confront any danger but, when he actually reached the fire, it flared up into a solid wall of flame and he disappeared completely from view.

The excursion was over.

CHAPTER TWO

Robert Colbeck was seated at the desk in his office when he heard a polite tap on the door. It opened to reveal a young detective with a nervous manner.

'The superintendent requests that you visit him at your earliest convenience, sir,' he said.

Colbeck was surprised. 'Are you sure that it was a request and not a demand?' he asked.

'I'm only repeating what I was told, Inspector.'

'What sort of a mood is he in?'

'He was very pleasant to me.'

'We *are* talking about Superintendent Tallis, aren't we?' said Colbeck, mystified. 'He's never been remotely pleasant towards anyone of your rank before. In fact, he enjoys being prickly towards everyone but the commissioner. Very well,' he went on, rising to his feet. 'Thank you for the message. I'll go at once. I've always wanted to witness a miracle.'

Colbeck walked along the corridor to the appropriate office, wondering what he'd find on the other side of the door. Ordinarily, it was an angry, brooding superintendent, wreathed in cigar smoke and ready to issue orders as if he were addressing soldiers on a parade ground. Could the man *really* have changed so much? Colbeck refused to believe it.

After knocking on the door, he opened it and went into the room. Three surprises greeted him. There was no hint of cigar smoke, the window was slightly open to admit an invigorating blast of cold air and – the biggest shock of all – Tallis actually smiled at him.

'Good morning, Inspector,' he said. 'It's good of you to come so promptly. Do please sit down.'

Colbeck couldn't believe what he was hearing. As a rule, Tallis deliberately kept him standing while he himself remained in his high-backed chair. Offering the inspector a seat was an act of consideration that he rarely showed, and he'd never before done so with a friendly smile on his face.

'You'll have to make allowances for me,' said Tallis, apologetically. 'I've only been back in harness for a few hours and it may take time for me to . . . settle into my old routine.'

Colbeck sat down. 'Welcome back, sir,' he said. 'We were delighted to hear that you'd made a full recovery.'

'It was in no small way aided by the reports I got of your successes. Yes, I know that I was supposed to forget all about Scotland Yard during my convalescence, but old habits die hard. I just *had* to know what was going on here. I kept a close eye on all your investigations,' said Tallis, 'and I was delighted to see that you managed so well without me.'

'It's kind of you to say so, sir.'

'To be honest, it was exactly what I'd expected.'

It was the superintendent's first day back at work and he looked alert and healthy. The previous December, he'd been abducted by a former soldier from his old regiment who nursed a grudge against him. Tallis was cruelly treated and deeply shaken by the experience, yet he wouldn't take time off to recover from the ordeal. As a result, he succumbed to the multiple pressures on him and was hopelessly unable to do his job. This time, he'd bowed to medical opinion and had a break for several months. Evidently, it had been productive.

'Let's not waste time in idle conversation,' said Tallis, briskly. 'A telegraph has just arrived and it asks – nay, it demands – that you leave for the Lake District immediately.'

'Was there a murder on the railway there?'

'There might well have been, though it's still in doubt.'

'What did the telegraph say?'

'Read it for yourself, Inspector.' Stretching out a hand, he gave it to Colbeck and allowed him time to read it. 'Puzzling, isn't it?'

'It's both puzzling and bizarre, sir. A crime was certainly committed – there's clear damage to railway property – but was this young man actually burnt to death?'

'Who knows?'

'He can't simply have vanished into thin air.'

'Strange things happen at Hallowe'en.'

'They don't always have such dire consequences,' said Colbeck. 'There's a peremptory tone to this telegraph. It's obviously sent by a man who expects his orders to be obeyed. Have you ever heard of Lord Culverhouse before, sir?'

'The name is vaguely familiar. I'm told that he's Lord Lieutenant of the county. That probably means he's one of those spiky, disagreeable individuals who doesn't suffer fools gladly and who loves throwing his weight about.' Tallis grinned, wolfishly. 'In the course of your work here, I daresay you've met someone exactly like that.'

In the census taken that year, Kendal was discovered to have a total of 12,029 inhabitants. None was more important and assertive than Lord Culverhouse, a man whose influence ran well beyond the boundaries of Cumberland. Tall, rotund and gimlet-eyed, he wore a full beard peppered with white hairs. Like most people who had dealings with him, Geoffrey Hedley was slightly intimidated. A lawyer by trade, he was a fleshy man in his early thirties, with dimpled cheeks more suited to a small child. Hedley spread his arms in a gesture of despair.

'I feel so guilty,' he admitted.

'It wasn't your fault, man.'

'To some extent it was, I fear. I was responsible for putting the idea into Alex's head. We were in our cups at the time and it's always fatal to make decisions in such a condition. I said – jokingly, as it happens – that we ought to do something very special for Hallowe'en and Alex seized on the idea at once. The next thing I knew,' said Hedley, 'was that he'd hired a train and named it the Phantom Special because it was going to take us on a journey into the unknown.'

'My nephew has always been rather headstrong,' said Culverhouse. 'There are no half-measures with Alex.'

'He was fearless. Most of us were shaking in our shoes, especially when the train ground to a halt in the middle of nowhere. Alex jumped out of our compartment in a flash. By the time I caught up with him,' recalled Hedley, 'he was pulsing with rage at the interruption to our outing. Before we could stop him, he went haring off in the direction of that blaze.'

'Why didn't you go after him?'

'Alex didn't give us the chance. He charged off as if he was in some kind of race. We'd never have caught up. The last we saw of him was when he disappeared in a wall of flame.'

'Then why was there no body?' asked Culverhouse. 'An untimely death presupposes a corpse. None was found and, though we searched high and low all day yesterday, there was no trace of Alex.'

'I know. I joined in the search party.'

They were standing in front of the fireplace in the library of Culverhouse Court, a magnificent country house just outside the town. On the wall behind the older man was a striking portrait of him in the dress uniform of a Lord Lieutenant. He looked proud, dignified and soldierly. Hedley tried to keep his gaze off the portrait. One Lord Culverhouse was more than enough to cope with. Two were overwhelming.

'There *was* one suggestion,' said Hedley, tentatively.

'What was that?'

'Someone wondered if the whole thing might be an elaborate prank devised by Alex.'

'That's arrant nonsense!'

'He does have a weird sense of humour, Lord Culverhouse.'

'Why did he hire this Phantom Special, then prevent it from reaching its destination? It doesn't make sense. Besides,' said Culverhouse, 'there's the small matter of Miss Haslam. I accept that my nephew is prone to moments of madness but even Alex wouldn't cause deliberate distress to his betrothed. The poor woman is distraught.'

'In retrospect, it's as well that she refused to take part in the excursion. The very notion frightened her.'

'Miss Haslam deserves peace of mind – as do we all. And the only way to achieve that is by calling in someone with the expertise to unravel this mystery.'

'That's well beyond the abilities of the local constabulary. They're as baffled as the rest of us.'

'I've gone above their heads and sent a telegraph to Scotland Yard, asking for the assistance of Inspector Colbeck, the famous Railway Detective.'

Hedley was impressed. 'Even *I* have heard of him.'

'We need the best man for the task.'

'But will he be available? A man with his reputation will be in constant demand. What makes you think you'll get a positive response to your request?'

'I took no chances,' said the other. 'As it happens, I'm well acquainted with the commissioner. To ensure success, I sent my telegraph directly to him.'

'In short, you pulled strings.'

'That's a deplorable expression. I merely adopted the right

tactics to get the desired end.' He struck a pose. 'I have every confidence that Colbeck will be on his way here right now.'

Victor Leeming was frustrated. He disliked leaving London and he hated doing so by means of rail. He was a man who loved his home comforts and knew that an unwelcome summons from Cumberland would be an inadequate replacement for the joy of sleeping with his wife and waking to see his children in the morning. There was a secondary cause of his frustration. He still had no real idea why they were suddenly rushing north. During the cab ride to Euston Station, Colbeck had only been able to give him the briefest details. The sergeant still had several questions to put to him but, when they'd bought their tickets and boarded the train, they discovered that they were sharing the compartment with six other passengers and a yapping dog. There was simply no chance of having a private conversation.

Colbeck had bought a copy of *The Times* and was soon engrossed in it. All that Leeming could do was to listen to the dog and watch the London suburbs scud past through the window. He braced himself for a long, tedious, uncomfortable trip. His fears, however, were unfounded. At a series of stops, their companions left the train one by one. Last to go was the woman with the irritating little creature who'd sat in her lap for the entire journey and kept up a positive fusillade of barks. As they set off yet again, Leeming had his first question ready, but he was too slow to stop Colbeck from seizing the initiative.

'There's a most interesting article in here, Victor,' he said.

'I'm not a reading man, sir,' grumbled the other.

'You ought to be. It's quite uncanny. This article might have been written specifically for you – and for those, like you, with a dislike of rail transport.'

'It's more than a dislike. I *loathe* trains.'

'You have an irrational fear of them.'

'Call it what you want, Inspector. Every time I get into one, my heart sinks and my stomach rumbles.'

'What about your mind?'

'I feel as if I'm on the verge of panic.'

'Exactly!' said Colbeck, folding the newspaper. 'That's what the article was about – the mental torment suffered by those who feel unsafe on the railway. Oddly enough, men are more likely to suffer than women. Some have even been driven insane and had to be confined in asylums.'

'I'm not that bad,' said Leeming in alarm. 'I just prefer to travel by coach. You know where you are when you've got a team of horses pulling you along.'

'Well, I won't bore you by reciting the advantages of travelling by rail. You've heard me do so many times. Just take a glance at this,' said Colbeck, handing him the newspaper. 'Read it at your leisure.'

'*What* leisure?'

Colbeck laughed. 'That's a fair comment. Anyway, I'm sorry that we were unable to talk until now. I can see that you're bursting to say something.'

'Why are we going all the way to Cumberland?'

'We have a crime to solve.'

'But we don't even know that a crime has been committed. From what you told me in the cab, we're being dragged out of London simply because a Hallowe'en excursion was cancelled.'

'There's more to it than that, Victor.'

'You said the telegraph gave very few details.'

'That's true.'

'Then why are we paying the slightest attention to it? More to the point, why did the superintendent take any notice of it? You know how much he dislikes sending us to a distant part of the country when there's so much crime to solve in London.'

'It was not Superintendent Tallis's decision. What I didn't know was that the man who dispatched the telegraph was a friend of the commissioner and the request first went to him. So you needn't blame the superintendent,' said Colbeck. 'The person you need to thank for sending us on this little jaunt is Sir Richard Mayne.'

Leeming was surly. 'It's going to be a lot more than a little jaunt,' he complained.

'Try to show some compassion, Victor. Instead of worrying about your own discomfort, think of other people. A mysterious fire appeared on a railway track, an excursion was summarily abandoned, and a man has unaccountably vanished. He'll have a family,' Colbeck pointed out. 'They'll be consumed by grief.'

Melissa Haslam lay stretched out on her bed and dabbed at her red-rimmed eyes with an already damp handkerchief. She was an astonishingly beautiful young woman but her face was now distorted by anguish and her mind was clouded by despair. All hope of happiness had been abruptly stolen away from her. She was quite inconsolable. Two days earlier she'd been thinking about her forthcoming marriage, but there was no longer a future husband. Her beloved Alex Piper had gone.

CHAPTER THREE

'The Lake District?' cried Caleb Andrews, aghast. 'Why on earth is Robert going there?'

'He isn't entirely sure, Father,' said Madeleine Colbeck. 'According to the letter he had delivered here by hand, he and Sergeant Leeming were sent off to solve a mystery concerning some event at Hallowe'en. It had to be abandoned because the person who organised it disappeared without trace. Foul play is suspected.'

Andrews grimaced. 'Don't talk to me about Hallowe'en, Maddy. It was the bane of my life. There were always some idiots who decided the best way to celebrate it was to sneak aboard the train I was driving to cause mischief, or pelt me and my fireman with rotten apples as we drove past. I used to hate working that particular night,' he said, resentfully. 'Some people have a twisted idea of fun.'

Though it was years since he'd retired from his job as an

engine driver for the London and North Western Railway, memories of his working life remained vivid. The problem was that he felt his long experience as a railwayman entitled him to act as an unpaid advisor to his son-in-law, and he was annoyed that Colbeck somehow never felt the need to call on him.

'Well,' he said, 'at least he's travelling with the best railway company in the whole country. A locomotive belonging to the LNWR will take him there speedily and comfortably.'

'I just hope that it brings him back home very soon.'

'By rights, he should never have gone. Gallivanting around the country is not the way a father should behave. His wife and daughter need him here. In the course of this year, he's travelled hundreds and hundreds of miles to arrest vicious criminals in faraway places. What's wrong with London?' he asked. 'We have more murders here than anywhere. Aren't our killers good enough for him?'

Madeleine laughed. 'You're so funny sometimes, Father.'

She was always pleased to see him and, since Colbeck was likely to be away for some time, she'd have to rely even more on the old man's company. Ostensibly, he'd called to enjoy some time with his granddaughter, but his real purpose had been to see Madeleine again. When his wife had died, Andrews had been shattered and only his daughter's unstinting love and support had carried him through a very difficult period. Every time he looked at her, he saw a younger version of his late wife. It always lifted his spirits.

'When do I get to play with my granddaughter?' he asked.

'When she's had her nap.'

'That girl is always sleeping. It's not healthy.'

'She seemed to be awake for twenty-four hours a day when she was first born. I'm glad of any respite. It's the one time I can get to my studio.'

'You're a mother, Maddy.'

'You don't need to remind me.'

'Helen must come first. You can always work on your painting when you've put her to bed.'

There was no point in arguing with him. It was unfair to expect him to understand the impulses that had made her an artist or to share the intense pleasure it gave her to stand in front of an easel to create something entirely new. She moved to the door.

'I'll order some tea.'

'In the old days,' he said, wistfully, 'you used to make it yourself. Now you have a servant to do it for you.' He looked around the spacious drawing room. 'You've come up in the world, Maddy. I'm proud of you.'

'Thank you, Father.'

'*I* must take some credit, mind you.'

'Why?'

'Well, if it hadn't been for that robbery on my train, you'd never even have met Robert Colbeck.'

It was true. Andrews had been the engine driver on a train that was brought to a halt by a gang. When he refused to do what the robbers wanted, he was badly beaten. Madeleine still shuddered when she recalled the incident.

'You were in a dreadful state when I got there,' she said. 'We weren't at all sure that you'd recover.'

He chuckled. 'It takes more than a bang on the head to finish me off,' he boasted. 'Besides, I had good reason to stay alive. I knew that one day I'd take you down the aisle to marry the clever detective inspector who caught those train robbers.'

Rail travel was such an unalloyed pleasure for Colbeck that he never minded how long a journey might be. There was always something interesting to see out of the window and he loved to plot his journey by referring to his copy of *Bradshaw's Descriptive Railway Hand-Book*. Leeming, by contrast, was suffering. The combination of noise, discomfort, boredom and a musty smell made the trip an ordeal for him. Though he tried hard to read the article in *The Times*, it failed to hold his interest. He didn't need a doctor to tell him that travelling by train could destroy the human mind. As Leeming put the newspaper aside, Colbeck glanced across at him.

'What did you think of that article, Victor?'

'It upset me, sir.'

'Would you rather borrow my copy of *Bradshaw*?' asked Colbeck, holding it up.

'I can't think of anything worse than reading that.'

'But it's an indispensable guide. Don't you want to know where you're likely to be staying in Kendal?'

Leeming sat up with interest. 'Well, yes. I do.'

'We're offered a choice between the King's Arms and the Commercial Hotel.'

'Which one serves the best beer?'

'That's one thing *Bradshaw* doesn't tell us,' said Colbeck. 'Besides, I'm sure there'll be more than those two places where we can be accommodated during the investigation. I promise you that the quality of its beer will be taken into account.'

'Tell me about the man who sent that telegraph.'

'He's the Lord Lieutenant of the county and his nephew went missing in peculiar circumstances.'

'What does a Lord Lieutenant do, sir?'

'From what I understand,' replied Colbeck, 'it's largely a titular appointment. The Lord Lieutenant has taken on the responsibilities that fell in the olden days to sheriffs. That means, for instance, that he's in command of the county militia. If there's a breakdown in law and order, he can call them out.'

'Superintendent Tallis would love a job like that.'

'He'd also enjoy wearing a splendid uniform with a rose and crown badge on the cap and shoulder boards.' They shared a laugh. 'At least, that's what the *old* superintendent would have done. The new one is rather different.'

'He'll be the same man-eating ogre underneath, sir,' insisted Leeming, ruefully.

'Suspend your judgement until you actually meet him again.'

Leeming lapsed into silence. After gazing through the window for a while, he made another attempt to read the article in the newspaper and sympathised with those who'd been, like him, hapless victims of rail travel. He was heartened by the fact that he was not alone in his misery. Casting *The*

Times aside once more, he pulled out the watch from his waistcoat pocket and looked at it.

'We've been on the way for *hours*,' he moaned.

'And there are still hours to go before we reach Oxenholme and change trains. I can, however, offer you some consolation,' said Colbeck. 'While we've been in transit, the search for the missing man has no doubt been going on with renewed intensity. It's possible that he's been found unharmed and we are therefore no longer needed.' Leeming smiled hopefully. 'In that case, we'll have the pleasure of catching the next available train and enjoying another long and fascinating journey.'

When she was told that Lord Culverhouse had called to see her, Melissa Haslam was initially reluctant to see him. She felt that she was in no state to speak to any visitor, preferring to stay in her bedroom. It took time, but her mother eventually persuaded her that she ought to talk to Culverhouse if only out of the respect due to his position in society. Melissa made an effort to pull herself together, then spent several minutes brushing her hair in front of the mirror and trying to master her emotions. When she at last felt ready, she and her mother went downstairs.

Lord Culverhouse was sitting in the drawing room. As soon as she came in, he was on his feet at once, crossing to squeeze her hands in greeting and offering her his sympathy. Melissa immediately jumped to the wrong conclusion.

'Does that mean you've *found* Alex?' she asked, lower lip trembling. 'Have you come to tell me that he's dead?'

'Not at all,' he said, quickly. 'The search continues and we remain hopeful that Alex is out there somewhere.'

'Then why has there been no sign of him?'

'I have a theory about that, Melissa, and it's supported by what Geoffrey Hedley told me. When he saw that fire blocking the line, Alex ran off to investigate.'

'I heard that a wall of flame suddenly shot up.'

'That's right,' said Culverhouse. 'Alex ran straight through it and, we believe, chased the man who'd caused that blaze in the first place. At some point, we feel, the rogue must have turned and fought with Alex, knocking him unconscious.'

'Then Geoffrey and the others who launched an immediate search should have found him.'

'It was pitch-dark, Melissa, and they had no lanterns. When he caught up with that man, Alex might have been a long way away from the railway track.'

'Then he'd still have been there in daylight,' suggested Bridget Haslam, a short, slight, agitated woman. 'Why didn't he simply walk back home or, at the very least, go to the nearest house and ask for help?'

'There's an answer to that, Mrs Haslam,' he said, 'and it bolsters my theory. If he had a severe blow to the head, he might have been badly concussed. Alex wasn't *able* to find his way back here because he was in a complete daze. He's just walked – or staggered – blindly around the countryside since the fight and may no longer even be in the county.'

'That's a dreadful thought!' exclaimed Melissa, bringing a hand up to her mouth.

'No, it isn't,' said her mother. 'It means that he could still be alive.'

'But he's spent two nights out in the cold and doesn't know where he is. Will he *ever* get his senses back again, my lord? Can Alex ever lead a normal life again?'

'It's only a theory, Melissa, and I hoped that it might comfort you. But I really came to pass on some important news. Since our search parties have so far failed, I have summoned a detective from London who is uncannily successful at solving crimes that take place on the railway.'

'That means you think Alex was murdered,' she gasped.

'If that was the case,' said her mother, putting an arm around her, 'they'd have stumbled upon the body by now.'

'Quite right, Mrs Haslam,' he agreed. 'What I came to ask your daughter was this. Think very carefully before you answer, Melissa. I know that you and Alex liked to go walking. It was one of the things that drew you together, wasn't it?'

'That's true,' said Melissa. 'We love to explore.'

'Is there a place that is particularly special to you, somewhere private that you often go to with him?' She shook her head. 'Are you quite sure? There are so many wonderful spots to visit – peaks, fells, moors, lakes and so on. You and Alex must have a favourite. If we knew where it was,' he said, 'we would see if he somehow found his way there by instinct.'

'There is no favourite place, my lord,' she confessed. 'When I'm with Alex, everywhere we go is special.'

'That's as it should be.'

'But tell me more about this detective from London. Can he really do what the search parties have so far failed to do?'

'I firmly believe that he can.'

'Yet we've already had police involved in the search.'

'They lack the expertise of a man like Inspector Colbeck. He'll be arriving this evening, and – here's an example of his thoughtfulness – he had the foresight to send a telegraph telling me which train he'd be on. I feel certain that Colbeck will be the answer to our prayers.' Culverhouse drew himself up to his full height. 'I've ordered Hedley to be on the platform to welcome him.'

'I'd like to meet him as well,' she said.

'All in good time,' he told her. 'He'll want to speak first to those who were actually on that Phantom Special. That's where his search must start.'

On the last leg of their journey, they had to go the short distance between Oxenholme and Kendal. Though it was an area of outstanding scenic beauty, the detectives were unable to enjoy the view because light was fading badly and a heavy drizzle was adding a second curtain between them and the passing landscape. While Colbeck was delighted that they were close to their destination, Leeming was simply glad that he'd survived the journey without joining the ranks of those driven into incurable madness by the rigours of rail travel.

'All *we* ever did at Hallowe'en,' he said, 'was to duck for apples.'

'It's a harmless but amusing tradition, Victor.'

'We could never afford to hire a train for the night.'

'I suspect that the good people of Kendal will regret that they did so. What began as an enjoyable excursion seems to have ended in disaster.'

'It's obvious that the missing man is dead.'

'I'm keeping an open mind,' said Colbeck. 'One thing is certain: alive or dead, it's our job to find him.'

The train began to lose speed and it was not long before it drew into Kendal Station and came to a halt. Gathering up their luggage, the detectives alighted onto the platform. Two men approached them at once. Geoffrey Hedley introduced himself and gave them a cordial welcome. The porter he'd brought with him took charge of the luggage. As they moved towards the exit, Hedley passed on the bad news.

'We still haven't found Alex,' he said. 'Dozens of us have been involved in looking for him but to no avail.'

'Who is coordinating the search?'

'I suppose that I am, Inspector, though I'm operating under instructions from Lord Culverhouse.'

'Did he take part in the excursion?'

'No, but I did. In fact, I was in the same compartment with Alex when the train came to an emergency halt. He's my closest friend. I simply can't believe that he's disappeared. By the way,' he went on, 'I've taken the liberty of booking you both in to the Riverside Hotel for the night. Needless to say, all your expenses will be paid.'

'Thank you,' said Colbeck.

'What's their beer like?' asked Leeming.

'We'll soon find out, Sergeant. Meanwhile, let's concentrate on our purpose for being here.' He turned to Hedley. 'What's your opinion?'

'To be honest,' replied the other, 'I'm struggling to remain optimistic. Lord Culverhouse has a theory and I pretend to endorse it when I'm with him, but I can't really subscribe to it.'

'Why not?'

'It's too fanciful. He believes that Alex chased after the person who started that fire but, when he caught up with him, was knocked out in a fierce struggle. Lord Culverhouse argues that his nephew is in a daze, wandering blindly about the countryside without having a clue where he is.'

'*I* feel like that after a long train journey,' said Leeming under his breath. He raised his voice. 'What exactly happened during the excursion, Mr Hedley?'

Having reached the waiting coach provided by Lord Culverhouse, they clambered into it. On the way to their accommodation, the lawyer gave them a succinct account of what had happened on the Phantom Special and of subsequent events. Colbeck was grateful to be dealing with someone so educated and articulate. In a matter of minutes, they'd heard all of the salient details.

'You say that Mr Piper was about to get married,' observed Colbeck. 'Why didn't his future bride travel with him on the excursion?'

'Miss Haslam is unduly nervous.'

'I'd say she made the right decision,' Leeming interjected. 'I wouldn't have wanted to grope around in the dark for hours on end, searching for the missing man. The excursion was a total failure.'

Hedley winced. 'I have to agree, Sergeant.'

'You told us that Phantom Special brought you all back here to Kendal,' noted Colbeck. 'I daresay that the engine is now in service again. What about the two carriages?'

'They're in a siding near the station, Inspector. They were part of some disused rolling stock that we chose because it was much cheaper to hire.'

Colbeck snapped his fingers. 'That's where we'll start first thing in the morning.'

'Why bother with two old carriages?' protested Leeming. 'What can they possibly tell us?'

'If you know how to listen, Sergeant, they can tell you quite a lot.'

CHAPTER FOUR

When a friend joined her for dinner that evening, Madeleine was reminded just how much she had – to quote her father – come up in the world. Until she'd met Colbeck, she'd led a typical working-class existence, with all its constraints and limited expectations. Her social circle was small, and the notion of meals cooked and served to her on a daily basis was unthinkable. Marriage had moved her out of the modest dwelling in which she'd been born into a fine house in Westminster. But it was in her friendship with Lydia Quayle that she'd realised how radically her life had changed.

While a train robbery had brought Colbeck into her life, an even more serious crime had introduced her to Lydia. The latter's father, a prosperous businessman and prospective chairman of the Midland Railway, had been found dead in a Derbyshire churchyard. As it happened, Lydia was estranged from her family at that time, living in London with an older woman and maintaining only fitful contact with her relations.

Convinced that Lydia might have information relevant to the case, Colbeck asked his wife to take part in the investigative process, a decision he kept secret from his superiors at Scotland Yard. Madeleine not only interviewed Lydia, she befriended her and was very supportive to the young woman whom she discovered was tormented by competing loyalties. When the murder had been solved, the friendship between them became even closer.

'Something puzzles me,' said Lydia. 'You told me that Robert was offered the position of Acting Superintendent. Why didn't he accept the promotion?'

'Robert is much happier as a detective inspector. He took on that role once before and he hated being chained to a desk. What he thrives on is action and that means freedom of movement. Besides,' said Madeleine, 'he was counting on the fact that Superintendent Tallis would eventually return to duty and didn't want to look as if he'd tried to usurp him.'

'You'd prefer your husband based at Scotland Yard, surely?'

'I want him to be happy in his work, Lydia, even if it means that he has to travel all over the country.'

'It's the wrong time of the year to visit the Lake District.'

'We know that. It would be lovely to take Helen on a family holiday in spring or summer.'

'Does Robert ever get holidays?'

Madeleine sighed. 'Yes and no . . .'

After all this time, she felt completely at ease with Lydia and able to confide in her. Madeleine had other women friends – Leeming's wife, Estelle, was one of them – but none was as close as the person sitting with her in the drawing room. What she admired about Lydia was her intelligence, her sense of independence and her easy social graces. For her part, Lydia had even more cause to be grateful for the friendship. It had helped her to liberate herself from the more possessive relationship into which she'd somehow drifted and which had become both uncomfortable and irksome. What Madeleine had, in fact, helped to give her was an entirely new and more fulfilling life.

'What are you working on at the moment?' asked Lydia.

'I'll show you when it's finished.'

'You're always so secretive about your paintings.'

'I'm superstitious, that's all,' said Madeleine. 'I'm afraid to let anyone see my work until a painting is finished.'

'I'll have to be patient, then. Do you think that Helen will inherit your artistic flair?'

'Oh, it's not really flair, Lydia. I had to study hard and learn from real artists. In any case,' she added, 'painting is a rather lonely way to pass the time. I'm hoping that our daughter will take after Robert. Who knows? When Helen has reached my age, we may even have female detectives?'

'Yes, please!' said Lydia with enthusiasm. 'That day can't come soon enough, if you ask me.'

The coach took them to the Riverside Hotel, a quaint seventeenth-century inn on the bank of the River Kent. It was too gloomy for the detectives to appreciate the finer points of its architecture, and they were not, as it happened, given much time to study its interior. They were simply able to leave their luggage in their respective rooms before they were hustled out by Hedley. With the three of them ensconced in the plush seating, the coach set off once again.

'Lord Culverhouse insisted on meeting you as soon as possible,' explained Hedley. 'He will doubtless press you to stay at Culverhouse Court, but I felt that you'd probably prefer to have more freedom.'

'We would, indeed,' said Colbeck.

'It's difficult to work when someone is looking over your shoulder all the time,' said Leeming. 'We'd feel hampered.'

'You made the right decision, Mr Hedley.'

'His Lordship may not think so,' warned the other.

'Where does he live?'

'Oh, it's not far away, Inspector. The house is in the middle of a large estate. Needless to say, he released some of his servants so that they could join in the search.'

'What about Mr Piper's family?' asked Leeming.

'They live in Ambleside. That's at the north end of Lake Windermere. They were aware that you were coming and hope to meet you tomorrow.'

'They're high on our list,' said Colbeck. 'The more we can learn about the missing person, the better.'

'Look,' said Hedley with slight embarrassment, 'there's something you should know. The Reverend and Mrs Piper have a rather jaundiced view of their son. They feel that he's let the family name down. Alex is no angel – I'm the first to

36

admit that – but he's not the complete rake his parents seem to think he is.'

'Rake?' echoed Leeming.

'He's had a rather colourful life and formed what his parents considered to be unsavoury attachments. I was the only one of Alex's close friends they deemed acceptable.'

'Why is that?'

'They felt I was a restraining influence.'

'Did Mr Piper live at home?'

'No,' said Hedley, 'he didn't. Alex stormed out after what he described as a spectacular row with them. He's had nothing to do with either of his parents since then. I've tried to act as a peacemaker between the warring parties but with little success. My hope is – or was – that his marriage would help to repair the rift with his family.'

'You sound as if you've given up hope of ever finding him,' said Colbeck. 'Is that the case?'

'The truthful answer is that I don't know. One moment, I'm convinced that he's still alive and that there's a perfectly logical explanation for his disappearance; the next, I fear that something dreadful has happened.' He made an effort to sound more positive. 'No, I refuse to believe that Alex is dead. He's one of nature's survivors. He *must* still be alive.'

'Then where is he?'

'I think he's being held captive by someone as a means of punishment. That's something else you should know about him,' said Hedley. 'Alex made lots of enemies.'

* * *

Dressed in black, the runner was invisible in the darkness. His pace was steady, unforced and methodical. After cresting the hill, he came down the incline with sure-footed confidence and, when he'd reached even ground, turned instinctively to the right. He jogged on until he came to the railway lines, running parallel to them for the best part of a mile. When he finally stopped, he crouched down by the track, pricked up his ears and listened intently.

When they got to the house, Lord Culverhouse was in the hall to welcome them. His first impression of the detectives was not encouraging. He thought that Colbeck was too much of a dandy and that Leeming was impossibly ugly and uncouth. Reading the situation at once, Colbeck decided that he could glean far more information if he spoke to the old man alone. He therefore suggested that the sergeant took a detailed statement in private from Hedley. Culverhouse agreed readily with the idea and had the two men conducted to the library. He led Colbeck to his study, a large, well-appointed room with a fire blazing in the grate. There was a pervasive smell of cigar smoke, reminding Colbeck of the superintendent. Culverhouse waved him to an armchair and sat opposite him, subjecting him to a penetrating stare.

'You're not exactly what I was expecting,' he said.

'Appearances can be deceptive.'

'I hope so. Your companion looks like the sort of person you should arrest on sight, not someone who's been entrusted with the rank of a detective at Scotland Yard.'

'The sergeant has many sterling qualities,' said Colbeck, loyally, 'among which are intelligence, tenacity and fearlessness. I can assure you that he is fully equipped to discharge his responsibilities as an officer of the law.'

Culverhouse sniffed. 'I'll take your word for it.' He glanced in the direction of the library. 'As he probably told you, Hedley is a lawyer. What do you make of him?'

'He's been extremely helpful. Having once worked as a barrister, I came into contact with many lawyers. Mr Hedley seems to have all of the virtues of the breed yet none of the abiding stuffiness.' Culverhouse smiled for the first time. 'He told me about your theory.'

'It's not as far-fetched as it may sound. I've read reports before of people who sustain a violent blow to the head that deprives them of all knowledge of who and where they are. Victims have been known to wander aimlessly for days.'

'I'm well aware of what can happen when someone's mind is disturbed,' said Colbeck, thinking of Tallis. 'Your hypothesis, however, is based on the notion that another person is involved.'

'It stands to reason, Inspector.'

'Does it?'

'Someone deliberately lit that fire.'

'I agree, but surely he'd have disappeared into the night so that he couldn't be identified?'

'My nephew must have found him somehow and tackled the villain. It's the sort of thing Alex would do. He'd never walk away from a fight.'

'Then why didn't he get the better of the man? According to Mr Hedley, your nephew was young, fit and had taken boxing lessons.'

'It's a plausible theory,' said Culverhouse, angrily, 'and I won't have it questioned. Even if there *was* no other person there, Alex could have charged off to search the area, tripped in the dark, banged his head on a rock and lost his bearings in every sense of the phrase.'

'You're quite right, Lord Culverhouse,' said Colbeck, trying to calm him. 'Yours is a suggestion that deserves respect. It would account for his sudden disappearance.' He changed his tack. 'Mr Hedley told us about your nephew's estrangement from his parents.'

'My brother-in-law was chiefly to blame for that.'

'Oh?'

'Foolishly, he expects his son to behave exactly as he did at that age.'

'I'm not sure what you mean, my lord.'

'Are you familiar with Tennyson's poems?'

'Yes, I'm a great admirer of his work.'

'Then you'll have read *St Simeon Stylites*, I daresay.'

'I have, indeed,' said Colbeck. 'Tennyson takes a rather mocking view of the privations he imposed on himself.'

'My brother-in-law is cut from the same cloth. He's a latter-day Simeon. I'm not saying that Rodney spent years living on top of a pillar with almost no clothes on, but he does have more than a touch of the martyr about him. Not unnaturally,' he went on, 'Alex rebelled against all that suffocating piety.'

'I gather that Mr Piper is a clergyman?'

'He's an archdeacon, Inspector. I love Rodney for my sister's sake, but I just couldn't bring myself to sit through one of his interminable sermons.'

'I begin to see why he and his son fell out.'

'It's a sad business. Alex is an only child. His parents are heartbroken that they lost him before reconciliation could take place. I've told them that he's still alive,' said the old man, 'but they refuse to believe me.'

'You are right to retain hope.'

'It's not hope I feel, it's a sense of certainty. Alex is out there somewhere, Inspector.' He pointed a finger at Colbeck. 'I'm counting on you and that unprepossessing sergeant of yours to find him.'

Leeming had spent the first couple of minutes in the library, staring up at the portrait of Lord Culverhouse in full fig. It was so lifelike that it unsettled him. Hedley didn't even glance up at it. He was too busy taking something out of the valise he was carrying. When the sergeant finally turned to him, the lawyer handed him a sheet of paper.

'That's a list of all the people on the Phantom Special,' he said. 'I've put a tick beside those who were in the last compartment with Alex and me.'

'Thank you, sir.' He looked at the names. 'I see that the ladies outnumbered the men in your compartment. Who was responsible for that?'

Hedley was evasive. 'That's just the way it worked out, Sergeant.'

'Both carriages seem to have been filled to capacity.'

'It was a very popular excursion. People are inclined to seek thrills at Hallowe'en.'

'There's not much of a thrill in ducking apples and getting your face soaked,' moaned Leeming. 'I'd have jumped at the chance of going to a haunted wood – except that you never actually got that far, did you?'

'No, we didn't. Alex's disappearance changed everything. When the train got to Birthwaite – that's the station near Windermere – we cancelled the waiting carriages and came straight back to Kendal.'

'How soon did the search resume?'

'I took a small party out at first light.'

'What was the weather like?'

'It was raining heavily,' said Hedley. 'If Alex was wandering around in a daze, as Lord Culverhouse believes, he'd have been drenched.'

'I can see why you don't agree with that theory. It leaves too many questions unanswered.' He looked up at the portrait again. 'If we lower our voices, he won't hear us.' Leeming resorted to a hoarse whisper. 'You told us earlier that you believed your friend might be being held as a punishment by someone. Wouldn't his captor demand a ransom?'

'I've been hoping that we'd have received one by now. It would at least prove that Alex is alive.'

'Not necessarily, sir – we were involved in a case where the kidnappers killed their victim immediately, then pretended he was still alive. Fortunately, we were able to catch them when they tried to collect the ransom.'

Hedley was adamant. 'I refuse to accept that Alex is dead.'

'It's an option that we have to consider,' said Leeming, solemnly, 'especially since you tell us that he had lots of enemies.'

'It's true.'

'Didn't that worry him?'

'Quite the opposite – he rejoiced in the fact.'

'It's not impossible that one or more of these so-called enemies might be responsible for his death.' He took out his notebook. 'I'll need some names, Mr Hedley. Who are the most likely suspects?'

Colbeck had to wait patiently while his companion embellished his theory about his missing nephew. In the course of doing so, Culverhouse provided a lot of useful information about the structure of his family and the exalted position he held in the community. Unlike his brother-in-law, the old man had no inclination towards martyrdom. Denial of any kind was foreign to him. His red cheeks, sizeable paunch and general air of self-indulgence made it clear that he was a confirmed sybarite. The gleaming whisky decanter on the man's desk seemed further proof of the fact and Colbeck wondered if his fondness for his nephew arose from the fact that Alex apparently shared his uncle's attitude to life. When Culverhouse finally ran out of steam, his visitor was able to get a question in at last.

'While I can see the logic of your theory,' he said, 'might I offer one of my own, please?'

'But you know nothing of what happened that night.'

'Nevertheless, I'd like to introduce an element that neither you nor Mr Hedley have touched upon. This isn't in any way an attack on your theory, Lord Culverhouse,' he added, hastily. 'Indeed, the two could coexist side by side.'

Culverhouse was tetchy. 'What are you babbling about?'

'The Kendal and Windermere Railway.'

'Damn you, man! You know nothing whatsoever about it.'

'On the contrary,' said Colbeck, 'I know a great deal. I'm aware, for instance, that the engineer was Joseph Locke and the contractor was Thomas Brassey, two gentlemen for whom I have the greatest respect and with whom I'm closely acquainted. The line was opened in 1847 as part of the Lancaster and Carlisle Railway but is now leased to the LNWR.'

'How did you learn that?' spluttered the other.

'I make it my business to keep abreast of developments in the railway system. My guess is that, since you occupy such a leading position in the county, you were instrumental in having the line built.'

'I certainly was. The main line to Carlisle skirted Kendal because they feared some expensive tunnelling would be involved. I didn't see why we shouldn't have the benefits of rail travel, so I led the campaign for the extension on which you have just travelled.'

'And you did so in the teeth of opposition, I believe?'

'There was a veritable outcry,' recalled Culverhouse. 'We were accused of shameless vandalism. No less a person than William Wordsworth lifted his pen in anger and poured scorn upon us. Being attacked by the poet laureate was a very disagreeable experience, I can tell you, but we couldn't let him stand in the way of progress.'

'Even after all this time, some people must harbour vengeful feelings towards you.'

'It's true, Inspector. I still get vicious poison pen letters, blaming me for allowing armies of holidaymakers to flood into the Lake District.'

'It's an area of unsurpassed beauty. People from all over the country should be entitled to enjoy it. Besides,' said Colbeck, 'many of the inhabitants here will have made a tidy profit as a result of railway access. Holidaymakers all need somewhere to eat, drink and spend the night.'

'That's a valid point, but my tormentors never consider it. They claim that I've let in ill-mannered hordes from the lower orders. I wouldn't dare to show my wife the vile correspondence I get. It's truly shocking.' The old man blinked. 'I begin to see what you mean,' he said. 'Alex was not picked out because of anything *he* did. Making him the target was a way of getting at his uncle. *That's* why it took place on the railway.'

'A railway closely identified with you.'

'Poor Alex is suffering because of me?'

'It's pure supposition at this point, Lord Culverhouse,' stressed Colbeck, 'but it mustn't be dismissed out of hand. The person who stopped that train must have known your nephew would be the only person on that excursion with the requisite courage to investigate the delay. He lay in wait to ambush him.'

'*That's* how Alex had that blow to the head,' said the other, banging his fist on the arm of the chair. 'Well done, Inspector! You've explained everything.'

'All I've done is to voice the possibility that the railway itself might have provoked what seems to be a deliberate attack on your nephew. Before we get too excited, it needs thinking through.'

'Excellent! I insist that you stay here as my guest so that we can discuss this at length over a glass of whisky.' He wagged a finger. 'That invitation is restricted to you, by the way. The sergeant can seek accommodation elsewhere. That face of his would only frighten the female members of staff.'

'Both of us will be staying at the Riverside Hotel,' declared Colbeck. 'It's not far from the railway station and ideal for our purposes.' He raised a palm to stifle any protest. 'It's all decided, my lord. We will, naturally, keep you informed of every stage of the investigation, but you must allow us to move about unhindered.'

'Can you guarantee that you'll find Alex alive?'

'No, I can't, I'm afraid. That's asking too much. What I can assure you is that we'll discover exactly what happened when your nephew disappeared into that fire.'

CHAPTER FIVE

Rodney Piper had spent so long kneeling in prayer that his legs seemed to have become paralysed, forcing his wife to lift him to his feet. Tall, stooping and emaciated, he had the unmistakeable look of an ascetic about him. His bald pate was a mass of wrinkles and his deep-set, anxious eyes looked as if they'd retreated into his head in a desperate search for safety. His wife, Emma, offered a stark contrast to his skeletal frame, being a full-bodied woman with a chubby face and an overall sense of solidity. As she helped him to sit on the edge of the bed, she kept a supportive arm around him.

'Take heart,' she said. 'Alex may soon be found.'

'But in what state will he be?' he asked. 'The only way to explain his disappearance is to accept that he's no longer alive. Our son has been killed by someone else or – we have to face this dreaded possibility, Emma – he died by his own hand. That would be an unbearable shame for us. We'd be the parents of a child who could not be buried in consecrated ground.'

His wife was roused. 'Don't even think of such a thing. Alex would never dream of committing suicide. He had a wonderful future ahead of him. There was his marriage, to start with, and he was on an excursion with all of his friends. He was there to enjoy himself.'

Her husband frowned. 'He was rather too fond of doing that.'

'Let's not think bad thoughts at a time like this. It doesn't help to bring him back. We should be regretting the incidents that forced him to move out of this house. If we're honest,' she said, softly, 'there were faults on both sides.'

'I could not let him treat us the way that he did, Emma.'

'Try to remember our delight when he was first born, and think of the many wonderful family outings we shared over the years. It's just that Alex saw life in a different way to us.'

'He turned his back on the church,' said Piper, resentfully, 'that's what he did. It was unforgivable.'

'Our son could be dead. Think well of him.'

'I'm rightly rebuked,' he said, penitently. 'I, of all people, should never speak ill of the deceased.'

'My heart goes out to Melissa. The news must have come as a devastating blow. All her dreams were invested in Alex.'

'So were ours,' he muttered.

'Let's hope that this man my brother has sent for will be able to uncover the truth. Until we know that, none of us can grieve properly. What was his name?'

'Inspector Colbeck.'

'The sooner we meet him, the sooner we'll get to some sort of peace.'

'I'm still undecided about the fellow.'

'But he's a famous detective and comes with the highest recommendation.'

'Yes, I know,' he said, 'and I'm sure that he'll be able to rescue us from this crushing uncertainty. But there's another side to it, Emma.'

'Is there?'

'He'll want to look closely into our relationship with Alex. That's my fear. Things I'd rather keep private will have to be exposed to scrutiny. I don't like that, Emma,' he continued. 'I value our privacy above all else. I don't want a complete stranger prying into our affairs.'

'It's because he's a stranger that he can be impartial,' she argued. 'Everyone else has taken sides. Our friends sympathise with us over the problems we endured and Alex was, in turn, supported by *his* friends.'

'Friends!' snorted her husband. 'His social circle consists of a gang of licentious good-for-nothings.'

'You can hardly describe Geoffrey Hedley in that way. He's a charming and thoroughly decent man.'

'In other words, he's the exception to the rule.'

'You're forgetting Melissa Haslam. She's a sweet young girl and comes from a good family. Everyone is saying that she's transformed Alex.'

'That's more than we could do,' admitted Piper.

'There are positive elements we must cling to, Rodney. Our

son was not the irredeemable wastrel you painted him as. I, too, said some harsh things to him and I regret them deeply now. The truth may be that we simply didn't understand him.'

Piper rolled his eyes. 'Oh, I understood him all too well.'

'You're doing it again,' she protested. 'Concentrate on the many good things Alex brought into our life. And please don't be afraid to talk openly to Inspector Colbeck. We can't hide our secrets away for ever, Rodney. The truth is bound to come out in the end.'

A smile had finally resurfaced on the face of Victor Leeming, making his unsightly features look less menacing. They were now back at the Riverside Hotel and everything there was to his satisfaction. Their rooms were comfortable, their meal had been delicious and – the deciding factor – the beer was exceptional. The sergeant was quaffing his second pint. Colbeck preferred a glass of wine with his meal and had promised himself a brandy before he retired to bed. Having eaten his fill, he sat back in his chair.

'Well, what's the verdict?'

'That's the best meal I'd had for ages, sir.'

'I wasn't talking about the food, Victor. I was referring to the case in hand. Judging by the amount you wrote in your notebook, you had a profitable time with Mr Hedley.'

'I'm not so sure about that.'

'What do you mean?'

'Well, he was very helpful and obliging but he was also cautious. Hedley measured his words carefully, so I was never sure what he was thinking. When I asked him who Piper's real enemies were,' recalled Leeming, 'I had to chisel the names out of him.'

'Lawyers are circumspect by nature.'

'*You* can be like that sometimes, sir.' Colbeck laughed. 'Anyway, I did manage to get four names out of him in the end. I ruled one of them out straight away.'

'Why was that?'

'It was a woman.'

'There have been many female killers in the past, remember.'

'Yes, I know. There was Martha Browne, that woman we heard about in Dorchester. She chopped her husband to death with a hatchet. The person I'm talking about, however, is far too ladylike to do anything like that.'

'She could always pay someone else to commit the crime for her. Who is the person named by Hedley?'

'Miss Caroline Treadgold.'

'What did he say about her?'

'Well, she and Alex Piper had what he called a "fleeting friendship". The moment he met Melissa Haslam, it fizzled out. Miss Treadgold was furious.'

'There's your motive,' said Colbeck. 'She was a woman scorned. Perhaps she wanted to strike back at him.'

'I have my doubts. To begin with, Hedley was very embarrassed at having to give me her name. I sensed that he was very fond of Miss Treadgold himself. What interested me was that he didn't criticise Piper for raising her hopes before dashing them. He just accepted it. If you want my opinion, I don't think she's a credible suspect.'

'Did she go on the Phantom Special?'

'No, sir, and I find that significant.'

'Why?'

'You'd expect her to seize any chance of getting close to Piper so that she could work on him. Hedley admitted that his friend had drunk a lot of champagne before they set off. Since Miss Haslam didn't go on the excursion,' said Leeming, 'Piper might have been vulnerable to an approach by Miss Treadgold. Hedley reckons that she vowed to get him back somehow.'

'Whatever the truth of the matter, she's someone of interest to us. I'll talk to her myself.' Colbeck drained his wine glass. 'Who were the other suspects?'

Referring to his notebook, Leeming gave him the names of the three men mentioned by Hedley and bewailed the fact that the lawyer had told him so little about the trio that he had no idea what motive each of them might have had to wreak revenge on Piper. Colbeck then took over, describing his conversation with Lord Culverhouse and explaining that he'd humoured the old man by pretending to accept his flawed theory of what had happened to his nephew. Leeming agreed that anyone wandering around in a confused state for so long a time would surely have been seen by someone. Colbeck's suggestion that the railway itself might be a key factor did not impress his companion. Anyone simmering with hatred at the building of the line, Leeming pointed out, would surely attack Lord Culverhouse, the man largely responsible for it, rather than his nephew.

The search for motives continued and, while Leeming moved on to another tankard of beer, Colbeck decided that a brandy was now in order. Leeming started to flag.

'I'm exhausted,' he said, stifling a yawn. 'It's time for bed, sir. We've been through all the possibilities.'

'Not quite, Victor.'

'I don't follow, sir.'

'We've missed out the most obvious explanation.'

'What's that?'

'Alex Piper was the victim of a supernatural event.'

'You told me you didn't believe in ghosts.'

'I don't,' said Colbeck, 'but most of the people on the Phantom Special did. Why? What was it that drew them to that particular spot at the dead of midnight? There's only one way to find out,' he added, raising his glass. 'We'll have to visit the place ourselves after dark.'

At the heart of what many believed to be a haunted wood was a clearing large enough to have accommodated all the people who went on the excursion. It was deserted now but a souvenir of the doomed Hallowe'en party was left behind. On the night before the Phantom Special set off on its fateful journey, Hedley had taken a pile of logs to the wood. Knowing how frightened some of the revellers would be, he'd laid a fire in the middle of the clearing so that it could be easily lit to provide warmth and illumination. The logs now stood forlornly, propping each other up on a cold and chilly night. Nobody was there to view the miracle. As the wind began to blow and the trees began to sway, an owl hooted. Far below, a tiny column of smoke began to rise almost imperceptibly from the logs. It was followed in due course by a dull glow that grew brighter and brighter by the minute. The smoke was gradually replaced by flame and the fire was eventually blazing merrily as if in celebration of something.

It was dawn when the search teams assembled. Hedley was the first there with a map spread out on a boulder. As each group arrived, he explained which area needed to be searched and sent them off. Everybody was wearing warm clothing and a hat. Grasped in their hands was a long walking stick that could be used for support and as a means of poking into the gorse and other shrubs. They were all experienced walkers with a good knowledge of the terrain, and most of them had joined the fruitless searches before. Undeterred by their lack of success, they were back again with increased determination to track down Alexander Piper, the young man with an unquenchable vitality about him who'd shown such daring when the train had been brought to a sudden halt.

Hedley was soon left with the team that he intended to lead. As they gathered around the map, he pointed out the area they were going to search, warning them that there would be some tricky climbing involved. They were about to set off when he saw someone alighting from a carriage and hurrying towards them. It was a female figure wrapped up so comprehensively against the cold that it was difficult to identify her. When he finally realised who it must be, Hedley sent the other members of the team ahead. He was left alone to welcome Caroline Treadgold. Out of breath when she reached him, she leant heavily on her walking stick.

'What are *you* doing here?' he asked in surprise.

'I've the same right to take part in the search as anyone,' she replied, tartly. 'Nobody was as close to Alex as me.'

'We don't need you, Caroline.'

'You try stopping me.'

'We have enough people as it is.'

Caroline curled a lip. 'Is *she* here?'

'No, she isn't. Melissa is still in a state of shock.'

'Then let's get going right away. We don't need that stupid little weakling. Alex preferred a *real* woman and that's why he chose me.'

Though the hearty breakfast had been welcome, Leeming didn't consider it adequate compensation for the ridiculously early start. When they reached the siding, Colbeck had to use a lamp to pick his way safely between the tracks. Unlike the search teams, neither of them was ideally dressed for the weather conditions. In his shiny top hat and immaculate attire, Colbeck looked far too elegant to be anywhere near the two dusty carriages waiting in the siding. Leeming scuffed both of his shoes as soon as they arrived and he couldn't understand how the inspector avoided a similar fate.

The carriages belonged to the railway company's discarded rolling stock but, since they were still serviceable, they were kept for the purpose of excursions. Colbeck's initial interest was in the compartment occupied nights before by Piper and his friends. After opening the door, Colbeck climbed up effortlessly into it but Leeming decided that he'd remain on the ground. Minutes later, Colbeck climbed out and closed the door behind him before moving on to the next compartment. When he'd thoroughly examined that, he went on to the last of the three compartments in the carriage then repeated the whole process with the carriage that had been nearer the locomotive. Only when Colbeck had finished his inspection did Leeming dare to ask a question.

'What were you doing, sir?'

'I wanted to satisfy my curiosity.'

'Why go into all six compartments? When you've seen inside one, you've seen them all.'

'That, Victor, is a misapprehension. Do you remember what Hedley told us about the early stage of the journey?'

'Yes, sir,' said Leeming. 'When the train first set off, everybody was scared by the sudden lurch forward – everyone except Piper, that is. He tried to rally them.'

'What happened further along the line?'

'There was a lot of jollity, I suppose. They'd all been drinking heavily. The light in the compartment was poor and I daresay some of the men took advantage of that.'

'Keep going.'

'That's it, sir. They were all enjoying themselves until the train lost speed then screeched to a halt in open country.'

'You've missed something out.'

'Have I?'

'Yes, and it may be turn out to be a clue.'

'Why?'

'Hedley told us that one of the lamps went out and they were more or less in the dark. The surprise is that both lamps didn't splutter and die because they had hardly any oil in them.'

'What about the other compartments?'

'Every lamp had been filled in those,' said Colbeck. 'I believe that someone may have tampered with the two in the compartment occupied by Piper. It may be that Piper himself was the culprit.'

'Why should he want the compartment in darkness?'

'It's for the same reason that he wanted to share it with a disproportionately large number of ladies. Hedley told us that Piper was in charge of allotting people to individual compartments. He chose,' said Colbeck, meaningfully, 'companions he most wanted close to him.'

'Are you saying what I think you're saying, sir?'

'Alexander Piper was a drunken, forceful, overexcited, red-blooded young man.'

'But he was due to get married fairly soon.'

'He wouldn't be the first bridegroom who was tempted to seek random pleasure before taking solemn vows that would bind him for life to his chosen partner. Miss Haslam was not on that train,' said Colbeck. 'Don't you think it odd that a man helps to organise an excursion that his future wife is unwilling to take part in? Would *you* have done such a thing shortly before your marriage to Estelle?'

'It would never have crossed my mind,' said Leeming, hotly. 'I think it was indecent and I'm shocked that Hedley went along with it.'

'Hedley was dazzled by him. You can hear it in his voice. It's almost a case of hero worship,' said Colbeck. 'Hedley was used to making allowances for the defects in Piper's character.

It's what close friends do. I believe that he's far too honourable to ape Piper's behaviour but, equally, he had neither the power nor the inclination to check his friend's excesses.' He put an apologetic hand on Leeming's shoulder. 'I'm sorry to get you up so early, Victor. I hope you'll now accept that coming here was well worth the effort.'

Alan Hinton had more cause than most detectives to be wary of the superintendent's return. He knew what it was like to be yelled at and threatened by Edward Tallis, a towering figure at Scotland Yard. As a rule, he tried to keep out of the way of his superior but, when Tallis was kidnapped, Hinton was sent off to Canterbury to join in the search for him. He'd received heartfelt thanks from the older man for his part in the rescue, then had to watch the dramatic decline in Tallis's mental health. Ironically, in trying to help the superintendent, Hinton only got himself yelled at with even more ferocity.

When he saw Tallis coming down the corridor towards him, therefore, his first instinct was to turn around and scamper out of the way. Steeling himself, he decided to carry on and hoped that he might get away with a curt nod from the other man. Tallis surprised him.

'Ah,' he said, stopping in front of the younger man and beaming at him. 'It's Hinton, isn't it?'

'Yes, sir . . . Welcome back.'

'Thank you. I feel rather like a new boy at school at the moment, but I'm slowly familiarising myself with my routine.'

Hinton looked at him closely. The change was remarkable.

Tallis looked healthy and clear-eyed. He'd lost weight, trimmed his moustache even more and seemed years younger. He also showed a genuine interest in Hinton.

'What are you assigned to at the moment?'

'I've been investigating a case of attempted arson in Finsbury, sir.'

'Have you made any progress?'

'We have two men in custody.'

'Excellent, excellent . . . you're one of Colbeck's protégés, aren't you?'

'I've learnt a lot from the inspector, if that's what you mean, sir.'

'We all have.'

Hinton couldn't believe that the man regarded as the resident ogre was so benign and approachable. Was it a sign of recovery or a form of relapse? Whichever it was, he decided to remain cautious when dealing with him.

'Actually, sir,' he said, 'I've been looking for Inspector Colbeck this morning, but nobody seems to know where he is.'

'He's in the Lake District at the moment, looking for a man who disappeared in mysterious circumstances. You'll know all about a situation like that, of course, because you were involved in the search for me when I was abducted.'

'Fortunately, we found you just in time.'

'I hope that Colbeck has equal success in Cumberland.'

'He rarely fails.'

'This case will tax even *his* fabled abilities, I fear. He and Sergeant Leeming will be working all hours.'

* * *

In order to get to Ambleside, he took the train to Birthwaite then transferred to a coach and paid the one-shilling fare. During a journey of well over four miles, Colbeck had the chance to see some of the most stunning views he'd ever encountered. Set among the mountains at the head of Lake Windermere, Ambleside was a small market town in the Vale of Brathay. It was built on a steep incline which gave it a curious irregularity that added to its charm. Even at first glance Colbeck was struck by its romantic aura and promised himself that he would one day bring Madeleine there to savour its beauty. Wansfell Pike loomed high above him and he could see a couple of climbers inching their way up it. From what he'd heard about Alexander Piper, he suspected that, as soon as he'd been strong enough as a boy, he'd probably taken on the challenge set by all the peaks in the surrounding area. There was obviously a daredevil streak in him that may have brought about his downfall.

Piper's parents lived in a rambling old house in the shadow of Loughrigg Fell. When Colbeck rang the bell, the door was opened by a servant, who straightened his shoulders when the inspector introduced himself. Inviting him in, he ushered the visitor along a corridor and into the drawing room. As he went in, a shock awaited Colbeck.

Rodney and Emma Piper were dressed from head to foot in black. In their opinion, any hope of finding their son alive had ceased to exist. They were already in mourning.

CHAPTER SIX

Left on his own at Kendal Station, Victor Leeming had been busy. He'd managed to talk to both the driver and the fireman of the Phantom Special, discovering that neither of them had really wanted to be involved in the excursion because it meant staying on duty for hours while – in their own words – a group of rich, rowdy, selfish, drunken young people went off to play silly games in a wood. Leeming liked their forthrightness, enlivened, as it was, by the odd expletive. When he'd taken statements from both railwaymen, he went off to interview the first of the three men Hedley had designated as possible suspects.

Cecil Dymock was a local doctor and, since he was examining a patient when Leeming arrived, the sergeant had to wait until the consultation was over. Insisting on seeing Dymock next, he had a row with a patient waiting for an appointment and annoyed that someone was jumping the queue. Leeming's status as a Scotland Yard detective carried no weight with him. It did so, however, with the doctor, who whisked the sergeant immediately into his consulting room.

'I'm sure you realise why I'm here,' Leeming began.

'Frankly, I don't. What I am certain is that you didn't come to have a boil lanced or an ingrown toenail dealt with. You're here on official business of some sort.'

'It concerns Alexander Piper.'

'So?'

'Your name was given to me as someone who'd fallen out with the gentleman.'

Dymock gave a hollow laugh. 'You surely don't think that I had anything to do with his disappearance?'

'I'm simply gathering evidence, Doctor.'

'Evidence of *what*, for heaven's sake?'

'Let me ask the questions, please.'

Leeming had taken against him on sight. Dymock was a stringy man in his forties with the kind of patronising manner that made the sergeant squirm. But that, he reminded himself, didn't mean that the doctor was in any way party to a murder. Colbeck had always emphasised the need to be objective when questioning a suspect and that's what he now strove to be.

'I'm told that you're a well-respected doctor,' he said.

'Spare me false compliments, Sergeant.'

'You are also an experienced climber and love to tackle the most difficult peaks.'

'It's my hobby,' said Dymock.

'It may be relevant to our investigation, sir.'

The doctor gaped. 'Are you telling me that you came all

the way from London to discuss climbing with me?'

'No, sir, we're here to discover how and why Mr Piper vanished on his way to a Hallowe'en party. Your name has been put forward because, I gather, you and the missing man were sworn enemies.'

'I loathed him. Piper was despicable.'

'Could you be more specific, please?'

'No, I can't,' snapped the other. 'I've nothing further to add about Alex Piper. What I will say is this. Our landscape is a joy to behold in daylight but, on a dark night, it can become treacherous. Freak accidents happen all the time. Even able climbers have come to grief in the mountains.'

He looked his visitor straight in the eye to signal that he would say nothing else. Leeming accepted defeat. Dymock was like so many professional men he'd questioned, masters of evasion who hid behind a wall of pomposity and who made the sergeant feel his social inferiority. Moving to the door, the doctor opened it wide.

'Thank you for coming,' he said with light sarcasm, 'but I must now attend to my next patient.'

While they were touched that he'd made the effort to visit them so early in the day, Rodney Piper and his wife were beyond the stage when reassurance had any effect on them. Even though Colbeck pointed out that he'd found missing persons who'd been lost for a whole week yet who'd still been alive when finally discovered, they refused to believe there could be hope. When they offered him refreshment, he was glad to accept.

The three of them were soon sipping cups of tea. Emma Piper somehow managed to hold back tears and her husband went off into a kind of trance, gazing at the crucifix on the mantelpiece. As he watched the man's lips moving, Colbeck could guess what words the archdeacon was sending up to heaven. All of a sudden, Piper shook himself.

'Oh!' he cried. 'Do please excuse me, Inspector. It was very rude of me to drift off like that.'

'You must do as you wish. I have no complaint.'

'Thank you.'

'I know it's a sensitive area,' said Colbeck, gently, 'but do you feel able to talk about your son?'

'We've done nothing else since we heard the grim tidings.'

'We feel so guilty,' said his wife. 'Mr Hedley will have told you that we were estranged from Alex. What he may not have confided is that he tried to bring us back together again.'

'As it happens he did mention his efforts to act as peacemaker but Mr Hedley was far too modest to trumpet his good deeds.'

'You've judged him aright,' said Piper. 'The tragedy is that, in losing our son, we lost our friendship with his best friend. If we had our time again, we'd behave differently. In spite of his shortcomings, Alex was still our son. I should have kept that fact inscribed upon my heart.'

'You did what you felt was right, Rodney,' said Emma. 'There was a point where bad behaviour could no longer be tolerated.'

'According to Mr Hedley,' said Colbeck, 'your son was given to impulsive action. He found living here with you in this beautiful little town far too tame an existence.'

'Tame?' repeated Piper. 'Is that what our lives really look like? Did Alex never see the passion that underlay our beliefs? In a sinful world such as this, *someone* has to stand up for righteousness. I felt that it was my duty to do so.'

For one scary moment, Colbeck feared that his host was about to unleash a sermon tailored especially for him, but the danger soon passed. Piper and his wife withdrew into a lengthy mutual silence. Colbeck studied them in turn. As predicted by his brother-in-law, Piper did have the gaunt, pale, spiritual look of a martyr suffering in the name of his faith. Emma Piper, on the other hand, was plump yet still attractive and appeared to be glowing with health. The couple finally became aware of their guest and apologised in unison for their bad manners.

'I'm so sorry,' said Emma. 'We keep doing that all the time, I fear. Rodney and I have so much on our minds.'

'That's understandable,' said Colbeck, tolerantly.

'Please excuse our poor hospitality,' added Piper. 'You come all the way from London to help us and we can't even behave politely. I promise you that we'll make an effort to concentrate from now on.'

'Thank you, sir.'

'I can see that you have many questions for us.'

'The first one concerns the forthcoming marriage,' said Colbeck. 'Did it meet with your approval?'

'There's no short answer to that, Inspector. The news took us rather by surprise and showed how little we knew of Alex's life. We have nothing against Miss Haslam as a person. She's a delightful young woman and we've always been on good terms with her family. My worry, however,' admitted Piper, 'is that she doesn't know how wayward our son can be. It's a dreadful thing to say about one's own flesh and blood, but I feel that Miss Haslam deserves a more serious and committed husband than Alex could ever be.'

'That was my reaction at first,' said his wife, 'but I came to the view that it might be the best thing that ever happened to our son. Melissa Haslam might have been the salvation of him. More to the point, the wedding would be a means of uniting us with Alex at last. That was important to me.'

'And to me, Emma,' said Piper. 'The very fact that he was prepared to renounce his bachelor life was heartening. My doubts may be quite illusory. I prayed earnestly that being a husband – and, in time, a father – would be the making of him.'

'We fear for poor Melissa. She's such a sensitive creature. This tragedy will scar her for life.'

'That depends on what we find,' said Colbeck. 'If it turns out that your son was killed in an unfortunate accident, it will be easier to bear. If, however, it transpires that he was a murder victim, Miss Haslam may be quite unable to cope with the enormity of the loss.'

Melissa Haslam and her mother had also turned to prayer. After a visit to Holy Trinity Church, they came out arm in arm and walked to the waiting carriage. Bridget Haslam had found a degree of comfort while on her knees at the altar rail, but her daughter was still assailed by demons. As they were driven away, she was more fearful than ever.

'I know the truth now,' she said, visibly shaking.

'How can you, Melissa?'

'It all became clear inside the church.'

'What are you talking about?'

'It's almost as if God felt that I should know the worst. Lord Culverhouse was wrong. Alex is not wandering from place to place. It's foolish to believe that he could be.'

'Then what did happen to him?'

'He was murdered,' said Melissa with conviction. 'He was killed in cold blood and, worst of all, a woman was involved.'

Tears began to cascade down her cheeks.

They had caught up with the rest of the search team and were part of a line that stretched out fifty yards or more. Moving forward together, they combed the area systematically. When he felt they needed a rest, Hedley called out to the others and they paused for refreshment. He'd brought water with him and offered the bottle to Caroline Treadgold. She shook her head.

'I need something stronger than that.'

'I can't provide it, I'm afraid.'

'No matter,' she said. 'In another half an hour, we'll reach The Jolly Traveller – not that I feel very jolly at the moment.'

'Why did you decide to join us?'

'I felt compelled to do so.'

'Aren't you afraid of what we might find?'

'However awful, I must know the truth.'

Hedley had a sip of water then put the cork back into the bottle. He looked at her with a mingled interest and affection.

'It's good of you to come, Caroline.'

'I had no choice.'

'Alex would've been grateful.'

'He had a lot to be grateful for,' she said, introducing a slightly sour note. 'But that's all in the past.' She became quizzical. 'How much did he tell you about me?'

'He told me very little and that, in itself, was unusual. When he'd had a drink or two, Alex loved to boast. But he never did that where you were concerned. It was months before he even confessed that you'd been seeing each other in secret.'

She smiled. 'I like secrecy. It excites me.'

'Well, you've rather abandoned it today, Caroline. When people see you crawling over the hillsides with us, they'll work out why you're here.'

'Alex would expect it of me, that's why.'

'Your secret will be out.'

'I'm proud of that, Hedley. For all I care, the whole world can know about it now. The truth is that he loved me and never really left me. In his heart,' she said, eyes glinting, 'I always had pride of place.'

Since Colbeck had set out for Ambleside early that morning, it was left to Victor Leeming to establish contact with the local constabulary. Arriving at the police station, he was met by Sergeant Bernard Ainsley. Bulky, broad-shouldered and moustached, the man gave him a guarded welcome. It was no more than Leeming had expected. Wherever they went, the detectives aroused hostility from the local and railway police, all of whom resented what they perceived as interference, because it meant they were considered unequal to the task of solving a particular crime. Leeming tried to ease the situation with an emollient smile but all that got back in return was a sustained glower from the older man.

'Don't bother with introductions,' said Ainsley, 'I know who you are and what you are.'

'May I at least know your name?'

'Sergeant Ainsley.'

'I'm sure we can count on your cooperation, Sergeant.'

'What you mean is that you'll steal all the intelligence that we've gathered and pass it off as your own.'

'We're not here to steal anything. Our job is quite simple. A man has disappeared. *You* can't find him. We will.'

'And how do you propose to do that? Go on, tell me. Did you bring a magic wand?' Leeming laughed. 'It's what you'll need if you expect to solve this puzzle before we do.'

'We were summoned here by Lord Culverhouse.'

'So?'

'As you know, he has a very personal interest in this case. What do you think he'd say if he realised that someone from the Cumberland constabulary is refusing to assist us?'

'We'll do as we're told,' grunted the other.

'Would you like to say that to Lord Culverhouse himself?'

Ainsley was cowed. Lowering his head, he took a step

backwards. Though he still wore a mask of hostility, he'd been brought to heel. Leeming had won. In mentioning Culverhouse, he had an effective means of control. He fired a first question.

'Have you examined those carriages yet?'

'What carriages?'

'The two that formed the Phantom Special, of course,' said Leeming. 'They're parked in a siding near the station.'

'Why should we bother with them?'

'They have a tale to tell, Sergeant. Earlier this morning, Inspector Colbeck searched every one of the six compartments. In the one in which Mr Piper travelled, he discovered that the oil lamps had been more or less emptied so that the light was likely to be extinguished at some stage in the journey. We're told that one of the lamps did exactly that, plunging the compartment into half-darkness and spreading fear. In short,' said Leeming, jabbing a finger at him, 'someone was bent on causing trouble. Why didn't you realise that?'

'We know our trade. This is no lawless backwater. It's a well-policed provincial town with a gaol as well as a house of correction. We're proud of our record and we don't deserve criticism.'

'That depends on how many other things you failed to notice. Let me go through them one by one, shall I?'

Ainsley struck back. 'How long have you been here?' he asked, pointedly.

'We arrived yesterday evening.'

'Yet you have the brazen cheek to claim that you know far more than people who've been looking into this case for days.'

'We're very well informed, Sergeant.'

'Really?'

'Mr Hedley has been our main source.'

'Ah, yes, we know all about Geoffrey Hedley,' said the other with an expressive sniff. 'He's been in here time and again to get his friend out of trouble.'

'What do you mean?'

'Piper has been a thorn in our flesh for years. Because his uncle is Lord Culverhouse, he thinks that he's above the law. Anybody else would have been prosecuted for drunkenness, causing an affray, damaging property and, most recently, knocking someone senseless in the King's Arms. In every single instance,' Ainsley went on, 'Hedley claimed that it was simply a case of high spirits. Behind the scenes, victims were paid off and quietly withdrew their charges. I'll wager that Hedley didn't mention that to you.'

'No, he didn't,' conceded Leeming.

'And there's a lot more I could tell you about Alexander Piper. He's been a real menace.'

'Is that why you're dragging your feet?'

Ainsley crooked a finger to beckon him closer.

'Can I tell you something in confidence?'

'Go on.'

'I don't want this reported to Lord Culverhouse.'

'You have my word on that.'

'Thank you,' said Ainsley. 'I'll do my level best to find Mr

Piper and use my full resources. But, if you want the truth, I was delighted when that arrogant bastard disappeared. I hope that he never comes back.'

The visit to Ambleside had given Colbeck much food for thought and he was glad that he had met the parents of the missing man. Even though he was visibly grieving, Rodney Piper insisted on driving his visitor to the railway station. As the dog cart rumbled along, Piper was philosophical.

'Fate can be very cruel,' he said, 'but we must abide by it.'

'In this case, we don't yet know the full truth.'

'*I* do, Inspector. Just as we were about to get our son back, he's gone for ever. We have to fit our minds to accept that.'

'I understand.'

Colbeck was in luck. When they reached Birthwaite, the train was just drawing into the station. There was a relatively short wait before he could take his seat and reflect on what he'd learnt in the course of his trip. Piper and his wife struck him as devout people who set moral standards so high that even the most dutiful son would struggle to live up to them. Their house was more like a small church than a place of habitation, and there was a pervading air of purity and self-denial. While the parents had answered all of his questions, there had been one awkward moment.

Colbeck had asked them if he might see their son's bedroom because it might give him some insight into the latter's character. Both of them were profoundly shocked. It was as if he'd wanted to lift the lid of Alexander Piper's coffin and peer in. It took Colbeck some time to placate them. When he'd left the house, he could see that Emma was still jangled. Having met Lord Culverhouse, he found it hard to believe that she was his sister. What sort of childhood did they have together? Why had it sent them off in opposite directions? Culverhouse had embraced all the pleasures of life while she had spurned them, drawing succour instead from a more puritanical existence. It was her misfortune to give birth to a child who shared his uncle's delights rather than those of his mother.

As the train headed back, Colbeck kept one eye on the passing landscape. Halfway back to Kendal, he caught sight of a search party steadily moving forward and searching intently. High above them on a peak was a tiny figure in black, staring down at the people below. Colbeck only had time to catch the merest glimpse of him because, like a startled animal, the man suddenly turned tail and ran swiftly away.

CHAPTER SEVEN

After his abrasive meeting with the first of the people named as possible suspects, Leeming approached the second one with more care. As it turned out, his fears were groundless. Cecil Dymock had been a testy doctor, insulted by the very idea that he should be questioned about the disappearance of Alexander Piper. Norman Tiller was altogether different. As soon as Leeming went into the bookshop, he was given a cordial welcome and a broad grin. Tiller was a slim, hirsute, stooping man of medium height and indeterminate age. Though he looked as if he was in his fifties, his voice and manner suggested he was much younger. His coat was shabby and his trousers baggy but he had a cheerful unconcern for his appearance.

Extending a palm, he gave Leeming a firm handshake.

'Norman Tiller,' he said. 'Most people call me Norm.'

'I'm Victor Leeming.'

'Pleased to meet you, sir – we don't get many visitors at

this time of year. Will you be staying in Kendal for long?'

'That depends.'

'On what, may I ask?'

'On what we manage to uncover,' said Leeming. 'I didn't give you my title, Norm. It's *Sergeant* Victor Leeming. I'm a detective from London, helping in the search for a man who went missing.'

'Alex Piper.'

'You knew him, I believe.'

'Everyone knew Alex. He made sure of that.'

Leeming looked around. The shop was small, cluttered and smelt faintly of damp. With no source of heat, it was also very cold. The walls were covered by well-stocked bookshelves and, even on a chilly day, there were some tattered volumes for sale on a rickety table standing outside the shop window. Tiller looked thoroughly at home in his surroundings. Literature was his natural habitat. Leeming appraised him.

'I was told that you were a poet,' he said.

'That's right, Sergeant. The Lake District is the nearest thing to the Garden of Eden. It cries out to be celebrated in verse. Do you like poetry?'

'I like reading nursery rhymes to my children.'

'And which poets do you read for your own pleasure?'

'Oh, I never get time to read anything,' said Leeming, 'unless it's a statement I've taken from a witness. I've already collected a few of those since I've been here.'

'The police need all the help they can get. That's why they sent for you, I daresay.'

'Actually, we're here at the behest of Lord Culverhouse.'

'Oh, of course – Alex was his nephew.'

Leeming wondered if he'd come to the wrong place. There was absolutely no trace of rancour in Tiller's voice when Piper's name was mentioned. The bookseller was a gentle soul, patently at ease with the world and living in what he felt was a paradise. The sergeant began to probe.

'Did Mr Piper ever come in here?'

'You're talking about Alex, I assume?'

'Yes, I am.'

'Then the answer is that he didn't. He's not the reading type. Alex is a man of action. His father, by contrast, did pop in here from time to time. The archdeacon would browse for hours and always bought something of an ecclesiastical nature.'

'What about Mr Hedley? Do you know him?'

'Having lived here all my life, I know most people in the town. Geoffrey Hedley has come in here in the past in search of books pertaining to the law. He's a charming fellow and always asks after my poetry.'

'If you run this shop, when do you find the time to write?'

'Whenever inspiration strikes,' replied Tiller. 'Sometimes, that's in the middle of the night. I've got up at all hours.'

'Doesn't your wife complain?'

'Luckily, she's a heavy sleeper.'

Leeming liked him and wished that he could talk with Tiller at length, but he was there to gather information. He also wanted to know why Hedley had singled this apparently innocuous man out as a potential suspect with regard to the disappearance of the lawyer's close friend.

'What did you think when you heard the news?' he asked.

'About Alex, you mean?' Leeming nodded. 'Well, my thoughts were with his family. I know that he fell out with his parents because his father mentioned it, so they will be doubly distressed – shocked to have lost a son and desperately sad that they had no time to settle their differences with him beforehand. You can imagine how tortured they must be.'

'You talk as if the young Mr Piper has gone for good.'

'I doubt if we'll see him alive again.'

'Why do you think that?'

'It's what everybody is saying.'

'Don't you have an opinion of your own?'

Tiller was blunt. 'Yes – I think he's dead.'

'Do you think he could have died by natural means?'

'It's unlikely, Sergeant. He was one of the fittest people you could ever meet.'

'Suppose he did come back alive?' asked Leeming. 'How would you feel about that?'

'I'd be grateful, for his parents' sake. Then, of course, there's Miss Haslam. I can't bear to think of her suffering,' he said, face crumpling. 'She's such an enchanting young lady and highly educated as well. Miss Haslam has been kind enough to buy the slim volume of verse that I once had published. She even asked me to sign it.'

'Inspector Colbeck, who is here with me, is hoping to speak with the lady later today.'

'She's bound to be in a delicate state.'

'He'll be very considerate.'

'That's good to hear.' Tiller eyed him shrewdly. 'And what's *your* view of this situation? Do you think that you'll ever find Alex?'

'It won't be for want of trying. Search parties are out there right now.'

'But are they looking in the right place?'

'Of course they are.'

'I wonder.'

Tiller crossed to a bookshelf and ran his finger along the titles. Finding the one he wanted, he took it out and blew off the dust. He then offered it to Leeming, who held up his hands as if fending off an attack.

'I don't want to buy a book.'

'I'm not *selling* it to you, Sergeant. It's a loan.'

'I told you – I never have time to read.'

'Oh, you'll find time for *this* book, I promise you. Read the first chapter just to humour me, and I promise you that you'll feel compelled to press on until you get to the last page.'

'Why?' said Leeming, taking it from him and opening it. 'What is it about?'

'It's about the *real* Cumberland, the one you can't see with the naked eye. Strange and frightening things have happened here in the past. Until you know what they are,' warned Tiller, 'you'll never be able to understand the true nature of this county.'

* * *

Entering the house, Colbeck felt as if he'd interrupted a funeral. Melissa Haslam's father was helping in the search, but her mother was there and she was pleased to meet the inspector. While she promised to do her best, she told him that she might not be able to persuade her daughter to come down from her room because Melissa just wanted to be left alone. Colbeck said that he was content to wait for hours if necessary, and he mentioned that he'd just been to see Piper's parents. That made Bridget Haslam's eyes light up with interest.

Settling down alone in the drawing room, Colbeck was pleasantly surprised when Bridget returned within minutes with her daughter in tow. Melissa was understandably tense and nervous. After introductions had taken place, she sat beside her mother on the sofa. Colbeck lowered himself into the armchair opposite them.

The two women looked at him wistfully, as if he represented the last possible hope of ever finding the missing man.

'I'm sorry to disturb you, Miss Haslam,' he said. 'I fully understand why you wish to be alone, but I wanted to offer you at least a modicum of reassurance.'

'There's good news?' she asked, brightening.

'Not exactly, I fear. By the same token, there's not bad news either. The search continues. Ignore the passage of time. We were once involved in the search for a child of ten who'd been swept overboard from his parents' boat. They blamed themselves for his death,' he explained, 'but I refused to accept that there was no point in an extensive search. A week later, we found him. He'd been washed up onto a tiny island and kept himself alive by drinking water and eating berries. Now,' he continued, 'I know that this case is very different, but the same principle applies. We *never* walk away until we've unearthed the full facts.'

'That's very comforting,' said Bridget.

'May I ask your daughter how she first met Mr Piper?'

'It was in church, actually,' replied Melissa with a wan smile. 'Alex was in the row behind me and I heard him singing. He had the most glorious voice.'

'His parents told me about it.'

'How are they, Inspector?'

'They are . . . still dazed by the turn of events,' he said, tactfully. 'Knowing that I'd be coming here, they sent their regards to you and your parents.'

'That's kind,' murmured Bridget.

'Did your fiancé ever talk about why he left home?' asked Colbeck, turning to Melissa.

'He just wanted his independence, Inspector.'

'I see.'

'Alex loved his parents, but they wouldn't let him lead the kind of life he wanted. He agonised over it for months. In the end,' said Melissa, 'he chose to move to Kendal. I suppose that I was the main beneficiary of that decision.'

'How long have you known him?'

'It must be four or five months. And yes, I know that it seems too short a time in which to make a decision that would affect the whole of my life. The truth is that, when I met Alex, I felt that I'd known him for ages.'

'He had that effect on me as well,' agreed Bridget, sadly. 'He was a remarkable young man – sensible, mature and trustworthy.'

Colbeck was startled. They were not words he'd expected to hear. Even his best friend had admitted that Piper had faults. Had Melissa's beauty brought about a complete change in him? It seemed apparent to Colbeck that it was no accident that Piper had happened to be in the church pew immediately behind her. It was a deliberate move. The hymns that he sung were a means of attracting her and making her acquaintance. He remembered something that Lord Culverhouse had told him.

'I believe that you and Mr Piper enjoyed walking?' he said.

'We loved to be out on a fine day,' she confirmed.

'And I used to go with them at first,' Bridget chimed in, 'but it was soon clear that Melissa needed no chaperone. She trusted him. Alex loved and respected her.'

'He was a true gentleman, Inspector.'

'That's why we had no qualms on that account.'

'Let's move on to the Phantom Special, shall we?' he said. 'You refused to go on the excursion, didn't you?'

Melissa twitched. 'I was too frightened.'

'Did you mind your fiancé going without you?'

'He couldn't back out, Inspector. It had been Geoffrey Hedley's idea at the start, but Alex got excited at the prospect. He wanted to prove that those ghoulish tales about the haunted wood were pure drivel.'

'Did you agree with him?'

'I did at the time.'

'And now?'

'I've come to think otherwise. There *is* some malign spirit out there and Alex paid for taunting it.'

'What's your opinion, Inspector?' asked Bridget.

'A malign spirit was certainly involved,' he said, 'but he was in human form. My interim judgement is that someone was anxious to stop Mr Piper from getting to his destination. Who that person might be, I don't know. But I give you my solemn word that I'll track down the villain and find out exactly what happened that night.'

'Is there *any* chance Alex may still be alive?' bleated Melissa.

'Anything is possible, Miss Haslam.'

'Just hearing you say that is a tonic,' said Bridget.

'I can't offer any guarantees, mind you.'

'We don't expect you to do so.'

'But I can deprive you of any fears that what happened was a supernatural event. Everything that occurred on that Hallowe'en excursion was devised by human hand.' Colbeck smiled. 'I very much look forward to arresting the person to whom the hand belongs.'

Geoffrey Hedley was returning from the search when he saw Lord Culverhouse's carriage coming towards him. He thanked Caroline Treadgold for her assistance then broke away from her. She went off briskly in the opposite direction. When the coach pulled up ten yards away, he walked obediently across to it. Culverhouse spoke to him through the window.

'Is there any good news to report?'

'I'm afraid not, my lord,' said Hedley, 'but we'll be out again this afternoon.'

'Who was that fetching young woman I saw you with?'

'Oh, that was just somebody who joined us.'

'She's uncommonly pretty, I must say. What's her name?'

'Miss Caroline Treadgold.'

'So *that's* who she is,' said the old man, pensively stroking his beard. 'I've heard lots of good things about her.'

'Really?'

'Why was she here?'

'She simply felt that she wanted to help.'

'That's a creditable impulse.' He changed the subject. 'I've just come back from the printers, by the way. As a result, there may be lots of other people who suddenly feel the same impulse.'

'Why is that, my lord?'

'I'm offering a reward.'

He held up one of the posters. The bold lettering declared that a reward would be paid to anyone who gave accurate information about the whereabouts of Alexander Piper. Hedley gasped at the amount on offer.

'That's exceedingly generous of you.'

'He's my only nephew.'

'Even so . . .'

'Someone has to open his wallet.'

'Does the inspector know about this?'

'It was his suggestion,' said Culverhouse. 'While you were

talking to that gruesome sergeant of his, we were exploring all options. Colbeck thinks that a reward of that size might smoke out the person or persons who've been responsible for whatever happened to Alex. Once they're out in the open, they can be arrested and interrogated.' He beamed. 'If all goes well, I won't have to pay a penny.'

'I hope that the plan works, my lord.'

'So do I. We must try *everything*.'

'The inspector seems to be full of initiatives.'

'That's why I demanded that he be sent here. Nobody else would have done.' He looked at the carriage in which Caroline was just departing. 'Incidentally, where did you say Miss Treadgold lived?'

'I didn't, my lord.'

'Then perhaps you'd do so now . . .'

'Yes, of course,' replied Hedley, concealing his reluctance. 'I'll be glad to give you the address.'

Leeming had never met anyone quite like Norman Tiller. The man had crafted the perfect life for himself, working contentedly among his books, writing his poetry, finding joy and satisfaction in everything around him. The sergeant was bound to compare himself with him. Days in London didn't unfold slowly and give him ample time to talk to anyone he chose. There was a hectic pace to everything that Leeming did. His was an existence that consisted of effort, danger, movement, stress, vigilance and orders he needed to obey. Tiller was clearly a popular figure. Everyone who passed the shop gave him a cheery wave. Several put their heads in to exchange a word or two. Tiller was a distinctive feature in the town whereas Leeming was nothing more than an anonymous face in a vast city, bedevilled by crime, grime and the stink of industry.

'I envy you, Mr Tiller,' he said.

'Why on earth should you do that?'

'You've got peace of mind.'

'Not when I'm in the throes of my latest poem,' said the other with a chuckle. 'It drives me mad for days until I finally get it down on paper and start to refine it. When I'm here in the shop, yes, I do enjoy a measure of serenity, but it's shattered when an idea gets hold of me. I'm a prisoner of the creative urge then.'

'I'm just a prisoner,' sighed Leeming.

'You do an important job, Sergeant. Be proud of it.'

'I just wish I lived in a place like this.'

'Then you'd probably be engaged in the wool, rope, carpet, leather or fish-hook trade. Or a strong man like you would be welcome in the marble works. Is that what you really want?' he asked. 'No, I don't think so. You were born to be a policeman so why don't you ask the questions that brought you here in the first place?'

'How well do you know Dr Dymock?'

'Oh, he's far too expensive for me. I try to keep healthy and stay well away from doctors.'

'But you must have come across him. What's he like?'

'People respect him.'

'I'm asking about his character, Norm. Is he kind, helpful and pleasant or is there a darker side to him?'

'I have heard complaints,' admitted Tiller. 'They say that he can be brisk at times, but that's usually the mark of a busy man. He's held in high esteem.'

'I found him testy.'

'Perhaps you caught him at the wrong moment.'

'I fancy that there's always a wrong moment where the doctor is concerned.'

'You must speak as you find, Sergeant.'

'I just did.' He glanced down at the book he'd been given. 'Will this tell me anything about that haunted wood?'

'It will only tell you about strange apparitions that have appeared there. That's because it was written by an antiquarian almost half a century ago,' explained Tiller. 'The real trouble in Hither Wood started much later – nine or ten years ago at most.'

'What happened?'

'Somebody went there alone at Hallowe'en and he's never been seen again. But he's been heard many a time. That's what the Phantom Special was doing,' he continued. 'It was taking those rich young folk to the wood so that they could hear the disembodied voice of a dead man.'

CHAPTER EIGHT

Caleb Andrews straddled two disparate worlds. When he was at home in the little terraced house he rented, he was surrounded by reminders of his long, arduous service on the railway system. His work clothing, his cap and his boots were kept in a large wooden box and there were lots of other souvenirs. Among them was a scrapbook containing newspaper accounts of the train robbery in which he'd been badly injured. Every article had praised him for his courage in standing up to the robbers. Reading them was a constant source of pleasure.

Whenever he visited his daughter, he entered a different section of society and dressed accordingly. Much as he enjoyed being able to savour what to him was luxury, there was always the nagging fear that he didn't really deserve it. What connected his two worlds was the painting he had of a locomotive he had once driven. It was one of Madeleine's early works and had been hung on the wall above the fireplace. Andrews still gazed at it for hours, suffused with pride at the fact that his daughter was such a gifted artist and recalling the many times he'd stood on the footplate of that particular locomotive.

He may have retired from the LNWR, but he kept in touch with all of his old workmates so that he could talk about the years when he felt that he was living a really useful life. It was the reason he often called at a pub near Euston where employees of the LNWR tended to gather for a pint of beer at the end of their shift. When he called in there not long after noon, Andrews was pleased to see two faces he recognised. One of them was Dirk Sowerby, who had been his fireman for a number of years, and the other was Vernon Passmore. They gave Andrews a warm welcome and the three of them were soon sitting at a table with a pint in their hands, gossiping happily.

Sowerby was a big-boned individual with a potato face, whereas the buck-toothed Passmore was unusually short and almost painfully thin. As usual, they soon began to tease Andrews.

'Are you still rubbing shoulders with the gentry?' asked Sowerby with a grin. 'You'll be moving up into aristocratic circles before long, I expect.'

'Why stop there?' said Passmore. 'Caleb will be invited to hobnob with royalty one day.'

'He'd need a knighthood to do that, Vernon.'

'That will come in time.'

'Laugh all you like,' said Andrews. 'As it happens, I did get close to Prince Albert on one occasion. I drove the royal train and, when I got to the end of the journey, he made a point of coming to thank me.'

'Did you invite him home for tea?' asked Passmore.

'He probably drinks nothing but champagne,' said Sowerby, 'but then I daresay Caleb keeps a good supply of that in his wine cellar.'

Andrews chortled. '*What* wine cellar?'

He didn't mind the ribbing in the least. It was all in good fun. Andrews was among friends. Sowerby and Passmore talked the same language and shared the same working experience. He felt completely at ease. The sense of belonging was wonderful.

'What were Piper's parents like?' asked Leeming.

'They fear the worst, Victor – so much so that they're already dressed in mourning attire.'

'It's far too early for that.'

'Not in their minds, alas,' said Colbeck. 'Unsurprisingly, they're racked with guilt about the estrangement with their son. The Reverend and Mrs Piper are good people in a desperate situation. It's not difficult to see why their son rejected their way of life – it verges on the monastic. Lord Culverhouse was right.'

'Was he?'

'Yes. There's more than a faint whiff of Simeon Stylites about Piper's father.'

Leeming sat up. '*Who?*'

They were in the pub where they'd agreed to meet in order to exchange information about their respective discoveries. Conscious of how much more work awaited them, they restricted themselves to a very simple meal. After gulping down a last mouthful, Leeming put the same question to him again.

'Who is Simeon Whatever-His-Name-Was?'

'He was a saint and a hermit,' explained Colbeck. 'He lived in the Middle East in the fifth century and was famous for undergoing extreme torment in a bid to please God.'

'What sort of torment?'

'I don't think it would appeal to you, Victor. For the last twenty years of his life, he lived on a pillar sixty feet high, staying up there in all weathers. People venerated him as a saint and made pilgrimages to see him.'

Leeming was aghast. 'He was at the top of a pillar in full view of those below? How did he . . . ?'

'I leave that to your imagination.'

'He must have had no privacy at all.'

'Simeon wanted his suffering to be *seen* by everyone,' said Colbeck. 'Tennyson wrote a poem about him. Anyway, the Reverend Piper is also a man who goes to extremes. No wonder his son wanted to live a more normal life.'

'It wasn't very normal, according to Sergeant Ainsley, and it certainly wasn't very Christian. But for his connections, Piper would've been arrested many times.'

'What manner of man was the sergeant?'

'He was a bit hostile at first, sir. Ainsley feels that we're treading on his toes. It's a pity. He's a good, old-fashioned policeman of the type I used to pound the beat with in uniform. We must try to win him over.'

'I agree.'

'He could be very useful to us,' said Leeming.

'Tell me about the possible suspects.'

'I've only spoken to two of them, as you know, and I really don't think we should bother with Miss Treadgold. The first person I spoke to was Cecil Dymock and got short shrift there. He was outraged at being thought of as a suspect and more or less threw me out of his surgery.'

'Actions speak louder than words.'

'Oh, he had plenty of words to say – unpleasant ones.'

'Why did Mr Hedley suggest his name in the first place?'

'It was because Piper and the doctor were locked in some kind of boundary dispute. Hedley didn't give me details.'

'That brings us to Norman Tiller.'

'You can forget about him, sir.'

'Why do you say that?'

'Mr Tiller – or Norm, as everyone calls him – is a bit like that saint you were talking about. He's given up what most people would call basic comforts and lives a very simple life in a tiny bookshop. The house itself is a limestone cottage in need of attention but Norm is too busy writing poetry to worry about mending a broken window or replacing some badly damaged brickwork. He doesn't even bother to sell books,' Leeming went on, lifting up the one he'd been given. 'He lends them.'

'How does he stay in business?'

'It's not a business to him. He just muddles along. Norm is a dreamer. He's found the secret of true happiness.'

'I thought *I'd* found that when the superintendent was on

leave.' They laughed in unison. 'What is the book he wanted you to read?'

'It's about the folklore and superstitions of Cumberland.'

'I'd appreciate a glance at it some time.'

'Have it whenever you want, sir.'

'Thank you,' said Colbeck, rubbing a thoughtful hand across his chin. 'If Tiller is so obviously not a suspect, why ever did Hedley claim that he was?'

'You'll have to ask him that.'

'I will, Victor.'

'But my visit was not entirely in vain,' said Leeming. 'I discovered something that could be of some importance. I know why that wood is supposed to be haunted.'

'My guess is that someone was once killed there.'

'That's what everyone believes. It happened nine or ten years ago when a man named Gregor Hayes went into that wood alone at Hallowe'en and never came out again.'

'How do they know?'

'They found some of his clothing scattered about.'

'That's not proof positive of a murder.'

'How else do you explain the fact that a man's voice is heard howling in that wood at every Hallowe'en? People who knew him well have sworn that it was the blacksmith.'

'What's Sergeant Ainsley's opinion?'

'I don't know, sir.'

'Try to find out. Since he's a local man, he'd have been here when it happened and might even have led the search.'

'Norm is convinced that a ghost haunts that wood.'

'Yes, but as you pointed out, Mr Tiller is a dreamer. I prefer an opinion from a policeman. They know how to keep their minds clear and grounded in reality.'

When he was told that his brother-in-law had called to see him, Lord Culverhouse asked that his visitor be sent into the study immediately. His surprise quickly turned to astonishment when he saw what Rodney Piper was wearing.

'Good gracious!' he exclaimed. 'Whatever are you doing?'

'I'm in mourning for my son.'

'His death hasn't been formally established yet. His father, of all people, ought to hold fast until the truth is finally known.'

'I already know it.' Piper tapped his head. 'In here.'

'That's an unreliable source of information, Rodney. I know that you feel you have direct contact with the Almighty, but I don't believe that he's furnished you with incontrovertible evidence of Alex's demise.'

'Please don't mock my faith.'

'It's your *lack* of faith that I deplore,' said Culverhouse, indicating a chair. 'And please sit down. You look as if you're about to fall over. Doesn't my sister feed you properly?'

'I prefer to eat sparely.'

'That's certainly not true of Emma. She always had a healthy appetite. Can I offer you a drink? Whisky, perhaps?'

'That's the brew of the devil.'

'We don't have any communion wine, I'm afraid,' said Culverhouse, mischievously. 'Forgive me, Rodney,' he added, quickly. 'Levity is hardly appropriate in a crisis like this. How is my dear sister?'

'Emma is bearing up as best she can.'

'Why didn't you bring her with you?'

'This is not a social visit. I came in search of advice.'

'That's a change. You're usually the one who likes to dispense it. It's part of your stock-in-trade.'

'There's no need to be offensive, Horace.'

'I take it back at once,' said Culverhouse, holding up both palms. 'Now please sit down before I force you into that chair.' Piper lowered himself gingerly onto the sofa. His brother-in-law sat beside him. 'That's better. I'm all ears.'

'First of all, I must thank you for having the foresight to employ Inspector Colbeck.'

'Only the best is ever good enough for me.'

'We've met him.'

'Then you must have seen that burning intelligence of his. Colbeck will sort everything out somehow.'

'We drew strength from his confident attitude.'

'I was impressed by that as well. But what's this about advice, Rodney?'

'It concerns Mr and Mrs Haslam. I'd like to speak to them. Do you think it's wise to call at the house uninvited?'

'Of course it is. It's what I've already done.'

'My position is rather different. When the betrothal took place, we were not on speaking terms with our son. It meant that our relationship with Miss Haslam's father had to be conducted by letter. Her father wrote to me,' he continued, 'and had the kindness to say how much he'd enjoyed a sermon I once preached at St Mary and St Michael Church in Cartmel. That somehow helped to break down the barriers between us.'

'What about Alex himself? When did he get in touch?'

'It was immediately before the engagement was due to be announced. Alex sent us a short note of apology for the way that he'd behaved towards us and said that his life had changed for the better in every way since he'd met Miss Haslam. He hoped that we'd soon get to meet her family.'

'And you did, Rodney, so why are you afraid to visit them again?'

'I feel I'd be trespassing on a house of mourning. Miss Haslam's loss is as great as our own. How would she feel if I went barging in there? It would only remind her of the unfortunate strife that existed between us and our son.'

'Melissa Haslam would welcome you, I'm sure. When I called there yesterday, she was able to talk to me. As for the parents, they too will be glad to see you. There is, after all, a bond between the two families. A visit from you will strengthen that bond,' said Culverhouse, 'provided you don't preach that sermon you gave in Cartmel, of course.'

'You have the most regrettable sense of humour, Horace.'

'My wife has been telling me that for almost forty years.'

'Emma did warn me about it.'

'Yet you still married her,' observed Culverhouse. 'That's clear evidence of the power of true love. You married her in spite of her disreputable brother. It was the same in the case of Melissa Haslam. Love triumphed once again. Regardless of volatility in your family, she was ready to become Alex's wife.'

'That's true.'

He put a hand on Piper's shoulder. 'And that still might happen, Rodney. Don't rule it out, because it's what I'm praying for.'

Edward Tallis was renowned for his conscientiousness. First to arrive each morning at Scotland Yard, he was invariably the last to leave, often taking work home with him. Since he lived alone, he was able to dedicate himself completely to the cases in hand. Having returned after a restorative break, Tallis was even more industrious than usual. Seated at his desk, he was so busy going through a pile of documents that he didn't hear the tentative knock on his door. When he looked up, he saw Alan Hinton standing in front of him.

'I did knock, sir,' said the newcomer. 'This came for you.'

'Thank you.'

Handing over a telegraph, Hinton turned to leave but he only got as far as the door before he was called back. Tallis waved the telegraph in the air.

'This has been sent by Inspector Colbeck,' he said. 'A full report will arrive in tomorrow's mail, but he informs me that a great deal of intelligence has already been gathered and that he is confident of success.'

'That's encouraging, sir,' said Hinton.

'I'm sure that Mrs Colbeck would like to hear what I've just told you. I believe that you know the lady.'

'Yes, I do, Superintendent.'

'Then you might pass on the news to her. She, too, will doubtless receive a missive from her husband tomorrow morning but she might appreciate advance notice, so to speak.'

Hinton was momentarily stunned. In the past, Tallis had never accepted that his officers had wives and families, and no reference was ever made to them. The fact that he'd actually mentioned Madeleine Colbeck was astounding. A loud cough from the superintendent signalled that he wanted an answer.

'I'm sure that she'll be delighted, sir,' said Hinton.

After thanking him, the young detective let himself out. An excuse to visit Madeleine was always seized upon because there was often a chance of meeting Lydia Quayle there. Hinton almost skipped along the corridor.

On his way to meet the third suspect, Leeming wished that Hedley had given him more details about the man. All that the lawyer had provided was a name and address, so the sergeant had no idea what to expect when he approached the house. Rebuffed by Cecil Dymock, he'd been warmly received by Norman Tiller who even gave him a book he felt might help the investigation. Of the two, Leeming thought the doctor a far more dangerous enemy to have than the obliging poet, but he was not discounting the latter yet. It remained to be seen how Walter Vine, the third man, would react to questioning by a detective. Leeming soon found out.

In response to the ringing of the bell, the front door of Vine's house was opened by a manservant. When he was given the visitor's name, he invited Leeming into the hall. It was as far as he got because a young man came striding down the staircase with a sense of purpose. Dark, good-looking and of medium height, he had one arm in a sling. He had clearly overheard Leeming introducing himself.

'I know why you're here,' he said, acidly, 'and I've no wish to speak to you or anyone else about Alex Piper. I was not even in the county when he disappeared, so you are wasting your time and mine by coming here.' He turned to the servant. 'Show the sergeant out, Murchison.'

The interview was over as quickly as that.

Caleb Andrews had spent well over an hour at the pub with his friends. When both Sowerby and Passmore eventually peeled off to go home, Andrews took the opportunity to walk into nearby Euston Station, a place from which he'd departed on the footplate of a locomotive on so many occasions. As he strolled around, his mind was a blizzard of happy memories, though some unhappy ones did assail him as well.

He recalled the first time he'd taken Madeleine there. She was only a young girl at the time and had hated the deafening noise, swirling smoke and abiding stink of the place. Frightened that she might be knocked over by the eddying crowds, she'd begged her father to take her home at once. It was ironic that someone who had once fled in a panic from a railway station went on to become an artist who specialised in painting locomotives or scenes related exclusively to railways. Madeleine had completely overcome her initial fear.

On his way back home, he reflected on the fact that Robert Colbeck had, to a large extent, helped her to conquer her dread of railway stations. Significantly, it was at a railway station that the couple had first met and, as their relationship became ever closer, Madeleine followed his career as he dealt primarily with major crimes committed on the railway system. There was more than one occasion when – to her father's envy – she was directly involved in the investigative process, showing a flair for the work that she didn't know she possessed.

Andrews was bound to feel a pang when he compared his experience with that of his daughter. For him, the railway had meant long hours and hard work as he gradually progressed from being a cleaner to a fireman and on to a fully fledged driver. Standing on a footplate with little protection, he was at the mercy of the weather. He remembered the fatigue in his body, the stink in his nostrils, the smoke in his lungs, the filth on his clothing and the ever-present danger of a job that had killed or maimed many other railwaymen. For all that, he'd loved the work and the people with whom he shared it.

For his daughter, however, railways were simply a source of inspiration. It did entail visits to various engine sheds and other locations, but bringing a locomotive vividly to life was something she did in the comfort of a studio where she could break off at any time for refreshment. Yet Andrews felt no bitterness. He was proud of his daughter's achievements, all the more so because she was keeping the family link with a railway system that had transformed the whole country in the course of his lifetime.

When he eventually let himself back into his house, Andrews was still wallowing in his memories. The first thing he did was to glance at Madeleine's painting above the fireplace. It never failed to excite him afresh whenever he studied it. There was something else that had special value for him. It was the award he'd received from the LNWR in recognition of the outstanding service he'd given the company. Taking out a key, he unlocked the little cupboard and lifted out the box in which it was kept, intending to hold the medal in the palm of his hand and gaze at it with pride. There was, however, a problem.

When he opened the box, it was empty.

CHAPTER NINE

Hoping to interview Caroline Treadgold, Colbeck went to her house, only to be told that she'd gone out for the afternoon with another search party. That confirmed how close her relationship with Alexander Piper must have been. Others involved in the search were predominantly male. Few women had joined in. After leaving a message that he'd return, Colbeck decided to make contact with Sergeant Ainsley with a view to weighing him up. When he called at the police station, he was invited into a room that Ainsley used as an office. It was small, cold, barely furnished and had an unfriendly feel to it. Posters were pinned to a board on one wall. The desk was littered with piles of paper.

After a formal handshake, the two men took a moment to appraise each other. Ainsley was exactly as Leeming had described him, a typical guardian of law enforcement in a small town and a man with the requisite physique for a job that entailed danger. For his part, the sergeant was unimpressed by Colbeck's gentlemanly air and striking elegance.

'You're not dressed for these parts,' he said.

'We left London in rather a hurry,' explained Colbeck. 'I'm afraid that I didn't have time to go home for climbing boots and outdoor wear.'

'The Lake District is a pretty place in spring and summer but, at this time of year, the weather can turn nasty.'

'That would hamper the search.'

'It's already hampered. They're looking for somebody they'll never find.'

'That's a rather negative attitude.'

'It's based on experience, Inspector. Ten years ago, I was involved in the search for Gregor Hayes. Just like Piper, he also vanished mysteriously.'

'Yes, I've heard the bare bones of the story.'

'We never found him. It will be the same in this case.'

'Do you see any parallels between the two victims?'

'Not really,' said Ainsley. 'Gregor was a blacksmith here in Kendal. He was a likeable man, the sort you could enjoy talking to over a pint. I suspect that Sergeant Leeming will have told you my opinion of Piper. Gregor worked for a living. Piper didn't. He was a . . . gentleman of leisure.'

'I can see that that would be grounds for resentment,' said Colbeck, 'especially as he used his position to misbehave with impunity. Did you never even get him into court?'

'Never – but, then, I was told not to try too hard.'

'Was that a case of interference by Lord Culverhouse?'

'The whisper in my ear came from Mr Hedley.'

'Let's go back to the blacksmith. What links the case of Gregor Hayes with this one?'

'That's what baffles me. The only link is Hither Wood. Gregor went into it and was never seen alive again. People believe that it's haunted by his ghost but, then,' added Ainsley, cynically, 'the ones who've dared to go there at Hallowe'en have usually been fortified by drink. That makes them very suggestible.'

'Piper scoffed at the idea of a ghost. He organised the Phantom Special to prove that there was no such thing.'

'He was just showing off.'

'Don't you have any sympathy for him?'

'I have sympathy for his parents and for his intended, of course. They must be suffering. From the moment I heard the news,' said Ainsley, 'I've tried to do what was expected of me and deployed my men accordingly, but please, I beg you, don't ask me to feel sorry for Piper.'

'You felt sorry for Gregor Hayes.'

'He was a friend. He used to shoe my horse.'

'A victim is a victim,' said Colbeck, sternly, 'whatever you may think about him or her. As such, they're entitled to sympathy. Thank you for what you've told me, Sergeant. It's been quite enlightening.' He put on his hat and adjusted the angle slightly. 'This investigation has suddenly become more complicated. It looks as if we have to solve the mystery of Gregor Hayes's disappearance before we can find out what happened to Alexander Piper.'

'I've spent ten years searching for the truth about Gregor.'

'Then I welcome your assistance. I know you see us as intruders, but we're only trying to shine a light into some very dark places. If you help us to do that,' he went on, 'everyone in this town and beyond it will reap the benefit.'

'You won't have cause for complaint about me.'

'Thank you. I'll need to see the records of the earlier case.'

'They're available whenever you wish to go through them,' said Ainsley. 'I think you'll see how thorough we've been. Before you study them, however, I suggest that I take you to the exact spot where Piper disappeared, then – while light still holds – we'll drive on to Hither Wood. You must see that.'

The first thing that Caleb Andrews did was to begin a frantic search. He went from room to room, opening every cupboard and rummaging through every drawer. When he'd first received the award, he'd been so proud of it that he slept with it under his pillow. It was then put on display on the mantelpiece until he realised that it distracted the eye from Madeleine's painting on the wall above it. The little cupboard was the obvious home for it. Tucked away in the corner of the living room, it would always be accessible and was protected by a stout lock.

His initial frenetic hunt yielded nothing. Andrews therefore made himself sit down in order to think clearly. The medal had gone. That meant someone had not only broken into his house, he'd also contrived to open the door of the cupboard and steal the medal. And yet, he reminded himself, nothing else had been taken. A burglar would surely have stolen whatever he deemed to be of value in the house. A small bronze medal with an inscription would be of no real use to him. Andrews began to wonder if he'd made a mistake. Perhaps the treasured object was still there, after all.

He'd had lapses of memory before, quite serious ones. Had he taken the medal out and forgotten to lock it away? It was more than a possibility. Moving slowly from room to room, he began a more rigorous and systematic search. The medal was irreplaceable. It simply had to be found.

Leeming returned to the bookshop. After his frosty reception at the home of Walter Vine, he went back to the one place where he'd been given a welcome. Norman Tiller looked up from the book he was reading and smiled.

'It's nice to see you again, Sergeant.'

'I needed to see a friendly face for a change.'

'You'll always find one here,' said Tiller. 'Have you had chance to look at that book I gave you?'

'Not really – I'll have a proper read this evening.'

'Good. It will open your eyes.'

'I really came back here to ask you about a man named Walter Vine. What can you tell me about him?'

'Very little, I'm afraid. He's not a customer of mine.'

'But you know who he is, I expect.'

'Yes, of course. Mr Vine is very much in the mould of Alex Piper, a young man of independent means who has a lot of energy to burn and free time to fill.'

'He refused to talk to me.'

'Why?'

'He didn't say. I was turned away from the house. It's obvious that he has no time for Mr Piper.'

'That's strange. They used to be close friends.'

'Why did they fall out?'

'I don't know, Sergeant, but, at a guess . . .'

'A woman was involved,' decided Leeming, 'and I think I know her name. It was Miss Haslam.'

'Oh, no, she'd hardly attract Walter Vine.'

'Yet she caught Piper's eye and you say that he and Vine were birds of a feather.'

'There's something I didn't tell you about Melissa Haslam. She has very watchful parents. They wouldn't let any suitor near her until they were assured that his intentions were honourable.'

'Then how did Piper slip through their guard?'

'His father is an archdeacon,' said Tiller, 'and likely to become a bishop. That means a lot to Melissa's parents. Also, their first encounter with Piper was in a church.'

'What about his reputation?'

'They were sublimely unaware of that, Sergeant. They're not the sort of people who listen to gossip. They'd consider it far too vulgar.'

'So who *was* this woman known to Piper and Vine?'

Even as he asked the question, Leeming realised that he already knew the answer. It was Caroline Treadgold.

Alan Hinton was so keen to deliver the message that he took time away from Scotland Yard to pay a short visit to the

Colbeck residence in John Islip Street. He was thrilled to see that Lydia Quayle was there, taking tea with Madeleine. Both women were pleased at his unexpected visit and he was invited to join them, but he explained that he had to return to work immediately. He passed on the message given him by Tallis.

'That's so kind of the superintendent!' said Madeleine. 'He'd never have done anything like that in the past. As far as he was concerned, I didn't really exist.'

'He's come back a different man,' said Hinton, 'though I'm not sure how long it will last.'

'Please thank him on my behalf.'

'I'll be sure to do so.' He turned to Lydia. 'And how are you, Miss Quayle?'

'I'm very well, thank you,' she replied.

'You certainly look well.'

There was a brief moment when both of them forgot that anyone else was in the room with them, and they let their affection for each other shine through. Madeleine pretended not to notice. She was happy that the friendship between the two of them had slowly burgeoned and was sorry that their visitor was unable to stay.

'Well,' said Hinton, 'I must be on my way, I fear.'

'Do call again whenever you wish,' said Madeleine.

'Thank you, but I can't promise that Superintendent Tallis will use me as a messenger boy again.'

'You don't need an excuse, Alan.'

'We're always delighted to see you,' added Lydia.

Smiling warmly, she held his gaze for a few seconds. Before

they could commune in silence for any longer, they were startled by a thunderous knocking on the front door.

'Whoever can that be?' asked Madeleine.

Opening the door of the drawing room, she looked out into the hall. Hinton and Lydia moved to stand behind her, their shoulders lightly touching. A maidservant came into the hall and opened the front door. Fearful and wild-eyed, Caleb Andrews barged straight in.

'I've been robbed!' he cried.

Colbeck had never been driven quite so fast or so furiously in a trap. Ainsley's bulk meant that his passenger was squeezed into what little remained of the seat. There was no time to admire the scenery. Colbeck's primary interest was in survival. They followed a twisting road that gave them occasional glimpses of the railway line. At one point, a train steamed past them. It was the signal for Ainsley to slow down slightly.

'If you always go at that pace,' said Colbeck, 'you must have needed horseshoes on a regular basis. That means you'd have seen a lot of Gregor Hayes.'

'I told you before. He was a friend.'

'Why did he go to Hither Wood in the first place?'

'It was because of a wager. Long before he disappeared there, there'd always been stories about the wood. Witches, demons, monsters – they'd all been reported at Hallowe'en. Few people dared to go there on that night.'

'The blacksmith did.'

'Gregor was never one to shirk a challenge. Besides,' said

Ainsley, 'there was a lot of money involved. He accepted the wager and went off to Hither Wood at Hallowe'en.'

'How could you be sure that he stuck to the terms of the wager? If he was on his own, nobody would have seen him enter the wood. Other people would've been too frightened to follow him in order to verify that he was obeying the rules.'

'Gregor Hayes was a man you could trust.'

'So you let him go off on his own?'

'That's what most of us were happy for him to do,' said Ainsley, 'but we had to satisfy the doubters. Gregor agreed. He insisted that we had observers. I was one of them and I put my men at strategic points around the wood. There's no way he could have sneaked out without one of us spotting him.'

'What, even in the dark?'

'We all had lanterns.'

'Were you armed?'

'Some of us had shotguns.'

'Why was that?'

'Three or four of my men were very superstitious,' said Ainsley. 'They thought there really were evil spirits in the wood. I refused to believe it. That's why I bet on Gregor to walk out of there unharmed.'

'But he didn't walk out at all.'

'No, he didn't. To win the wager, he had to stay in there alone for two hours. After two and a half, there was still no sign of him and we started to get worried. I ordered my men to search for him and we went into the wood.'

'Even with lanterns, you couldn't have seen all that well in the dark. How long were you in there?'

'Well past dawn,' replied Ainsley, 'and by that time, a lot of other people had joined us. There were dozens of us combing our way through Hither Wood. Gregor had definitely been there because items of his clothing were found, but there was no trace of him.'

'Did he have a family?'

'Yes – he had a wife, three children and one grandchild.'

'Who broke the news to them?'

'I did,' said Ainsley, clearly moved, 'and it was the most difficult thing I've ever done in my life. I felt so guilty at urging him to accept the wager. It's the reason I've put my heart and soul into searching for him. The family is owed that.'

He used the whip to get more speed out of the horse.

Andrews was too upset to make sense. Madeleine helped her father into the drawing room and made him sit down, urging him to get his breath back before continuing. Lydia and Hinton were sympathetic onlookers. When he felt ready to go on, the old man tried to speak more slowly and clearly. He obviously felt that he was reporting a major crime. At the end of his recital, Madeleine held his hand.

'Are you *quite* sure it isn't in the house?' she asked.

'I told you, Maddy. I searched high and low.'

'Your eyes are not what they were, Father.'

'I know you think that I put it somewhere then forgot where it was,' he said, 'and I believed that myself for a time.

I was wrong. Somebody got into my house and stole that medal.' He rounded on Hinton. 'Thank heaven you're here! You must take this case on at once. You've no idea how important that award is to me. It's one of the most valuable things I have.'

'I appreciate that, Mr Andrews,' said Hinton, 'but I have to have a case assigned to me by the superintendent. I can't just pick and choose what crimes to investigate.'

'Don't you understand how much this means to me? Ideally, I'd like my son-in-law in charge, but he's not even in London at the moment. That's why I'm appealing to you.'

'Alan is right,' said Madeleine. 'In any case, I'm not entirely certain that the medal *was* stolen. I'd need to search the house myself.'

'It does seem odd that a thief would take that one item and nothing else,' Lydia remarked. 'What do you think, Alan?'

'That's a point worth making. Thieves usually take whatever they can sell for money. Why leave everything else untouched? It doesn't make sense.'

'Report it to Scotland Yard,' demanded the old man.

'No,' said Madeleine, firmly, 'I have to go through the house myself first. It's full of nooks and crannies. I'm fairly certain that I'll find it.'

'It's not there, Maddy,' howled her father, stamping his foot. 'I just *know* it.'

'Then let me suggest this,' said Hinton, intervening gently. 'If your daughter's search *is* fruitless, I'll look into the case unofficially, so to speak.'

'That means working in your own time,' said Lydia.

He looked at her. 'I've done that before, remember.'

'You certainly have – *I* was the beneficiary.'

'I'd just like some *action*,' insisted Andrews. 'I don't feel safe in my house any more. It's a horrible feeling.'

'You can always stay here, Father,' said Madeleine. 'For the moment, we must let Alan go and hope that we don't have to take advantage of his kind offer. While *you* stay here with Lydia, I'll take a cab to the house and go through every inch of it. Meanwhile,' she continued, helping him to his feet, 'you can go upstairs to the nursery to see your granddaughter. Helen will soon cheer you up.'

When they got to the place where the fire had been seen on the line, Ainsley brought the horse to a halt. He and Colbeck got out of the trap. They were in an isolated spot with hills rising on one side and a veritable forest on the other. Anyone wishing to disappear quickly in the darkness had a choice of routes. Charred branches had been moved off the line and left some yards away. Colbeck knelt down to examine them, removing a glove to pick up some of the ash and hold it to his nose. Ainsley looked on in silence.

'Where was the train?' asked Colbeck, getting up.

'Fifty yards or more in that direction,' said the other, pointing towards Kendal. 'The driver was taking no chances. He stopped well clear of the fire.'

'So Mr Piper sprinted all the way here, did he?'

'That's what witnesses told us.'

'It's confirmed by what Mr Hedley said.' He turned to his companion. 'I wonder if I might ask you a favour?'

'What is it?'

'Hold my hat and coat.'

'But it's cold out here, Inspector.'

'I daresay I'll soon warm up.'

Taking off his hat and coat, he handed them to Ainsley and jogged the best part of sixty yards up the track, moving easily with long, fluent strides. To the sergeant's amazement, Colbeck turned around, bent down as if about to start a race then set off. Quickly gathering speed, he ran at full pelt towards him. When he got to the point where the fire had been raging, he carried on before gradually slowing down to a halt. After looking around carefully in every direction for a while, Colbeck walked back up the track. Ainsley was surprised that he wasn't breathing heavily after his exertions. When Colbeck reached him, the sergeant handed over his coat.

'What the devil were you doing?' he asked.

'I was conducting an experiment.'

CHAPTER TEN

Victor Leeming found the bookshop both intriguing and restful. He felt so relaxed that he had to remind himself that he was there in connection with an unexplained disappearance. As they chatted, Tiller pottered about, writing the titles of new books in his ledger before putting them onto the relevant shelves.

'It may look like chaos in here,' he said, cheerfully, 'but I do have a system. If any customer wants a book on a particular subject, I can put my hand on it at once.'

'What about prices?'

'Oh, I never write those on any second-hand books. I work out what someone can afford to pay and decide that way. If a customer like Geoffrey Hedley came in here, I'd tend to move the price up, whereas I'd make allowances for someone with more limited resources.'

'What sort of price would *I* have to pay?'

'A fair one.'

'I won't put you to the test. On my wage, I can't spend money on books. I've got a family to feed.'

'They must come first.' Tiller looked him up and down, then lowered his voice. 'Why don't you be honest about it, Sergeant?'

'What are you talking about?'

'We both know what brought you here.'

'I thought you'd be a useful person to talk to, that's all.'

'You were *sent* here,' said the other, flatly. 'Someone gave you my name, didn't they? I was picked out because . . . well, Alex Piper and I were not exactly friends.'

'That's the first I've heard of it.'

'Then perhaps you should know the details. As you can see,' said Tiller, indicating the shop with a wave of his hand, 'I don't ask much from life. This is enough for me – this and the freedom to write my poetry.'

'It obviously means a lot to you, Norm.'

'It means *everything*.'

'Ah,' said Leeming, 'I think I know what you're going to tell me. This is to do with Miss Haslam, isn't it?'

'In one sense, I suppose that it is, but I don't blame her.'

'What happened, Norm?'

'I'm not the only poet in this town, you see. There's a handful of us and we get together now and then to read our latest work to each other. We hire a room at the King's Arms,' said Tiller. 'It's nice and private. We enjoy our evenings there. At least, we did until a recent meeting.'

'What happened?'

'Things were getting a little rowdy in the bar. We could hear voices raised and drunken laughter. Someone then barged into our room.'

'I think I can guess who it was.'

'Alex Piper.'

'What state was he in?'

'He was swaying all over the place.'

'Couldn't you just ask him to leave?'

'I did but he was determined to say his piece first. Miss Haslam had obviously shown him that anthology I sold her, because he was holding it aloft in mockery. Then,' said Tiller, teeth clenched, 'he had the gall to read from the book. It was a tender love poem and he ridiculed it.'

'Didn't someone try to stop him?'

'Hedley did his best to drag him away, but he was shrugged off. Piper wanted to humiliate me and he succeeded.'

'That must have upset you.'

'It was agonising.'

'How did you feel?'

For a split second, Tiller's eyes blazed. 'I felt as if I could kill him,' he snarled. He held up both hands in apology. 'That was wrong of me, I know, but my poems are more precious to me than anything I own. To have one of them derided in front of my friends was unbearable.'

'Did you tell Miss Haslam what happened?'

'I couldn't.'

'She was engaged to marry that man. I think she has the right to know what sort of person he really was.'

'It was not my place to shatter her dreams.'

'I wonder why Mr Hedley made no mention of this.'

'Like me,' said Tiller with a shrug, 'he probably thinks it best forgotten.'

'But you *haven't* forgotten it, have you?'

The reply came in the form of a low animal growl.

'No, Sergeant. I haven't.'

Before she went to the house, Madeleine called at the home of the person who came in to clean her father's house and do anything else that was needful. Feeling that she was under suspicion, Rene Garrity, a motherly, middle-aged woman, pointed out that she had no key to the cupboard where the medal was kept and no desire to own such a thing. When Madeleine had soothed her ruffled feathers, the cleaner said that Andrews was always forgetting things or putting them back in the wrong places.

It was a salutary warning. Madeleine went straight on to her father's house and let herself in with the key. She found several items that needed to be restored to their original places. Evidently, her father was more forgetful than she'd realised. After taking a deep breath, she began her search.

Though it was not large, Hither Wood was dense. Trees were closely packed together, and undergrowth filled the remaining few gaps. It was difficult to walk along any of its narrow paths without making contact with trailing branches or spiky shrubs. Light was also restricted by the canopy. As Colbeck followed his guide, he could see the problems posed by the wood. Reaching the middle, they were suddenly in an open area of tufted grass. They stopped to survey it.

'This is where it happened,' said Ainsley. 'Gregor had brought a couple of blankets to keep himself warm.'

'Were they still here?'

'Yes, and so were the clothes he'd taken off.'

'Why should he do that in cold weather?'

'I don't know, Inspector.'

'Isn't it more likely that someone else took them off him?'

'But there was nobody else here,' argued Ainsley. 'As I told you, we looked *everywhere*.'

'How many trees did you climb?'

'Well . . .'

'None at all, I'll warrant. Somebody high up in those branches would be invisible in the day, not to mention the night. You only looked down here, didn't you?'

'Yes, but we covered every inch.'

'You might have been looking in the wrong direction.'

'I don't agree,' said Ainsley, smarting at the rebuke. 'Even if someone *was* out of sight up there, that doesn't explain what happened to Gregor. If he'd been killed, we'd have seen the body down here on the ground.'

'Not if he was hidden away,' said Colbeck, looking upward. 'Even a heavy man, as I presume the blacksmith was, could be hauled up into a tree by a stout rope. There might, of course, have been two assassins. That would have made the task much easier. And bear in mind that time was on their side.'

'Was it?'

'To win the bet, Mr Hayes had to stay here on his own for two hours. That gave the attackers ample time to murder, truss him up and conceal the body high among the foliage.'

Ainsley removed his hat to look upwards. Loath to accept Colbeck's theory, he offered one of his own, suggesting that a lone killer had been to the wood in advance to prepare a hiding place for himself and his victim.

'Days later,' he confided, 'we did find a trench dug out and cleverly covered. I think that's where Gregor must have been concealed.'

'It's not impossible,' said Colbeck. 'At least we agree on the involvement of a human agency. Did you have any suspects?'

'Not really,' admitted the other. 'Gregor was a popular man. Everyone liked him. That led me to believe that it might be the work of a tramp sleeping here in Hither Wood. Some of these vagrants can be vicious. He might have killed Gregor to steal any money he had.'

'If he was a vagrant, he's more likely to have stolen his clothes and blankets. They'd be more use to him than money. What could he spend it on out here? Were there any reports of itinerants in this area at the time?'

'There were, actually.'

'Did you try to round them up?'

'Of course we did. We found three in all and I put the fear of death into each one of them. But, under questioning, they were obviously innocent, so we had to let them go.'

'You should have been looking nearer home.'

Ainsley bristled. 'Don't tell me my job, Inspector.'

'It's just a friendly observation,' said Colbeck. 'I accept that the blacksmith was well liked but his very popularity might have been a source of bitterness for someone.'

'I don't believe that.'

'Will you accept that it had to be someone who knew about that wager? In other words, they had time to get here in advance and lay in ambush.'

'There were between twenty or thirty of us in all. I spoke to each and every one who'd placed a bet. None of them could possibly have sneaked off here that night,' stressed Ainsley. 'Their wives and families would have noticed them missing. Ten years of searching has taught me one thing, Inspector. The killer didn't come from Kendal.'

'Perhaps not,' said Colbeck, 'but the money needed to retain his services might well have done. Hired killers tend to be expensive. We should be looking for someone with money.'

Madeleine's search was handicapped by nostalgia. Instead of being able to work her way through the house, she kept stumbling on items that revived fond memories. There were wooden toys that her father had carved for her and a shawl that had once belonged to her mother. Most evocative of all were the letters she found in a box in the front bedroom. They'd been written to her father before the couple had married and they brought tears to her eyes.

Vowing not to be distracted again, she pressed on with renewed determination. Madeleine was more painstaking than her father had been, looking under rugs and behind curtains, going carefully through her mother's sewing bag, checking the pockets in all of her father's clothing and even climbing on a chair to look at the top of cupboards. Because she knew that he had fits of absent-mindedness, she found herself taking every item of china and cutlery out of their respective places so that she could look behind them.

It was all to no avail. She had to admit defeat.

As soon as light began to fade noticeably, Geoffrey Hedley signalled to his team that it was time to call off the search for the day. There was a long walk back to Kendal and they didn't wish to clamber over uneven terrain in the dark. Hedley fell in beside Caroline Treadgold, who was clearly struggling to keep pace with the others. He offered his arm to her.

'Would you like some support?' he asked.

'I can manage, thank you.'

'We've got some tricky inclines ahead of us, Caroline. On the way here, I saw you stumble on one of them.'

'You should have been looking for signs of Alex,' she scolded, 'not watching me.'

'I'm worried about you. If it were left to me, you'd be waiting at home until we came back. It's not just the effort you've had to put in,' he said, 'it's the possibility that we might find Alex in . . .'

'I know what you're going to say. He might be dead and even mutilated. I've prepared myself for that shock,' she told him. 'I've got stronger nerves than you might think, Geoffrey.

I just want to feel that I've done what I can to find Alex, no matter how taxing it may be on my body.'

'I admire your bravery.'

As they walked on for a few minutes, Hedley was conscious that he was gradually slowing his pace to match hers. It was obvious that Caroline needed help but she was too proud to ask for it. He was disappointed, wanting the sheer pleasure of touching a woman for whom he harboured such affection. In the circumstances, it would be inappropriate to let his feelings show. All that interested Caroline was finding the man she'd loved. Hedley would need to allow a long time to elapse before he could begin to approach her. For the moment, he had to content himself with walking beside her.

'What about Inspector Colbeck?' she asked, breaking the silence. 'Why aren't he and the sergeant out here with us?'

'They have their own methods of searching, Caroline.'

'Do you trust them?'

'Lord Culverhouse certainly does.'

'I'm asking *you*.'

'I trust them to do their very best,' he said, 'but I must admit that I am wavering slightly. There's no doubting the inspector's intelligence and record of success. This case, however, is unique. It means that he's just flailing around. Well, that's how it appears, anyway.' He tried to sound more confident. 'Colbeck has brought qualities to the search that the rest of us lack. My judgement may well be unfair on him. It's possible that he will, after all, be able to justify his reputation.'

* * *

The return journey was made at a more sedate pace. Since he knew the road well, Ainsley was not worried about the way that shadows were lengthening as light was being chased out of the sky. The sergeant was silent and somnolent. Colbeck had the feeling that his companion was sulking at the implied criticism of the way that he'd organised the search of Hither Wood. The visit there had been instructive and Colbeck was glad that they'd gone. Ainsley, on the other hand, seemed to be regretting the decision to take him there.

It was when they reached the place where the fire had been lit on the railway line that the sergeant found his voice.

'Do you need to stop here again?' he asked.

'I don't think so.'

'What did you discover earlier on?'

'I discovered that I'm not quite as young as I used to be,' confessed Colbeck with a grin. 'There was a time when I could run like the wind.'

'You looked fast enough to me.'

'Yes, but I took longer to recover from the effort. That's why I stayed further down the track. As I looked around, I was giving myself time to get my breath back.'

'You didn't tell me what your experiment was.'

'No, I didn't.'

'Why was that?'

'I hadn't evaluated the result at that point.'

'Have you done so now?'

'I think so,' said Colbeck. 'I believe that the person who started that fire did so to entice Mr Piper. Everyone else

123

on that train was consumed with fear, including the driver and the fireman. Put yourself in their position. They're on a locomotive in the pitch-dark and they suddenly see a huge blaze ahead of them. It's no wonder they brought the train to a halt.'

'Hedley told me that Piper was enraged because he thought someone was trying to wreck the excursion.'

'I think that he was provoked on purpose. Piper did exactly what *I* did earlier. He ran at top speed towards the fire and, when he got there, he was travelling at such velocity that he could have gone through the flames unharmed.'

'And then what?'

'He was completely vulnerable.'

'I don't follow, Inspector.'

'Then you should have tried sprinting that distance yourself. You build up such momentum that it's difficult to stop. I found that out, yet I was completely sober. Piper, however, was inebriated. A headlong dash over sixty yards,' said Colbeck, 'would have left him shaky and exhausted. He'd be no match for the person or persons waiting for him.'

'You've forgotten something – Mr Hedley and others went after him.'

'Yes, but they were far too slow. By the time they got to the other side of that blaze, Piper had been hustled into those trees. That's why the spot was chosen. It offered almost instant escape for whoever was waiting for him.'

'It's an interesting theory,' conceded Ainsley, 'but I'm not entirely persuaded, and you haven't answered the big question.'

'What's that?'

'Is Piper alive or dead?'

'When I find out,' said Colbeck, 'I'll let you know.'

A cab took Madeleine back home and she let herself into the house. Lydia was alone in the drawing room. She rose to her feet at once.

'You were gone a long time, Madeleine.'

'There was a lot to search.'

'I should have come with you. Two pairs of eyes are better than one.'

'You wouldn't have known where to look. What took the time was putting things back in their rightful places. Living on his own, Father has become very careless.'

'I thought that a cleaner came in regularly?'

'Yes, that's Mrs Garrity. I spoke to her before I even went into the house. She confirmed what I feared. Father is becoming absent-minded. He's losing things all the time because he can't remember where he put them.'

'Oh dear!'

'We suggested that he move in with us, but he's wedded to the idea of independence. Also, he's afraid that he'd be a burden if he came here. That's just not true.'

'He could spend more time with Helen. He obviously dotes on her, and she, in turn, clearly loves her grandfather. I've heard her chortling ever since he went up to see her and he's been laughing merrily.'

'He won't laugh when I tell him that I couldn't find his

medal,' said Madeleine. 'It's nowhere in the house.'

'That's going to distress him.'

Hearing footsteps in the hall, they turned to the door. It opened to reveal Andrews with a look of hope in his eyes.

'I thought I heard the front door open,' he said. 'Why didn't you come straight up to see me, Maddy? You know how desperate I was for news.'

'The tidings are not good, I'm afraid.'

His face fell. 'It's not there?'

'Robert couldn't have searched the house any more thoroughly. I even climbed up into the attic and that was an achievement in this dress.'

'Someone stole it,' he said, vengefully.

'We don't know that, Father.'

'How else could it leave the house?'

'Perhaps you inadvertently took it out yourself, Mr Andrews,' said Lydia. 'You may have wanted to show it to friends, perhaps, or even taken it to be valued.'

'I'd have remembered.'

'Would you?' asked Madeleine. 'Mrs Garrity said that you get very confused at times.'

'She had no right to criticise me,' he said, angrily.

'She was simply being honest.'

'So it's *my* fault now, is it? I'm a stupid, forgetful, scatterbrained old man who can't be trusted on his own. What else did Mrs Garrity tell you? Did she think I was in danger of walking out of the house one day without any trousers on?' The two women laughed. 'It's no joke,' he cried. 'I've lost

126

something that reminds me of my long service on the railway. It's my badge of honour and I want it back.'

'Of course,' said Madeleine, guiding him to the sofa with an arm around his shoulders. 'And we will ask Alan Hinton to look into it. In fact,' she continued, turning to Lydia, 'that might be something *you* could do. You know where Alan lives.'

'I'll send him a note this very evening.'

'Thank you,' said Andrews. 'I'm glad that someone believes me at last. We're dealing with a serious crime.'

The more he got to know Kendal, the more Leeming came to like the town. It compared favourably with London. The air was cleaner, the people were friendlier and there was none of the foul stink of the capital. The town had its share of factories and workshops, but the industrial clamour was almost negligible when set against London's continuous uproar. In his opinion, Kendal was a far healthier place to bring up his children, though they might struggle to understand some of the richer local accents. On balance, his sons might be better off where they were. With all its faults, London was, in Leeming's opinion, still the greatest city in the world.

As soon as he'd seen it, he'd liked the look of the King's Arms and was disappointed they were not staying there. Having an excuse to visit it, he quickly took advantage of it. A barmaid was cleaning the tables when he entered. Leeming asked for the landlord and she scuttled off to find him. Hugh Penrose soon appeared though it was difficult to see him at first. The landlord was of such diminutive stature that he stood less than a foot above the bar counter. Stepping onto a wooden box, he was suddenly closer to Leeming's height. Penrose had an unusually deep and melodious voice.

'I'm Hugh Penrose,' he said, hand on his chest. 'You wish to speak to me, sir?'

'Yes,' replied the other. 'I'm Victor Leeming, a detective from Scotland Yard sent to investigate the strange event at Hallowe'en.'

'I know who you are, Sergeant. You and the inspector are staying at the Riverside Hotel. You'd be far better off here. We offer the best food in Kendal.'

'I'll take your word for it, sir. I'm really here to ask you about a group of poets who meet occasionally in a private room.'

'They're an odd collection, I must say, but business is business and they're always well behaved. The group is run by a man named Norman Tiller.'

'It's because of him that I'm here.'

'Oh, I see.'

'He told me that there was a spot of trouble here at their last meeting. Somebody forced his way in.'

'That would be Mr Piper, the gentleman who's missing.'

'Were you on duty that evening?'

'There's rarely a time when I'm *not* on duty, Sergeant. It's the curse of the hotel trade. There's never any time to rest.'

'It's the same in the police force. Holidays are something that other people have. Let's go back to Mr Tiller. He seems such a nice, quiet sort of man.'

'He's the salt of the earth.'

'What about Mr Piper?'

'He's different,' said Penrose, glancing round to make sure that he wasn't overheard. 'He was a born troublemaker, the kind of man who can't hold his drink and who has this urge to cause trouble for the sheer sake of it.'

'That's what he did when the poets were last here.'

'He did. It was very upsetting. The problem is that you can't just throw someone like Alex Piper out on his ear. He has connections. You have to handle him delicately.'

'What exactly happened that night, Mr Penrose?'

The landlord stepped off his box and all but disappeared.

'You'd better come into the back room, Sergeant.'

CHAPTER ELEVEN

Colbeck arrived back at the police station with Sergeant Ainsley to find Geoffrey Hedley there. He'd come to deliver his report on the day's search. Both men listened to it with interest, though neither was surprised that no clues had been found as to the whereabouts of the missing man. Ainsley took notes throughout and thanked Hedley for his diligence. When it was Colbeck's turn to question him, he suggested that the pair of them adjourned to the Riverside Hotel. Wearied from hours of trudging the hills, Hedley was only too glad to agree.

They sat either side of a table in the lounge. After giving him time to relax, Colbeck started to gather information from the lawyer.

'You told us that Miss Treadgold joined you today.'

'That's true, Inspector.'

'Were you expecting her to do so?'

'Not at all,' replied Hedley. 'Caroline . . . Miss Treadgold, that is, has no love of traipsing around the countryside. She's a lady who values the comforts of life.'

'What made her sacrifice them today?'

'She was anxious to help.'

'That was testimony to the affection she felt for Mr Piper, I believe,' said Colbeck.

'It was, indeed.'

'I'm hoping to see the lady myself very shortly but, before I do that, there's something that troubles me. Why did you tell Sergeant Leeming that Miss Treadgold might be considered as a possible suspect in whatever scheme was devised to capture – or even kill – Mr Piper? Was it a serious suggestion?'

'No – I don't believe she was involved in any way.'

'Then why did you mislead my colleague?'

'I didn't do that,' said Hedley. 'I simply felt that I should put her name forward before anyone else did. Miss Treadgold is very beautiful, and she arouses intense envy in some quarters. It's only a matter of time before someone points an accusing finger at her.'

'On what grounds would they do that?'

'Her relationship with Alex was not the private matter it should have been. He couldn't resist waving her like a flag he'd captured from the enemy. Many people – I was one of them – felt that it might well end in marriage one day.'

'Why didn't it?'

'He met Melissa Haslam and fell in love.'

'Did he think her more acceptable to his parents?'

'That never entered his head. He simply believed that she

131

was the right person for him. Lord Culverhouse agreed. Miss Treadgold was rather cruelly dismissed. Everyone knew that she wouldn't surrender him without going into battle.'

'These military metaphors are very colourful,' said Colbeck, 'but they hardly represent reality. I've met Miss Haslam and a less combative creature would be hard to find. She wouldn't take up arms against anyone.'

'Caroline Treadgold would,' said Hedley. 'I admire her forthrightness, but others would probably interpret it as a form of aggression. They see her as a jilted lover with an axe to grind. There'll be loud whispers about her determination to get even with Alex.'

'Thanks to your advice, I'll ignore them.'

'You must make your own estimation of her.'

'Oh, I intend to, Mr Hedley. But I was curious to know why she crept into your list of suspects. Dr Dymock, Mr Tiller and Mr Vine sound as if they're more likely culprits.'

'Each of them fell out with Alex.'

'With respect to your friend,' said Colbeck, raising an eyebrow, 'he seems to have fallen out with half the town. I can see why he never considered a career as a diplomat.'

'His father wanted him to take holy orders,' said Hedley with a wry smile. 'The last thing the church needed was a renegade priest.'

'Thank you for your honesty, sir. It's refreshing. As for the three men you named, I await Sergeant Leeming's report on them. I, as you will imagine, have not been idle. I spent much of the afternoon in the company of Sergeant Ainsley.'

He went on to give Hedley an edited version of what had happened at the two places where he and the sergeant had stopped. Colbeck said that he felt much more able to tackle the case now that he had a clearer idea of its geography. He ended with a question for his listener.

'When we reached that clearing in Hither Wood,' he said, 'there were the remains of a recent fire in the middle of it. That surprised me. In the wake of the events at Hallowe'en, I thought everyone would be too fearful to go anywhere near the place, let alone light a fire there.'

'It was something that we'd planned to do ourselves,' explained Hedley. 'I laid that fire on the eve of the excursion on the Phantom Special. I thought it would be something to crouch around on a cold night and that we'd have a degree of light from it. But I'm amazed that someone actually *lit* the fire,' he added. 'Nobody had any reason to go into Hither Wood.'

'One thought occurred to me.'

'What was that?'

'Guy Fawkes Night is almost upon us. Bonfires will be lit everywhere to mark the death of an attempt at regicide. Could something similar have happened in the wood?' asked Colbeck, keen to see his reaction. 'Was that fire also in honour of an execution?'

Having dismissed her father's fears as a product of increasing forgetfulness on his part, Madeleine had come to share them. The medal must have been stolen. She immediately absolved Mrs Garrity of any blame. The cleaner was honest, hard-working and very reliable. An intruder must somehow have got into the house and she could therefore understand her father's disquiet.

'I'm sorry, Maddy,' he said. 'When I was a younger man, I'd have taken on any burglars. I was as hard as iron in those days. But I have to be more careful now.'

'Yes, of course.'

'I just hate the feeling that the house has been *watched*.'

'It's being watched now,' she said. 'While I was there, I took the trouble to speak to Mr and Mrs Kingston because they live directly opposite. Now that Mr Kingston is on crutches, he rarely goes out. His wife told me that he spends most of the day sitting by the window. I asked him to keep a special eye on your house.'

'Thanks for doing that. I'll make a point of speaking to Alf Kingston myself.'

'You've done *him* enough favours over the years. It's high time that he did one for you. However,' she went on, handing him the notebook and pencil she'd just retrieved from Colbeck's office, 'let's do some initial detective work.'

They were seated alone in the drawing room. Lydia had left them and promised to make contact with Alan Hinton, but Madeleine was not going to wait for him.

'Write down the answers,' she instructed. 'I'm just going to do what Robert would do, were he here.'

He lifted the pencil. 'I'm ready, Maddy.'

'When did you last see your medal?'

'Oh, it was some time ago, I think . . .'

'Was it weeks, months, longer than that?'

'It was a month or more, I reckon.'

'Put that down as your answer.' He scribbled away. 'Now then, *why* did you take it out?'

'It needs a polish from time to time, Maddy.'

She was amused. 'It would hardly get tarnished when it was kept in a box with a velvet interior.'

'I have a routine.'

'Write that down as well.' She waited until he'd finished. 'Now, is there any *other* reason that would make you unlock that cupboard and get the medal out?'

'Well, I have taken it out from time to time.'

'Why is that?'

'They've asked to see it.'

'Who have?'

'I've shown it to friends.'

'How many of them?'

He looked guilty. 'A lot.'

Leeming felt that his visit to the King's Arms had been rewarding. He'd tasted the beer, learnt a great deal about Norman Tiller and met the smallest landlord in the county, if not in the whole of England. Penrose had turned out to be a mine of information about Kendal and its inhabitants. Since it was now evening, the sergeant made his way back to the Riverside Hotel. He was astounded to learn that Walter Vine was waiting for him in the lounge. His arm still in a sling, the man was seated in a high-backed leather chair.

'Ah, there you are!' he said as if he was talking to a naughty dog that had just come into the house with muddy paws. 'Sit down a moment.'

'If you wish,' said Leeming, obeying the command.

'I've simply come to explain something.'

'You did that at our last meeting, sir.'

'That was regrettable. When I realised why you were there, I was angry that you'd dare to link my name to the disappearance of Alex Piper. What I told you was correct. I was over a hundred miles away at the time. A dozen witnesses would vouch for me.'

'There's no need for them to do that, Mr Vine. I accept your word without question.'

'Oh, I see,' said the other, taken aback. 'So my innocence is already recognised, is it?'

'Nobody is accusing you, sir.'

'Somebody must have given you my name. It was that creepy lawyer, Hedley, I daresay. He must have told you that Piper and I were sworn enemies.'

'As a matter of fact, he didn't. That information came from another source that I'm not prepared to disclose. You and Mr Piper were friends, I gather.'

'That was a long time ago.'

'Can't you even spare an iota of sympathy for him?'

'No, I can't.'

'But you'd like to know what fate befell him, surely?'

'I just want to know if he's dead.'

136

Leeming sat back and appraised him, conscious that he was probably looking at another version of Piper. There was a difference, however. Where the latter had, allegedly, been pulsing with life, Vine seemed cold and subdued. Leeming looked at the sling and saw the dressing on the arm beneath it. It was not the kind of wound that he'd be likely to collect from a mere fall. That it was still giving him pain was obvious. Vine kept wincing.

'Are you a fencing man, sir?' asked Leeming.

'I was in my younger days.'

'What about shooting?'

'You're being infernally intrusive,' snapped the other. 'I've done what I needed to do, so please tell Inspector Colbeck that neither he nor you has a need to pester me any further.' With an effort, he swung himself up on his feet, touching his wounded arm gingerly as he did so. 'Good day to you, Sergeant.'

'Goodbye, sir.'

But he was already talking to Vine's back as the man headed for the door with long strides. Though it had been a brief and disagreeable encounter, it had told Leeming something that might have a bearing on the case. Walter Vine and, reportedly, Alexander Piper were both handsome, debonair young bachelors drawn together by common interests. When they shared an interest in a particular woman, however, the friendship turned into a feud. Leeming was now certain that the person who'd split them apart was Caroline Treadgold.

* * *

Arriving once more at the Treadgold residence, Colbeck had to wait some time before he could speak to Caroline because she was resting after the effort of taking part in the search. He contented himself with learning more about her background. She came from a moneyed family and her only sibling was a younger sister. Her parents were of one mind, supportive, anxious and slightly embarrassed to have such an outspoken daughter. While they drew back from direct criticism of Piper, it was evident that they felt he'd let their daughter down badly.

When she finally appeared, Colbeck saw how much trouble she must have taken with her appearance and he was duly impressed with the result. Caroline was no longer the weary, tousle-haired, wind-blown young woman who'd returned home earlier. She exuded energy. He noticed immediately how much more worldly she was than Melissa Haslam could ever be. Her parents offered to stay but she told them, politely yet firmly, that it was unnecessary. Caroline waited until they'd gone before she spoke to her visitor.

'Geoffrey Hedley said that you wished to speak to me, so let me make one thing clear at the outset. I was not,' she went on, meeting his gaze confidently, 'involved in any way with Alex's disappearance.'

'Why should you imagine that I believed you were?'

'Other people do, Inspector. They view me as a scarlet woman. You've probably heard some of them say so.'

'I didn't come to Kendal to pick up idle tittle-tattle.'

'That's reassuring to hear.'

'Since you were close to Mr Piper, I simply felt that you might tell me things about him that nobody else could.'

'It's more than likely.'

'But my first question is this – why didn't you travel on the Phantom Special?'

'I wasn't invited to do so.'

'You strike me as the kind of person who'd be undeterred by the absence of an invitation. Had you really wished to go, you'd have been on that train.'

She smiled. 'You're very perceptive, Inspector.'

'So what held you back? I can't believe that it was out of consideration for Miss Haslam that you decided to stay away from the excursion.'

'It certainly wasn't,' said Caroline. 'I have nothing against Miss Haslam as a person. She has many fine qualities. But the fact remains that she deprived me of the man I love.'

'Your anger – if that's what it was – should have been directed at him rather than at her.'

'I agree. And it was, believe me.'

'Mr Hedley told me that, in effect, you were set on winning him back.'

She thrust out her chin. 'I'm not ashamed of that.'

'That depends on what lengths you were prepared to go.'

'Are you married, Inspector?'

'Yes, I am, and eternally grateful to be so.'

'A man as striking and urbane as you must have made many hearts flutter at one time. Your wife must have emerged triumphant out of a prolonged tussle with her rivals.'

'You flatter me, Miss Treadgold. There was no stampede for my attention. The lady who is now my dear wife was drawn to me because I arrested the man who'd tried to kill her father.' Caroline gasped. 'I'd have preferred our friendship to have started in a more romantic setting, but my profession tends to take me into the more hazardous areas of life.'

'Some women might find that very exciting.'

'Is that what appealed to you about Mr Piper? It's common report that his antics flirted with criminality. He seems to have believed that he was a law unto himself.'

'I did find that arousing,' she confessed. 'Everyone else in this town behaves like Geoffrey Hedley. They lead such dull, repetitive, uneventful lives. There was nothing uneventful about Alex, I can tell you.'

'And yet he was prepared to reject that life in the end. Choosing to marry Miss Haslam was an act of renunciation.'

'You're wrong. Deep down, he'd always be a rebel.'

'What do *you* think happened to him?'

She hunched her shoulders. 'I honestly don't know,' she said. 'I wish I did. I pray to God that you find out for us.'

Colbeck could see how moved she was. It was the first glimpse he'd had of what was underneath the carapace of coolness and easy charm behind which she sheltered. Caroline was as much a victim as Melissa Haslam. Invisible blood had been shed by both women.

'We know that he had enemies,' said Colbeck, 'but who were his friends – apart from Mr Hedley, that is?'

'Geoffrey was more than his friend. He worshipped Alex.'

'What about Walter Vine?'

'You *have* been busy, haven't you?' she observed.

'We try to be thorough.'

'Then you'll know that Alex and Walter fell out, and can probably guess why. Until that happened, they'd been bosom friends. In fact, Walter was much more of a natural ally for him than Geoffrey could be.'

'Yes, it's a curious friendship. Mr Hedley seems to be a beacon of respectability whereas Mr Piper was not. Was it simply a case of the attraction of opposites?'

'Alex led the kind of life that Geoffrey coveted but lacked the bravado to emulate.'

'Mr Hedley had the restraints of his profession.'

'Most of his restraints are self-imposed, Inspector.'

'That may be so,' said Colbeck, 'but, to be candid, I'm more interested in you than in him. Did you ever meet Mr Piper's parents?'

'No, I didn't.'

'Was that deliberate?'

'Not on my part,' she replied. 'I would've been happy to meet the archdeacon and his wife. Alex preferred to keep me away from them because the nature of our relationship might have scandalised them.'

'Did it scandalise *your* parents?'

'No, it didn't, because they never understood how close we were. In their eyes, Alex was an agreeable suitor for their daughter. He was always on his best behaviour in their company. That's why they were so shocked when he chose

Melissa Haslam in preference to me. They felt that it was in the nature of a betrayal.'

'I sensed their pain when I spoke to them.'

'They'll recover in time.'

'And what about *you*, Miss Treadgold? Do you believe that you will recover in time?'

Her eyelids fluttered and she was at a loss for words.

Having sent a message to him, Lydia Quayle made sure that she was back at the house before Alan Hinton called. Madeleine told her what she'd learnt from her father about the stolen medal.

'He polished it regularly?' asked Lydia.

'It was a kind of ritual.'

'Why is it so important to him?'

'It reminds him of a past he hasn't really put behind him. Father still sees friends from the LNWR. It's almost as if he's still working alongside them.'

'There's no harm in that, Madeleine.'

'I agree. I'm glad he keeps in touch with them.'

'Friends are important.'

It was a wistful comment. Lydia had often compared her situation with that of Madeleine. At least the latter still had a parent alive. Lydia's father had been murdered and her mother had died. Of the members of her family, only her younger brother was now in touch with her. The rest of them were still estranged.

The arrival of Alan Hinton prevented her from veering towards self-pity. She and Madeleine were grateful that he'd come so promptly and with such obvious enthusiasm to help. Retrieving the notebook, Madeleine read out the answers her father had given her. Though he listened carefully, Hinton's gaze never left Lydia.

'Did Mr Andrews name any of the people to whom he showed that medal?' he asked.

'Yes,' said Madeleine, 'he gave me half a dozen names but there were other people who saw it as well. My father likes to meet his friends for a drink when they come off duty. There are usually fifteen or twenty people in that pub. He's never been one to hide his light under a bushel,' she went on with a smile. 'When he first got his award, he showed it to everyone there.'

'His friends wouldn't steal from him, surely?' said Lydia.

'We don't know that they were all friends,' Hinton pointed out. 'Seeing his achievement, some of those railwaymen might have been jealous.'

'But would one of them actually break into his house?'

'It's possible.'

'That would mean someone picked the lock on the front door,' said Madeleine, 'and had the skill to open a locked cupboard. How would he know where the medal was kept?'

'Perhaps he'd seen your father take it out from the cupboard to show it to him. However,' said Hinton, 'we must not jump to any conclusions until we have more evidence. It may just be the work of a skilled burglar.'

'That brings us back to the question that Father asked,' said Madeleine. 'Why take only that when there were other things of value in the house?'

143

'I don't know.'

'What's the next step?' asked Lydia.

'Well,' said Hinton, thinking it over, 'I'll need to talk to Mr Andrews and get the names of friends who've been into the house and seen where he keeps that medal. Then I need to cast the net wider by finding out if anybody has been in there recently to do some work – a carpenter, perhaps, or a builder.'

'Father didn't mention anybody,' said Madeleine, 'but that means nothing. He freely admits that his mind is like a sieve sometimes. It may well be that the medal wasn't stolen, after all, and that would make me feel that we'd wasted your time, Alan.'

'Oh, it won't have been wasted, I assure you.'

He exchanged a meaningful glance with Lydia.

Still seated in the lounge at the hotel, Leeming opened his pad and studied the notes he'd made on the case. Having already amassed a sizeable amount of information, he knew that he'd have to ferret out far more before their work was done. When he was joined by Colbeck, he registered his complaint at once.

'I'd hoped to be back in London in time to light a bonfire for my children on November 5th.'

'There's no earthly chance of that happening, Victor.'

'I'm terrified we'll still be here by Christmas.'

'If it's necessary,' said Colbeck, 'we'll be here into the new year – though I certainly don't anticipate it.'

'I'll need a new notebook at this rate.'

'Good – that's a sign of progress.'

'Most of what I've learnt is irrelevant.'

'No, it isn't. Every time you've spoken to someone new, you've discovered additional details of what life is like in this part of the world.'

'It's a lot different from the way we live, sir.'

'That's why we have to get inside the minds of the local inhabitants and see the Lake District as they do. For instance, they're far more likely to believe in ghosts and phantoms than Londoners.'

'I discovered that from dipping into the book Tiller gave me. According to that, there are weird things going on all over the county.'

'We'll discuss them over dinner.'

'I can't wait for that,' said Leeming. 'I seem to have been on my feet all day. I've been looking forward to a good meal, plenty of beer and an early night.'

'You'll certainly get the food and drink, Victor, but you must forget the early night.'

'Why? I'm exhausted.'

'We both are,' said Colbeck, 'but duty comes first. Before we can retire to our beds, we must make the effort to visit Hither Wood at midnight. It's there that the story of Alexander Piper's disappearance really began.'

CHAPTER TWELVE

When he heard the details of another day of failed searches, even Lord Culverhouse found it difficult to maintain the belief that his nephew was still alive, albeit too dazed to know who or where he was. Geoffrey Hedley had called at Culverhouse Court to pass on the grim tidings. He apologised profusely for the lack of success.

'You might as well call off the search,' decided the old man. 'Alex is simply not there.'

'I don't like the idea of giving up, Lord Culverhouse.'

'We're not doing that,' said the other. 'We're handing over to detectives who are experienced at solving crimes because that's what we obviously have here – a ghastly crime.'

'I accept that now,' said Hedley.

'Alex's body is out there somewhere. I'm relying on Colbeck to find it for us so that we can get to the truth of this whole affair. My sister must be in despair.'

'Everyone who loved Alex feels the same.'

'If only he hadn't devised that lunatic scheme about the Phantom Special!' He turned on his visitor. 'Didn't you tell me that it was *your* idea originally?'

'I'm ashamed to admit that it was.'

'I can see that my nephew would be exhilarated by the venture but what would someone like you hope to get out of it?'

'We all went because of our friendship with Alex.'

'A real friend would have tried to stop the whole thing.'

'Once an idea possessed him,' said Hedley, 'that was that.'

The old man fell silent for a while, cheek muscles taut and eyebrows knitted in meditation. A deep sadness had drained the colour out of his face. He suddenly found his voice again.

'Isn't there *any* chance he may still be alive?'

'I sincerely hope so.'

'What does Sergeant Ainsley think?'

'He fears the worst.'

'Never learning the truth is my idea of the worst that can happen. It would be a terrible thing for my sister and her husband if they were left in ignorance about the fate of their only child for the rest of their lives. And the same,' he said, face clouding, 'would be true for the rest of us. I mean, it would be so . . . *unnatural*.'

'We must look to Inspector Colbeck for answers,' said Hedley. 'When I met him at the police station, he'd just come back from Hither Wood.'

'What was he doing there? Alex vanished miles away.'

'Gregor Hayes didn't. He disappeared in the wood.'

'That was donkey's years ago.'

'The inspector thinks that that case may have relevance to this one. I fail to see any connection myself, but he obviously does, and he told me that he's prepared to go into a haunted wood at midnight in order to prove it.'

Victor Leeming had not liked the idea when it was first put to him. Now that it had become a reality, he liked it even less. They were setting out in darkness into what he feared was a wilderness. Colbeck was driving a borrowed dog cart with lanterns attached to it to yield at least a suggestion of light. Having memorised the route he'd taken with Ainsley, he felt that he could find his way to Hither Wood without too much difficulty. Leeming didn't share his confidence. When they hit the first of many potholes, he was thrown inches into the air.

'Be careful!' he yelled.

'Get used to it, Victor. There'll be worse to come.'

'Then why not wait until daylight?'

'Hither Wood holds no fears then.'

'How long will it take us?'

'Never mind about that,' said Colbeck. 'The journey will give us plenty of time to review what we discussed over dinner. Which of the suspects should occupy prime position?'

'I'm not sure.'

'Somebody must look the most likely culprit.'

'I'm wondering if it should be Norm Tiller.'

'I thought you liked him.'

'I do – he's very friendly. He talks to people as if he really cares about them. Dymock didn't do that and neither did Vine. They treated me like dirt.'

'Both had good cause to hate Piper. The doctor's problem was that Piper moved into the house next door and immediately began a bitter boundary dispute with him. Tempers obviously flared up over that.'

'Yes,' said Leeming, 'but doctors swear to save lives, not to take them. Much as I'd *like* Dymock to be the villain so that I could arrest him, I don't think he's guilty.'

'What about Vine?'

'As I told you, I think he got that injury from a duel with Piper. When I asked him if he was interested in fencing or shooting, I could see that I'd touched on a sore point.'

'There's your chance to arrest Dr Dymock.'

'What cause would I have?'

'Well, it's more than likely that *he* treated Vine's wound. He must have guessed how it was sustained. Dymock was therefore party to an illegal duel.'

'We can't prove that, sir.'

'Perhaps not,' said Colbeck, 'but it might be mentioned to the doctor, if only to give him a nasty shock. I wonder if Miss Treadgold realised that two men were fighting over her.'

'From what you told me about her, I think she'd more or less goad them into it.'

'I doubt it. She wouldn't want Piper to get hurt.'

'But he *won* the duel.'

'She couldn't be certain of that beforehand.'

'No, I suppose not.'

'We're back with Mr Tiller again.'

'I'm going on what the manager of the King's Arms told me,' said Leeming. 'He'd always known Tiller as a meek and mild poet. When that meeting was interrupted by Piper, however, the poet turned into a roaring lion.'

'I'd like to meet Mr Tiller myself.'

'He's better company than either Dymock or Vine.'

'Yet you're picking *him* out as a potential killer.'

'He was wounded to the quick. Remember that.'

Leeming broke off as one wheel explored an even deeper pothole and the whole cart lifted at a sharp angle before righting itself with a thud. How much more of it he had to endure, Leeming didn't know but he was already praying for early deliverance from the ordeal. They'd left the town now and were enveloped by an inky darkness. The lanterns did nothing to penetrate it. Drizzle began to fall and a sudden wind whipped it up into their faces. Leeming kept thinking of the warm bed he'd been compelled to forsake. He was suffering.

Norman Tiller sat alone at a table in the King's Arms. Most of the other customers had gone but not before they made sure they'd a word with him. Tiller was seen as much as a resident philosopher as a poet, and had something of interest to say on any subject under the sun. A barmaid was clearing empty tankards off the tables and the landlord was locking the shutters. Penrose drifted across to the hunched figure at the table. Tiller seemed to be in a private world.

'Wake up, Norm,' he said, gently shaking him. 'It's time to go.'

'I wasn't asleep,' said Tiller. 'I was working on my latest poem. I have to get it absolutely right in my mind before I put pen to paper.'

'What's it called?'

'The *Phantom Special*.' He laughed at the look of alarm on the other man's face. 'I'm only teasing you. Its real title is *Peace on the Lake*.'

'Good – that won't upset anybody.'

'It's a poet's duty to cause upset from time to time,' said Tiller. 'We tell the truth about our existence here on earth and it's sometimes a rather ugly truth.'

'Save it until tomorrow, Norm. It's too late now.'

'Don't worry. I'm going.'

Tiller hauled himself to his feet and bent over slightly so that he could look deep into the landlord's eyes.

'What did he ask you?'

'Who are you talking about?'

'Sergeant Leeming.'

'Ah, him . . .'

'I know he came here. I told him about that meeting of the poets we had. The sergeant is too good a detective not to have wanted the story confirmed. He came here, didn't he?'

'That's right. I told him the truth.'

Tiller heaved a sigh. 'I was afraid that you would.'

'I also told him that, in all the time you'd come in here, you'd never once caused us the slightest trouble.'

'How did the sergeant react?'

'He was surprised. To be honest, we all were, Norm. We'd never seen you like that before.'

'I'm sorry about that, Hugh. It was wrong of me.'

Penrose eased him towards the door. 'Go home,' he advised. 'Write your poem on the way. As for the sergeant, I told him you'd always be welcome here – whatever you did.'

'Even if I'd done to Piper what the bastard deserved?'

'Yes – even then.'

'Thank you.'

Tiller stumbled off into the night.

Their first stop was at the point along the line where the fire had been lit to bring the Phantom Special to a halt. Even with a lantern in his hand, Leeming could see very little. Colbeck told him that he'd sprinted roughly the same distance beside the track as Piper.

'Well, don't ask *me* to do that,' said Leeming, anxiously. 'I'm not running blindly into the unknown.'

'It's what we do on a regular basis.'

'Yes, but we always have more light than this.'

When Colbeck explained why he'd run so far and so fast, Leeming could see the purpose behind it. All of a sudden, he shivered involuntarily.

'Oh!' he cried.

'Are you all right, Victor?'

'No, sir, I'm afraid.'

'That's not like you. As a rule, you're quite fearless.'

'Well, I'm not this time. It scared me.'

'What did?'

'I thought you'd have felt it as well.'

'I didn't feel a thing.'

'Well, I certainly did,' said Leeming. 'My whole body went ice cold and I shivered as if I was stark naked. I've never had that feeling before.' He looked around. 'We're being watched, Inspector.'

'Nobody can see us in the dark.'

'Yes, they can, and it frightens me.'

Night was always the worst time for Melissa Haslam. Ever since she'd received the news, she'd hardly slept a wink. Her parents had tried to persuade her to remain hopeful, but it was only a half-hearted appeal. They knew what their daughter had now come to accept. There would be no wedding to the man she loved so desperately. It was all over.

Because their relationship had been relatively short, there were few love tokens to act as mementoes. There was the gorgeous ring that Alexander Piper had bought her to signal his commitment and there were a few letters expressing his devotion to her. As she sat on the bed, she read them yet again by the flickering light of the lamp but, instead of acting as consolation, they only deepened her remorse.

Melissa blamed herself. If she'd gone on the excursion with him, the tragedy would never have happened. She'd have stopped him from running off like that. In refusing to go with him, she was leaving Piper vulnerable. Her place was beside him and she was too frightened to be there. Melissa had been wrong. In putting her fears before his safety, she'd been acting selfishly. She almost deserved the misery now afflicting her.

What caused her the most searing pain was that she still didn't know what had happened to him. Human beings couldn't just disappear instantly. And yet that was what seemed to have happened to Piper. Several people, she'd been told, saw him run into the flames. Had they swallowed him up and spat him out as so much smoke? Or had some trap been laid for him? That possibility was, in a sense, more worrying because it showed that the man she adored had ruthless enemies. Sublimely ignorant of the life he'd led before he met her, Melissa couldn't believe that the kind, caring, loving man she knew would do anything to upset other people. It was simply not in his character.

One faint hope remained. During their brief meeting, Robert Colbeck had given her a feeling of confidence in his abilities. He might not be able to bring Alexander Piper back to her, but the inspector might at least find out the elusive truth about his disappearance. Melissa could then start to mourn properly.

By the time they neared their destination, Leeming had shaken off his earlier fears. The book he'd been given by Norman Tiller had been to blame. It had given him the impression that a demon was hiding behind every bush and that a ghost haunted every stand of trees. No such things existed, he told himself, and he vowed to return the book to its owner. Leeming was weighing the three suspects in the balance when Colbeck added another name to the list.

'Perhaps there's a fourth, after all,' he said.

154

'I thought you said that Miss Treadgold was innocent of any involvement.'

'She is, Victor.'

'Then who are you talking about?'

'Geoffrey Hedley.'

Leeming was astounded. 'But he's Piper's best friend.'

'Is he?' asked Colbeck. 'Consider this. When I saw that the oil had been emptied from those lamps in one of the carriages, I assumed that Piper had been responsible. It could equally well have been Hedley. He helped to set the excursion up and knew that he'd be in the last compartment with his friend. Since those carriages were parked in a siding in the darkness, it would have been easy for him to slip into the second of the two and empty the oil out of the lamps.'

'But what was his motive?'

'I think he had more than one, Victor. My impression is that he was tired of being at Piper's beck and call, satisfying his friend's every whim and getting him out of trouble whenever he got himself arrested. That role turned sour for him.'

'I'm surprised that he played it so long.'

'Then there was the way Piper treated Miss Treadgold. It was deplorable. You noticed how fond of her Hedley seemed when you talked with him about her.'

'Yet he picked her out as a suspect.'

'He explained that to me, Victor. He gave us her name before others did the same, but he never believed that she was in any way guilty. It's not impossible,' Colbeck went on, 'that he was disgusted by his friend's brusque dismissal of a woman

155

who'd been so close to him and was determined to wreak revenge on her behalf.'

'Then there was Miss Haslam.'

'What about her?'

'Hedley must have pitied her,' suggested Leeming. 'He knew all of Piper's dark secrets and could imagine the sort of husband he'd be. Perhaps he wanted to save Miss Haslam from what would have been an unhappy marriage.'

'I don't think she came into the reckoning at all. The only woman in whom Hedley had any real interest was Caroline Treadgold. I could hear the affection in his voice when he talked about her.'

'Yes, I noticed that.'

'As long as Piper was alive,' said Colbeck, 'Hedley couldn't get near her. Now that he's out of the way . . .'

Leeming pondered. 'No,' he said at length, 'I still think that Tiller is our chief suspect. What's that proverb you sometimes quote at me? "Beware the silent man and the still water." That sums him up perfectly.'

'I'm shifting my interest to Hedley.'

'But he's been so helpful to us, sir.'

'That's what aroused my suspicion,' said Colbeck. 'He's been *too* helpful. That way, he's been able to shape our thinking and make us look in the direction he wants. Dymock and Vine couldn't do that, and neither could Mr Tiller. None of them was a close associate of Piper's.'

They'd reached the edge of Hither Wood and it loomed over them. When they got out of the dog cart, Colbeck tethered the horse to a bush. With a lantern apiece, they found a path and went carefully along it. Leading the way, Colbeck was able to warn Leeming about any minor hazard. The wood was eerily silent until an owl suddenly screeched from a high branch above their heads. Startled at first, they laughed with relief and heard the flutter of wings as the bird flew away.

The drizzle had now subsided, and the wind had died. When they came to the heart of the wood, they stepped into the clearing and looked around at the high, intimidating walls of trees. They stood there in silence for several minutes. Colbeck was contemplative but Leeming was unsettled.

'Why did you bring me here?' he complained.

'I wanted to see what it must have been like for Gregor Hayes. On such a night as this, he came here on his own to brave the ghosts that are supposed to haunt this place.'

'He went on to become one of them.'

'He's certainly here,' said Colbeck, 'but I won't believe that his ghost is. Somewhere in among those trees, Hayes's body is buried. On the night he ventured in here to win a bet, he had company. They were waiting for him.'

'Who were?'

'I don't know, Victor, but I wouldn't be at all surprised if the same people disposed of Alexander Piper. I get the feeling that he might be hidden away here as well.'

'But he disappeared miles away.'

'If he was murdered there, he could easily have been transported here immediately afterwards. That's why his body was never found when they searched the whole area where the Phantom Special had been forced to stop.'

'Please don't tell me we'll look for him now.'

'We'd need daylight and spades before we do that,' said Colbeck, smiling. 'We're finished here, Victor.'

'Thank goodness for that!'

'But I'm glad we came. I just wanted to get the feel of the place in the dead of night.'

'Gregor Hayes probably said the same thing.'

'He came here in search of money.'

'What were *we* searching for?'

'Enlightenment.'

Glad that they were going, Leeming led the way this time, threading his way through the undergrowth with the lantern held high. He counted his blessings. They had survived. There were no apparitions, no sense of danger and no mocking laughter in the dark. But for the screech of an owl, Hither Wood hadn't disturbed them in the least. They could now return to their hotel and climb into warm, cosy beds.

There was only one problem. When they emerged at last from the trees, they discovered that their horse and dog cart were no longer there.

'Where has it gone?' asked Colbeck.

'The horse must have pulled free.'

'He was tied too securely.'

'Do you mean that somebody *stole* the cart?'

'I'm afraid so.'

'Who else would be stupid enough to be out here in the cold at this time of night?'

'It might have been someone who followed us, Victor.'

'We didn't hear anything.'

'We weren't supposed to.'

Leeming looked around. 'We can't stay out here.'

'I wasn't intending to do that.'

'So what *do* we do?'

'We travel by Shanks's pony.'

'We can't walk all the way back!' he wailed. 'It must be more than ten miles.'

'Then it's just the healthy exercise we need,' said Colbeck, trying to make it sound like a bonus. 'Let's get started, Victor.'

'I don't have the strength, sir.'

'Yes, you do.'

'Why did I let myself get dragged out here?'

'You ought to be glad you came. We've just made an important discovery.'

'Yes – our feet will be very sore in the morning.'

'No, Victor. We are making progress.'

'That's not what I'd call it,' grumbled the other.

'Somebody is worried,' said Colbeck. 'They're afraid that we'll find what they wish to keep hidden away. In stealing our means of transport, they've just confirmed that we're on the right track. Doesn't that encourage you?'

Darkness hid the expression on Leeming's face.

CHAPTER THIRTEEN

Since the disappearance of her son, Emma Piper had enjoyed only fitful sleep. Unable to rest during the day, she was tormented at night by fears that she and her husband had somehow failed Alexander. They should have made greater efforts to heal the breach. It was distressing to recall that the only news they had of what Alexander was doing was contained in letters from her brother. During what was a critical time in his life, they'd not even set eyes on him.

Rodney Piper was even more tortured by regret than his wife, but he somehow managed to fall asleep at night. Sheer fatigue eventually overwhelmed Emma and she drifted off beside him. It was not long before she was in the grip of one of her nightmares, tossing and turning endlessly as if trying to escape from someone. Without warning, she came suddenly awake and realised how cold she was. Emma also noticed that her husband was no longer there. That alarmed her.

Dragging herself slowly to her feet, she felt for her slippers, put them on and reached for her dressing gown. Emma padded out of the bedroom and down the stairs, one hand on the banister to support her. She knew instinctively where she'd find him. When she went into the drawing room, she could see his outline. Lost in prayer, he was kneeling on the hearthrug in front of the crucifix on the wall above the mantelpiece. He was reciting prayers that she couldn't hear properly.

Emma waited until his voice died away and then spoke.

'Come back to bed, Rodney.'

'My place is here.'

'You can pray just as well upstairs.'

'No, I can't, Emma. It has to be here.'

'We both need our sleep. Stop punishing yourself.'

'It's no more than I deserve,' he admitted. 'I failed Alexander as a father and as a spiritual guide. I must repent.'

'We weren't to know that this would happen.'

'God has given us a sign.'

'Please, Rodney,' she said, taking him by the elbow. 'Let me help you up. It's cold down here and you've only got that nightshirt on. You're not in the best of health. Don't make the situation worse.'

'I'll do what I have to, Emma,' he said, pulling gently away from her. 'I'm grateful that you came down for me, but my place is here at the moment.'

'Then so is mine.'

Lowering herself down, she knelt beside him and winced at the pain in her knees and her hips. They remained there together, eyes closed, hands clasped, lips moving and words floating up to heaven in the gloom.

Colbeck had suggested an alternative. Instead of a long, testing walk back to Kendal, they could make the much shorter journey to Birthwaite Station and curl up there until the first train arrived in the morning. Leeming rejected the idea. Since the station would be closed, the best it could offer was a wooden bench exposed to the elements. If they kept on the move, he argued, they'd at least be relatively warm. They set off at a brisk pace.

'What will happen on Bonfire Night?' asked Colbeck.

'Everybody will enjoy it but us.'

'I was thinking of your family. I know that you planned to have a fire for the boys.'

'Oh, they'll still have that,' said Leeming, 'but it will be lit by their uncle instead of by me. Detective work is not for a man with a family.'

'You sound like the superintendent.'

'Left to him, we'd be on duty all day.'

'Madeleine would never stand for that and nor would Estelle. They do like an occasional glimpse of their husbands.'

Leeming grimaced. 'Chance would be a fine thing.'

Scrunching their way along in the dark, they felt completely alone. They heard occasional sounds of animals in the undergrowth and saw some low-flying birds from time to time but otherwise they were totally isolated. While Colbeck found that stimulating, Leeming was fearful.

'Are you sure that this is the right way?' he asked.

'It's the road we came on, Victor. It runs parallel with the railway for the bulk of the journey.'

'Who stole our horse and cart?'

'Think of our suspects and take your pick.'

'It wasn't Norm Tiller. I'm sure of that. He'll be at home in bed with his wife. This is far too mean a trick for him.'

'What about the doctor?'

'He's mean enough but how could he possibly know that we'd be coming out here this late?'

'That's a crucial point. Walter Vine wouldn't have been aware of our travel plans either and, with his arm in a sling, I doubt if he'd relish being driven along this bumpy track.'

'That brings us to Hedley, though I'd disregard him.'

'Why?'

'On a night like this,' said Leeming, 'he'll be gazing up at Miss Treadgold's window. Hedley is the sort of man who might actually like Tiller's poetry, whereas Piper hated it so much he had to mock the man who wrote it. That shows the difference between the two friends. When Piper had an impulse, he did something about it.'

'Hedley, on the other hand, is too repressed to follow suit. And yet he's the one person who knew that we'd come to Hither Wood at some point because I mentioned it to him. Has he been watching us to see when we'd make our move?'

'Lawyers are supposed to keep on the right side of the law, sir.'

'There are exceptions to the rule. So,' said Colbeck, 'none of our four suspects will have trailed us in person, but they could have hired someone else to follow us. They might even have installed someone at the hotel who dined within earshot of us earlier this evening.'

Leeming snapped his fingers. 'That's what must have happened. We've been spied on.'

'It was only a suggestion.'

'Maybe, but it has the ring of truth. All we have to work out is who is paying the spy.'

'I'd love to know, Victor.'

As they strolled on, they discussed each of their suspects in turn again and got so embroiled in their discussion that they forgot all about their aching limbs and the distance they still had to go. They might have been out for a bracing walk along a promenade. Shapes were deceptive in the dark but, when they came round a slight bend in the road, they both saw something ahead of them that looked vaguely familiar. Before they could confer, they heard a loud neigh and knew at once that they'd found their horse and cart.

Leeming ran quickly towards the animal and grabbed its bridle before it could run away. Colbeck came over and patted the horse gratefully. They could now ride back to the hotel.

'It must have escaped outside the wood,' said Leeming, 'and made its way here.'

'I disagree.'

'How else could it have got here?'

'It's a clever animal but I don't believe that it could untie itself from one bush, walk here, then tether itself to another.' He indicated the reins securely tied to a bush. 'Somebody else brought him here.'

'We've got him back. That's the only thing I care about.'

'Then you should be more alert.'

'Why?'

'Haven't you noticed where we are?' asked Colbeck with a sweeping gesture. 'We're at the exact spot where that fire was lit to stop the train. You can still see the embers.'

'Oh, yes, I recognise it now. We stopped here earlier.'

'And what happened?'

'I had a fit of the shivers,' recalled Leeming. 'I thought we were being watched.'

'Do you have that same feeling now?'

'No, I don't.'

'Neither do I.'

'What's going on, sir? It's uncanny. Is someone playing games with us?'

'Oh, it's a lot more serious than that, Victor.'

'Why steal our horse and cart then give it back?'

'We were given a warning to stay well clear of that wood.'

'What happens if we ignore the warning?'

'It will be interesting to find out.'

They got into the cart and set off. Leeming wanted to get back to the hotel as fast as possible but Colbeck limited the horse to a steady trot. He didn't wish to push an already tired animal too hard and, at a slower speed, he'd have more chance of avoiding potholes that suddenly appeared in front of them. They were soon discussing their suspects once again, trying to decide which one of them had organised the theft of their cart.

As they passed a stand of trees, they were too preoccupied to notice that someone was crouched beside them. When the cart had rattled past, the man stood up, waited for several minutes then ran slowly along in their wake.

Though it was a bleak day, Caroline Treadgold forced herself to get up early, consume a hasty breakfast then be driven to the point where the search teams were gathering. To her dismay, she saw that they were being dispersed by Geoffrey Hedley. She got quickly out of the vehicle. Quivering with indignation, she rushed up to him.

'What's going on?' she demanded.

'The search is being abandoned.'

'You can't just stop looking for Alex.'

'Lord Culverhouse decided that it's a futile exercise.'

'But he was the one who insisted on it,' she said. 'His nephew is out there somewhere. I can't believe that he's lost interest in finding him.'

'That's not what happened, Caroline.'

'Then what did? I insist on knowing.'

After calming her down, Hedley told her how the decision was made, stressing that he disagreed with it but had to accept what Lord Culverhouse had decreed. From now on, it would be left to the detectives to find out what had happened to the missing man. Caroline was not appeased.

'We *have* to continue,' she said, 'if only as a gesture.'

'It's a rather forlorn one, I'm afraid.'

'I couldn't forgive myself if I just gave up. And neither

could you, Geoffrey. You used to hang on Alex's every word. Have you forgotten that?'

'No, of course I haven't.'

'Then show some loyalty to him.'

Hedley was stung. 'Nobody can doubt my loyalty, Caroline,' he said, hotly. 'My friendship with Alex meant everything to me. If it were my decision to make, I'd be out there day after day leading a search party. It would at least give me the feeling that I was *doing* something.' He took a deep breath then recovered his composure. 'I do apologise. I just found your comment monstrously unfair.'

'Then the apology should come from me, Geoffrey,' she said, quietly. 'Alex relied on you for everything. I'm sorry that I forgot that.' There was an awkward pause. 'What was it that attracted him to Melissa Haslam?' she resumed. 'Is she more beautiful than me? Is she more intelligent, more interesting?'

'In my opinion, she's none of those things.'

'Then however did that woman come to replace me?'

'In fairness to Miss Haslam,' he said, 'I should point out that she was unaware that she was replacing anybody. She had no knowledge of the relationship between the two of you. Had she done so . . . well, things would have been rather different.'

'In short, Alex pretended that I never existed.'

'That's not true, Caroline. He often expressed regret about the way he'd treated you.'

'Why didn't he tell me directly?'

'That was his way, I'm afraid.'

'Did you condone it?'

167

'No,' he said with feeling. 'I thought he treated you rather shabbily and I told him so. Yet he still had feelings for you. Did you know that he once fought a duel on your behalf?'

'A duel!' she cried. 'Alex might have been killed or, at the very least, arrested. When was this?'

'A week or so ago – someone taunted him by making derogatory remarks about you. Alex challenged him at once. I acted as his second. Vine slunk off home with his arm almost sliced off.'

'I thought it might have been Walter Vine. The moment that Alex and I . . . parted company, Walter began chasing me in earnest. I had a great difficulty in shaking him off. He took the rejection badly.'

'That's why he was insulting you, Caroline.'

'And Alex took him on?'

'He said that it was a matter of honour.'

Caroline was partially mollified. The information had shown her that he'd still cared deeply for her and was ready to risk serious injury – if not worse – to defend her name. She knew Vine well enough to be aware of his character.

'*He* could be behind Alex's disappearance,' she claimed.

'I did mention his name to Sergeant Leeming.'

'Did you tell him about the duel?'

'No, I didn't.'

'Then I think that perhaps you should. It's an important factor. Walter Vine hates a defeat of any kind. Since he was humiliated by Alex, he'll have wanted revenge.'

'I'm sure that Inspector Colbeck will realise that when he discovers that the duel took place.'

Hearing about Vine's unexpected visit to the Riverside Hotel, Colbeck's curiosity had been aroused. That morning, therefore, he set off to speak to the man himself. He was given a rather offhand welcome.

'I've already spoken to the sergeant,' said Vine, flicking a dismissive hand, 'so there's no need to bother me any further. Besides, I have an appointment with my doctor very soon.'

'I won't keep you long, sir.'

'You won't be allowed to, believe me.'

'I must say, Mr Vine, that I find your attitude difficult to comprehend,' said Colbeck. 'A man has disappeared and there's a likelihood that he's come to serious harm. I would have thought it was common decency to lend your help to a police investigation.'

'If it was anybody but Alex Piper, I'd be glad to assist you. Since it happens to be him, I have no interest in the case.'

'Why is that?'

'Speak to that sergeant of yours. He'll tell you.'

'I'd rather *you* did that, sir.'

'This is starting to get rather boring,' said Vine with studied disdain. 'I bid you good day, Inspector.'

'Would you rather we had this conversation at the police station? That's where this will end if you don't start to cooperate with me.' He looked Vine in the eye. 'Well?'

The other man glared at him but Colbeck didn't flinch. He

remained cool and watchful. In the end, Vine backed down.

'Oh, very well,' he said, pretending to yawn. 'I'll humour you, if I must.'

'Why are you so hostile to Mr Piper?'

'I loathe the man.'

'That wasn't always the case, was it?'

'Have you never fallen out with an old friend, Inspector? It happens to all of us. Relationships fade with time. Qualities I once admired in Alex slowly disappeared and were replaced by altogether nastier traits.'

'How did he feel about *you*?'

Vine tensed. 'I beg your pardon?'

'Did Mr Piper start to find you wanting?'

'What is this?' protested the other. 'Are you interrogating me or planning to write my biography?'

'I'm simply gathering information.'

'Well, I object to the way that you're doing it. Be more respectful or I'll be in touch with your superior to get you reprimanded.'

'That's highly unlikely,' said Colbeck, easily. 'You'll find that I have the complete backing of Scotland Yard and that all you'll get is confirmation of that. My superior takes a poor view of people who dare to threaten his officers as you've just done.'

Vine was apoplectic. 'Who the devil do you think you're talking to?' he howled. 'It might interest you to know that I'm a person of standing in this town.'

'I've arrested lords, ladies and Members of Parliament in my time, sir. Criminals come from every class of society.'

'Are you daring to call me a criminal?'

'If you took part in an illegal duel – as I suspect you might have done – then you *are* a criminal and liable to arrest.'

Vine was instantly silenced. Turning away, he walked to the other side of the room and made an effort to control his temper before swinging round on his heel. About to issue a stout denial, he thought better of it when he saw the determined look on Colbeck's face. Clearly, his visitor could not be browbeaten. Vine tried to sound reasonable.

'We seem to have got off on the wrong foot,' he said, 'and I take my share of the blame for that. As for my injury, it was the result of a nasty accident in the stable and no concern of yours. The simple fact remains that I am not connected in any way whatsoever with Alex's disappearance, though I'm honest enough to admit that I hope it's a permanent one.'

'That's a very brutal standpoint.'

'It's nevertheless the one that I choose to take.'

'What exactly did Mr Piper do to upset you so much?'

'That's a private matter.'

'Not if it has a bearing on this investigation. I need every scrap of information that I can gather regarding the missing man. That being the case,' Colbeck emphasised, 'privacy doesn't exist. So let me rephrase my question. Did your differences with Mr Piper arise out of the fact that you each had an interest in a certain lady?'

Vine looked hunted.

Leeming's first task that morning was to visit the police station where he learnt, to his surprise, that Lord Culverhouse had called off the search. Sergeant Ainsley approved of the decision. Leeming was there to study the records of the search for Gregor Hayes. They were locked in a cupboard in Ainsley's office. Handing them over, he told his visitor that he was available for questioning about anything he might find as he reviewed the case. He then left Leeming alone. Even a cursory glance at the material told him that Ainsley had obviously been efficient. The records had been scrupulously kept in legible handwriting and revealed a man who'd led the police investigation with almost missionary zeal. He'd even included a diagram of Hither Wood with the areas that had been searched clearly marked.

Leeming went through the case records and learnt many new and interesting details in the course of doing so. When he'd transferred the relevant information to his notepad, he went off to talk to the sergeant. He found Ainsley helping to manhandle an obstreperous prisoner into a cell. When the man was safely locked away, he kicked at the bars and issued a stream of expletives. Ainsley raised a warning fist to silence him and the prisoner retreated to the corner of the cell.

'I'm sorry you had to hear such vile language, Sergeant,' said Ainsley, 'though I daresay you're used to it.'

Leeming nodded. 'I'm afraid that I am.'

'This man has a pretty wife and two lovely children. I've seen all four of them together in church. He'd never dare to swear like that in front of his family. And yet the moment he sees a police uniform . . .'

'It pours out of him like so much vomit.'

'Exactly – let's go into my office, shall we?'

They went back to the room and closed the door behind them. Referring to his notebook, Leeming asked a series of questions to clarify certain points in the records. Ainsley provided all the detail asked for and reiterated his belief that there was no real connection between the disappearances of the local blacksmith and Alexander Piper. Though he was not persuaded of that, Leeming pretended to agree. Obeying Colbeck's instructions, he said nothing about their visit to Hither Wood at midnight.

'I wonder if I can ask you about something else,' he said. 'I've met Mr Tiller a couple of times and he told me about an incident at the King's Arms.'

'Yes, he's part of a group of poets that meets there.'

'They had an intruder at their last meeting. You won't need telling who it was. As a result, there was such a violent argument that the landlord had to send for you.'

'I knew it was serious when that happened. Small as he is, Hugh Penrose can usually handle any trouble, but Norm Tiller was in a rage. Piper was goading him.'

'That was cruel.'

'He could be very cruel, Sergeant.'

'The landlord said that, in the end, you broke up the argument. Piper was sent packing.'

'That's not quite what happened,' said Ainsley. 'First of all, I got them to stop shouting at each other then I had a quiet word in Piper's ear.'

'What did you say?'

'I told him the one thing guaranteed to sober him.'

'And what was that?'

'I threatened to report the incident to Miss Haslam and he could see that I meant it. First of all, of course, he had to warn me that he could have me dismissed from the police force if he wished then he staggered out. If I hadn't stopped him, he'd have been attacked by Norm Tiller and I'd have had to arrest *him*, one of gentlest men I've ever met.'

'And did Piper try to get you forced out of office?'

'No, thankfully,' said Ainsley. 'I arrived at the station next morning to find Mr Hedley waiting for me with the usual soft soap about his friend being the injured party and how it was better for all of us if the whole matter was quietly forgotten.'

'He seems to have spent his entire life, running after Piper and cleaning up the mess he leaves behind him.'

'When I told Hedley that an apology was in order, he said that Norm ought to give it as soon as possible.'

'But the apology should have come from Piper.'

'Getting it out of him would have been like getting blood from a stone. It simply never happened. Norm just wanted the whole thing forgotten. Even though it will be a tight squeeze, future meetings of the poets will be held at his house.'

'What drove Piper to bait him like that?'

'Envy, I expect. He was annoyed that Miss Haslam had bought a copy of Norm's poems and said how good they were. In Piper's eyes, Tiller is just a scruffy bookseller who barely makes enough money to survive. The idea that his future wife was so fond of the poems that she insisted he read them made

Piper furious. He'd obviously heard that the poets used to meet at the King's Arms, so he thought he'd have some fun at Tiller's expense. You know the rest.'

'How could he be so vindictive?'

'It's typical of his behaviour.'

'But his father is a clergyman.'

'That doesn't hold him back,' said Ainsley. 'A few years ago, Piper came into a lot of money and started to flex his muscles. He left home, bought a house here and did exactly what he wanted. When he met Melissa Haslam, we hoped that he might turn over a new leaf and become a credit to Kendal instead of being a troublemaker. It never happened.'

'Thank you, Sergeant,' said Leeming. 'You've been very helpful. And thank you for letting me see the records of that earlier case.'

'There's something that isn't in the records, but which might be of interest to you.'

'Oh, and what's that?'

'Tiller wrote a poem about Gregor's disappearance.'

'Why did he do that?'

'Read it and you'll find out.'

CHAPTER FOURTEEN

Notwithstanding the consequences of a disturbed night, Emma Piper insisted on going to see her brother that morning. She and her husband were driven to Birthwaite and travelled on the train to Kendal. Neither of them stayed awake for the entirety of the journey. Even though they were troubled by aches and pains, they took it in turns to fall asleep. When they reached their destination, they took a cab to Culverhouse Court and were given an effusive welcome by Emma's brother. When he'd summoned her, Lady Culverhouse, his tall, stately wife, came in to greet them, then took her sister-in-law off to the drawing room, leaving the two men together in the study.

'Can I offer you anything, Rodney?' asked Culverhouse.

'No, thank you. We've had breakfast.'

'You're even thinner than on your last visit. Is my dear sister not looking after you properly? Is she trying to starve you to death?'

'Don't be silly,' said his brother-in-law. 'I'm simply keeping to the vows of denial that I made.'

'Well, at least sit down, man. You look exhausted.'

'I am,' confessed Piper, settling into a chair. 'We had another bad night. Sleep is impossible when you have something of this scale on your mind.'

'That's true, Rodney. The body may weaken but the brain keeps whirring away. However, unless I'm mistaken, you came here for the latest news of the search, didn't you?'

'Yes, we did. We feel so detached from it all. I feel as if I should be out there now with everyone else.'

'That's no longer possible, I'm afraid. I've bowed to the inevitable and had the search teams sent home.'

'You can't do that!' protested Piper.

'The decision has already been made.'

'Alex may still be out there somewhere.'

'If he was, we'd have found him by now. They've looked into every nook and cranny.'

'Then the search has to be widened.'

'We've already covered miles,' said Culverhouse. 'I've had daily reports from Geoffrey Hedley. He's made sure that every inch of the ground has been examined. There hasn't been the slightest clue found that has any relation to Alex's disappearance.'

'What does Inspector Colbeck think?'

'I haven't spoken to him yet.'

Piper was appalled. 'You cancelled the search without his advice? That was very foolish.'

'I'm sure that Colbeck will agree with me.'

'It would have been simple courtesy to consult him first.'

'He believes that Alex was the victim of a crime,' said Culverhouse, 'and is concentrating on the search for the person who committed that crime. Only when *he* is unmasked will we know the full truth.'

'I must speak to the inspector again.'

'Let him get on with his work, Rodney. I promised him a free hand and that's what he must have. It's wrong for us to put any pressure on him.'

'I simply want to know what progress he's made.'

'It's slow but steady.'

'Alex is our son. We're entitled to know how the investigation is going. There's something else that troubles me. If I talk to Inspector Colbeck, I can discuss the symbolism of what happened at Hallowe'en.'

'What symbolism?'

'Alex disappeared when he ran through a wall of flame,' said the other. 'It's almost as if someone arranged a descent into hell for him.'

Caleb Andrews was a man of combative disposition. In spite of that, he'd been popular among most of his workmates on the railway and respected by the others. He had, he believed, no real enemies and yet someone had apparently disliked him so much that he'd deliberately stolen an item that had given Andrews intense pride. Whenever he was alone, he kept wondering who the thief could possibly be. Aware of her father's obsessive concern, Madeleine tried to distract him as much as she could. When she was unable to spend time with him, she made sure that her daughter kept him occupied. In his role as a doting grandfather, Andrews almost forgot the stolen medal. He was nevertheless keenly aware of Madeleine's strategy. In a quiet moment together, he thanked her.

'I know what you're doing, Maddy, and I'm grateful to you. But it never goes away, I'm afraid. Ever since I discovered the theft yesterday, it's there all the time at the back of my mind.'

'I understand that.'

'Who could hate me that much?'

'Don't think that way, Father.'

'It worries me.'

'I still have hopes that the medal has been mislaid in the house. If we search together, we might actually find it.'

'We've both looked everywhere, Maddy. It's not there.'

'The box it was kept in is.'

'That's true.'

'Why didn't the thief take it with him? It's the obvious thing to do. I'm wondering if you took it out of the cupboard to clean and forgot to put it back. Somehow it went astray but the box remained locked away.'

Andrews frowned. 'Am I really *that* forgetful?'

'There's only one way to find out,' she said. 'We go back to the house together and we search it side by side. I thought I'd looked everywhere yesterday, but I keep wondering if I missed one or two places.'

'What about Alan Hinton?'

'If we fail, we'll hand over to him, though we must

remember that he can only give his help now and then. If the superintendent knew what he was doing on our behalf, he'd be very angry. His detectives are deployed to solve serious crimes.'

'This *is* a serious crime!' shouted Andrews.

'Yes, I know,' said Madeleine, 'but Alan has just finished dealing with a case of attempted arson and is now involved in an investigation of a bank robbery. To the superintendent, those crimes will seem far more important than the loss of your medal.'

'Robert wouldn't take that attitude.'

'Unfortunately, he's not here. Alan Hinton is and he's kind enough to offer his help. Meanwhile,' she went on, 'you need have no fears about the house itself while Mr Kingston is keeping it under surveillance.'

Alfred Kingston was an angular man in his late sixties with a broken leg that obliged him to move around with the help of crutches. Seated in the front window, he watched people come and go in both directions. On the table beside him were a pencil and a scrap of paper. A stocky man of middle height came into view and stopped directly opposite. He knocked on the door of Caleb Andrews' house and waited. When there was no response, he knocked even harder then peered intently through the window. Deciding that there was nobody at home, he turned on his heel and walked away.

After grabbing the pencil and jotting down a rough description of the man, Kingston took out the watch from his waistcoat pocket and made a note of the time.

* * *

When he made the appointment to see the doctor, Colbeck didn't mention that it was in connection with an investigation. Cecil Dymock was therefore expecting a new patient to walk in. After a polite handshake, he motioned his visitor to a chair.

'What seems to be the trouble?' he asked.

'I'm very confused, Doctor.'

'Have you had a bang on the head recently?'

'I've had several,' replied Colbeck, 'and they've all been self-inflicted. The next stage will be tearing my hair out. My confusion arises from the fact that I'm the detective inspector leading an investigation into what could well turn out to be a case of murder and certain people in this town simply refuse to assist me. You are one of them, Doctor.'

Dymock bristled. 'I've already spoken to Sergeant Leeming about that.'

'With respect, sir, you made a point of *not* speaking to him. When people do that, our natural assumption is that they have something to hide.'

'That's an outrageous accusation.'

'Perhaps you'd explain why.'

'Let me be frank. Alex Piper and I were neighbours. From the moment he moved in,' said Dymock, 'there was trouble. He claimed to own land that is patently mine, and held riotous parties in his house that went on into the small hours. With all that noise going on, my wife and I couldn't sleep.'

'Didn't you complain?'

'Yes – on several occasions.'

'How did Mr Piper respond?'

'He laughed in my face. When I went to the police, Sergeant Ainsley said that he'd have a quiet word with Piper but could not guarantee it would have any effect. Lord Culverhouse is Piper's uncle. He casts a long shadow.'

'Yes, I've met His Lordship.'

'Then you'll be aware of the power he yields here.'

'Did you complain to him?'

'I sent him a letter. He never replied.'

'That must have been disappointing.'

'It was insulting.'

'I take it that Lord Culverhouse is not one of your patients.'

'No, he isn't,' said Dymock.

'So you had no leverage with him.'

'I didn't but his nephew certainly did.'

'And he obviously used it to gain advantage over you. I can see how maddeningly unfair that must have seemed to you, Doctor, but it's hardly a good enough reason to refuse even to discuss what happened to Alex Piper.'

'Don't wait for an expression of sympathy, Inspector, because it won't be forthcoming.'

'It was curiosity that I was hoping for, sir. Aren't you interested to know what has happened to him?'

'He's gone for good and that makes me very happy.'

'How do you *know* he's gone for good?'

'Well . . .'

'You said it with such confidence that you must have information that we don't. How did you come by it?'

'I'm only saying what everybody else is.'

'You were rejoicing in the fact,' said Colbeck, 'and it distresses me. A highly educated man like you should surely be able to put aside his prejudices and feel sorry for a family that's in a state of anguish because they simply don't know what happened to their son. Since you seem to have privileged insight into the case, why don't you put them – and me, for that matter – out of our misery by telling us the truth?'

Dymock regarded him with a blend of dislike and caution. He could see that Colbeck couldn't be sent on his way as easily as Leeming had been. Walking behind his desk, he sat down and thought for a few moments before he spoke.

'You are right, Inspector,' he conceded. 'Perhaps I have adopted a vengeful position when impartiality is called for. I give you my word that I don't know what happened to Piper. I've just assumed – as we all have – that some harm has come to him and that we may never discover what it was.'

'Oh, I'll discover what it was,' said Colbeck, evenly. 'I've already collected a lot of valuable evidence. Those involved in what is clearly a plot will all be brought to justice.'

Dymock swallowed hard. 'I wish you well.'

'May I ask if Walter Vine is a patient of yours?'

'That information is confidential.'

'It also happens to be rather important. Are you aware of the penalty for refusing to help a police inquiry?' Dymock's face hardened. 'It's a simple question. Is he or isn't he?'

'He was at one time,' admitted the other.

'Why did he look for medical help elsewhere?'

'Because I asked him to do so when I learnt that he took

183

part in those deafening parties held in Piper's house. As it happened, I very rarely saw Mr Vine. Most of the time, he was too young and healthy to need a doctor.'

'He needs one at the moment,' said Colbeck. 'Do you have any idea who has replaced you?'

'No, I don't.'

'How did he react when you asked him to leave this practice?'

'He pretended that he was about to leave in any case and made some stinging criticism of my work.'

'That was very discourteous of him.'

'Yes,' said Dymock, 'I caught sight of Vine a few days ago as he rode past me. He had his arm in a sling. I presumed that it was a riding injury of sorts. Half his life appears to be spent in the saddle.' He pulled a face. 'One can't always choose one's patients. In some cases, I have to stretch my tolerance to extremes. Walter Vine pushed it to breaking point.'

Even though it had been necessary, Leeming had hated having to get up early that morning. Given the effort spent the night before, he could have stayed in bed until noon. There was one immediate bonus. As he'd left the hotel, he'd seen masses of textile workers going off to their respective factories. These were the people who kept Kendal throbbing with activity. The detectives had so far dealt largely with middle-class inhabitants and, in the case of Lord Culverhouse, with a member of the aristocracy. Leeming found it refreshing to see droves of what he regarded as real human beings, men and women whose destiny it was to keep the machines turning so that they could produce goods ready for dispatch and maintain the town's reputation for quality. If he lived there, he mused, he might have been working alongside them.

He got to the bookshop to discover that Tiller had gone off to market, leaving his wife in charge of the premises. Ruth Tiller was a slim, shy, pretty woman who was younger than her husband. Whenever she mentioned his name, a smile of pleasure flitted across her face. After introducing himself, Leeming took the opportunity to ask about their domestic life.

'Do you have any children?'

'No, but we look after David, who's very much like a child. He's Norm's younger brother. It's sad, really. David lives in a bookshop, yet he can't actually read. But, in spite of his problems, he's no trouble. He helps our servant with chores.'

'Does your husband always do the shopping?'

'Oh, yes,' she said, 'he has an eye for fruit and vegetables. I usually buy a bruised apple or a rotten cabbage by mistake, but Norm would never do that. Besides, he enjoys the bustle of the market whereas I find it a bit frightening.'

'Why is that, Mrs Tiller?'

'There's so much pushing, shoving and shouting. I hate being jostled.'

'What about the cooking. *You* do that, surely?'

'My husband usually helps. People think that he just sits around all day and dusts off his books, but he does a lot of work in the house as well. I couldn't manage without him.'

'My wife has to manage without *me*,' said Leeming, sadly.

185

'My work takes me all over the country so I'm very often not even there. It's unfair on her, really.'

'I'm sure she's very proud of the work you do, Sergeant.'

'I think she'd rather have me doing a job that allowed me to sleep in the same bed every night.' He glanced around the shelves. 'Where did Norm get all these books from?'

'Oh, he's always collected them. He's travelled all over the place to buy books. Norm went to an auction in Maryport once and came back with over two hundred.'

'Do you go off on his expeditions?'

'Sometimes,' she said. 'I went with him to Maryport because it's where I was born and where I first met him. I was very young at the time.'

'What interested you about him?'

'He was different. Maryport is a coal town and most of the lads there work in some part of the industry. They're strong and loud and usually up to mischief. Norm isn't like that. He's quiet and thoughtful. Moreover, he has principles. That's why he was in Maryport in the first place.'

'Tell me about his principles.'

'He loves this county because of its beauty and hated it when they built the Maryport and Carlisle Railway. It was already well established when he came to demonstrate against the latest extension,' she explained. 'The first time I ever saw him, he was carrying a banner that asked us to stop letting railways ruin our landscape.'

'What about the railway here?'

'Oh, he objected to that as well. We were together then. I

carried a banner alongside him and went to the talks Norm gave to people who felt the same as him.'

'I didn't realise he was an agitator.'

'He wasn't, Sergeant. He was just expressing an opinion. Mr Wordsworth did the same. He wrote a poem attacking the idea of a railway here. Norm wrote one as well.'

It was a new side to the bookseller and Leeming wanted to hear much more about it. Before he could ply her with further questions, however, Tiller returned from market with two large wicker baskets filled to capacity with fruit and vegetables.

'What are *you* doing here, Sergeant?' he asked.

'I came to see you.'

'Then you're just in time for a cup of tea. Here you are, Ruth,' he went on, handing her the baskets, 'I think that's everything you asked for. Put the kettle on, please. The sergeant looks as if he's thirsty.'

Since the search parties had been disbanded, Geoffrey Hedley was no longer committing his daylight hours to tramping across the countryside. Instead, he went to the police station to see what information he could pick up about the investigation. Sergeant Ainsley took him into his office.

'The person you should be asking is Inspector Colbeck,' he said. 'Only he can tell you what's going on.'

'I went to his hotel in the hope of speaking to him but both he and Sergeant Leeming left there early this morning.' Hedley shrugged. 'I've no idea where they are.'

'What's your opinion of them, may I ask?'

'Their reputation speaks for itself.'

'I've been a policeman far too long to put my trust in someone's reputation. I judge people by what they do now, not because of some triumph in the distant past.'

'Are you saying you have no faith in Inspector Colbeck?'

'Not at all, sir,' replied Ainsley. 'He's obviously a very clever man. It's just that I find his methods a little strange.'

'Could you explain why, please?'

'Well, let me give you an example. The first thing he did was to examine the railway carriage in which Mr Piper – and you, of course – both travelled on that excursion. He even checked how much oil there was in the lamps in the last compartment.'

Hedley was startled. 'Really – what did he find?'

'They'd been tampered with, he claimed. So much oil had been taken out that there was a likelihood that one or both of the lamps would go out in the course of the journey.'

'One of them *did* go out, as it happens.'

'I don't see any significance in that. All it proves is that someone forgot to put fresh oil in the lamps before the train set out. After all,' said Ainsley, 'the carriages are out of use most of the time. What the inspector sees as vital evidence could easily be a case of laziness on the part of a railwayman.'

'I'm inclined to agree with you,' said Hedley.

'In other ways, the inspector has done the right things. He's talked to all of the right people and has even identified a few suspects – thanks to help from you, sir.'

'I merely named people with a grudge against Alex.'

'There are rather a lot of those in Kendal.'

'These were men with a particular reason to want some kind of retribution.'

'And I can understand why, sir,' said Ainsley. 'However, I don't know that I'd have put Norm Tiller's name forward as a suspect. He did once lose his temper with Mr Piper but that's as far as it went.'

'Then I have to disagree with you, Sergeant. I witnessed the row at that meeting of the local poets. Alex had drunk too much. I'd tried to stop him but he ignored me. The next morning, he felt he'd gone too far. I suggested that he offered Tiller an apology but he refused to do that.'

'Yes, I know. He dared to demand an apology from Norm Tiller.'

'That's what I was ordered to ask for, Sergeant. In fact, I followed my own instincts. When I went to the bookshop, I made my own apology for Alex's behaviour.'

'What did Norm say to you?'

'He hardly said a word,' replied Hedley, 'but I could see that he was still simmering with anger. He refused point-blank to accept any apology. That's why his name went on the list I gave to Inspector Colbeck. Only one thing would appease him and that was Alex's death.'

Norman Tiller was in an almost jovial mood as he and his visitor drank their cup of tea. He regaled Leeming with anecdotes about his visits to the town market over the years and he chortled as he recalled some of the characters he'd met. A few of them had actually inspired poems of his. It was only when

189

his wife went off into the kitchen that Tiller's mood changed.

'What have I done *this* time, Sergeant?' he asked, softly.

'You've done nothing, as far as I know.'

'Then why have you come back?'

'I'm interested in some of your poems.'

'Let's be honest,' said the other. 'By your own admission, your interest is limited to nursery rhymes and I don't write those. Who've you been talking to?'

'I had a word with Sergeant Ainsley, as it happens.'

'I thought so. You wanted to know how that argument at the King's Arms ended.'

'I went in search of more detail,' said Leeming, 'but you were not the only person we talked about. The sergeant told me about his friendship with Gregor Hayes, the blacksmith.'

'They were very close.'

'I could tell that. He still has hopes of solving that case.'

'We'd all be grateful if he did that.'

'How well did you know Mr Hayes?'

'I only saw him when I took my horse to be shoed,' said Tiller, 'and we always had a chat. But I wouldn't say that I really knew Gregor. He was an important figure in this town, the kind you take for granted until they disappear. Then you realise how much you miss them.'

'Is that why you wrote a poem about him?'

Tiller was momentarily stunned. 'Who told you that?'

'Sergeant Ainsley happened to mention it. That's why I came here. I'd like to read it out of interest.'

'But you never knew the man.'

'I know of him and he fascinates me. Also, I'd like to see how you described his disappearance.'

Tiller was abrupt. 'Well, you can't, I'm afraid.'

'Why not?'

'I wasn't happy with the poem, so I tore it up.'

'That was a bit impulsive, wasn't it? Why go to all the trouble of writing it if you then destroy it?'

'It failed to meet the standard I set myself,' said Tiller. 'Most of my poems are like that. I do endless versions of them until I reach the point when I have to accept that they're simply not good enough. Out they go. You have to be brutal if you want to preserve the quality of your work.'

'That's a pity,' said Leeming. 'I just hope you've kept another poem I'd like to take a look at. Your wife was telling me how you've been involved in protests about the building of the railways in the Lake District.'

'That was years ago.'

'Perhaps it was, but you have the poem to remind you of the time when you fought against the Kendal and Windermere Railway. If I'd lived here, I'd have done the same. I hate railways,' said Leeming. 'That's why I'd love to see your poem. Do you still have it?'

The bookseller said nothing, but it was clear from the glint in his eye that his visitor's request was being turned down.

CHAPTER FIFTEEN

Aware of their intense suffering, Colbeck made a point of calling on the Haslam family. It seemed odd that, in such a relatively small community, they knew nothing about the rumours surrounding Alexander Piper but, having met them, he could understand why. Their house was isolated from Kendal and the only time they ventured into the town on a regular basis was when they went to church. When their daughter had been befriended by Piper, her parents had taken him largely at face value, assuming that the son of an archdeacon would be honourable and above reproach. All that concerned them was Melissa's happiness and she had been radiant. Unfortunately, the dramatic events at Hallowe'en had made her dreams of an idyllic marriage disintegrate.

When he called on the family, therefore, Colbeck made a point of spending some time alone with Melissa, doing his best to offer some reassurance. While promising her that he would find out exactly what had happened to her betrothed, he was conscious that the truth might well cause her even more sorrow. Melissa produced one surprise.

'Our friends have been so kind,' she said. 'We've had cards and letters of condolence from everyone, but there was a glaring exception.'

'Oh – and who might that be, Miss Haslam?'

'Mr Hedley.'

'That's because he's been heavily involved in the search,' suggested Colbeck. 'They leave not long after dawn and only get back when light is fading.'

'He could still have written to me.'

'That's true and no more than you should expect.'

'Geoffrey was there. He'd have travelled in the same compartment as Alex. He could tell me the things I'd like to know. Of all the men on that excursion, Geoffrey is the only one I'd trust.'

'What about some of the women on that train?'

'There were only a handful of those. According to Alex, most of the people on the Phantom Special were men. By and large, women were too frightened to go. I was one of them.'

Colbeck felt sorry for her as he realised that she'd been duped by her fiancé. Melissa had been told that the excursion was an almost exclusively male affair whereas there were several young women aboard the train.

'Will you be seeing Geoffrey Hedley today?' she asked.

'I expect so, Miss Haslam.'

'Then I'd be grateful if you'd pass on my concern.'

'I'll make a point of doing so,' said Colbeck, 'though it may well be that he's kept his distance from you because he fears that you're in too fragile a state to receive visitors.'

'I'd happily speak to *him*.'

'Then I'll pass on the message.'

'Thank you, Inspector. And let me say that I do appreciate your taking the trouble to come here at a time when you're in the middle of leading the investigation.'

'I have, alas, been in this situation many times, Miss Haslam,' he said, 'so I know the importance of keeping grieving families well informed. It's the reason I'm now going on to visit Lord and Lady Culverhouse to see what comfort I may be able to offer to them.'

Though she was always pleased to see Madeleine's father, Lydia Quayle was glad to have arrived at the house when the old man was preoccupied with his granddaughter. Now she could have a private conversation with her friend. Madeleine was unusually despondent.

'What's the trouble?' asked Lydia.

'The medal has definitely gone,' said the other. 'I still had hopes that it was there but, when father and I searched the house from top to bottom this morning, there was no sign of it. It's pointless expecting it to turn up out of the blue.'

'I'm so sorry, Madeleine.'

'Father is afraid he'll never see his medal again.'

'At least wait until Alan has looked into the case. During the time he's been at Scotland Yard, he's arrested quite a few thieves. Alan has a knack of finding clues.'

'We certainly need his help.'

'How is your father now?'

'Strangely enough, he's more settled in his mind. Now that he's been back to the house, he feels he'd rather sleep there tonight. He chided himself for being afraid to stay under his own roof yesterday. During the day, of course,' said Madeleine, 'he has no qualms because I asked a neighbour to keep watch on the house. We were able to speak to him earlier on.'

'Had he seen anything suspicious?'

'As a matter of fact, he had, Lydia. A man had banged on the front door twice then peered through the window. Mr Kingston didn't recognise him, so he wrote down a description of him and told us that he just didn't trust him.'

'You're lucky to have a good neighbour like that.'

'Mr Kingston has always got on well with my father. He used to work on the railway himself but only in the ticket office. He loved to hear about the adventures my father had, especially the story about how Robert and I first came to meet as a result of the train robbery. Oh,' said Madeleine, 'I almost forgot. I had a lovely long letter from Robert this morning.'

'What does he say about the investigation?'

'It's far more complicated than he thought it would be. But he's confident of success in the end. You know my husband, Lydia. He always strikes an optimistic note.' Madeleine pursed her lips. 'I wish I could say that about Father.'

Victor Leeming never needed any persuasion to step into a bar but, on this occasion, he was not there in search of a drink.

He'd come to the King's Arms to speak to its landlord, Hugh Penrose. Leeming asked him how many people belonged to the group of poets that used to meet there.

'Why do you want to know that, Sergeant?' asked Penrose. 'Are you thinking of joining them?'

Leeming grinned. 'I can't string more than a few words together,' he confessed, 'and even then, they're usually in the wrong order.'

'To answer your question, there are six or seven of them.'

'Can you remember their names?'

'Why? Do you want their autographs?'

'I want something a lot more important than that,' said Leeming, taking out his notebook and pencil. 'I'm ready.'

Penrose rattled off seven names and also provided details of each poet's occupation. As a result, the sergeant first headed off to the shop owned by Reginald Garside, one of the town's barbers. He found him carefully trimming the beard of a customer. Garside was a tall, bony, middle-aged man who'd spent so much time bent over in the course of his work that his spine had acquired a permanent stoop.

Luckily, no other customers were waiting. When the bearded man had paid and left, Garside turned to Leeming.

'What can I do for you, sir?' he asked.

'I'd like you to answer a few questions, if you will. I believe that you belong to a group of poets.'

'Well, yes, I do but I'm a barber, really. Norm Tiller is the real poet in this town. I'm just a dabbler, Mr . . .'

'It's Detective Sergeant Leeming. I'm in Kendal to look into the disappearance of Mr Alexander Piper.'

'My customers talk of nothing else. Most of them reckon he was carried off by a phantom of sorts. This part of the country is full of them.'

'You mentioned Mr Tiller a moment ago.'

'Yes, he's a wonderful man. To my shame, I had very little education, but I've always wanted to write poems. He encouraged me.'

'What sort of things do you write about?'

'I'm a kind of nature poet like Mr Wordsworth, though I'd never be able to match him, of course. He's even better than Norm.'

'You've read Mr Tiller's poems, then?'

'I've done better than that, Sergeant. I've heard him reading them out to us. It's what we do, you see. When we meet up together, we take it in turns to read something we've written. I was hopeless when I started but I've slowly got better.'

'How many of his poems have you heard?'

'Dozens of them, I suppose,' said Garside. 'He lets us write out copies of some of them so that we can take them home to study them. Unlike me, he has a real talent yet he's so modest about it.'

'That's what impressed me about him.'

Leeming had the feeling that he might have had the good fortune to stumble on the right person at the first attempt. It would save him having to locate and question a local butcher, an engineer, a chimney sweep and three men who worked in a woollen factory. The urge to write poetry had driven each one of them into the group run by the bookseller.

'The landlord at the King's Arms mentioned the last time you met there,' said Leeming.

Garside sighed. 'Oh, yes, it was dreadful.'

'Tell me about it.'

'Hasn't Hugh already done that?'

'I want to hear from someone who was a victim of the intruder. You admire Norm Tiller's work. It must have been awful to hear someone poking fun at it.'

'It was so spiteful,' said Garside.

Then he went on to give his version. The barber's respect for the bookseller was obvious. The latter had obviously become his mentor. He'd copied out a number of the man's poems and claimed to be able to recite some of them by heart.

'Are they that good?' asked Leeming.

'*I* think so. Norm has the gift of language.'

'Which is your favourite?'

'It's difficult to say.'

'Try.'

'All right, then – there's one about witches that I like to read aloud. It scares my wife, but I love it.'

'He wrote one about the disappearance of Gregor Hayes, the blacksmith,' said Leeming. 'I don't suppose you have a copy of that poem, by any chance?'

Colbeck arrived at Culverhouse Court to learn that Alexander Piper's parents were also there. He was delighted by the coincidence because it saved him another journey to Ambleside. Shown into the drawing room, he found all four of them seated.

Since Lord Culverhouse was near his sister, Colbeck could see the striking contrast between the two of them. In her plain, black dress, Emma Piper looked more like one of the servants than a member of the Culverhouse family. Rodney Piper was the same spectral figure Colbeck had met once before.

As he'd done so with Melissa Haslam, he told them that he felt confident of finding out exactly what had happened to Alexander Piper, though he warned them that it might take time. He poured scorn on the notion of supernatural intervention of any kind and assured them that, having visited Hither Wood at midnight, he refused to believe that it was haunted.

The archdeacon was critical. 'I'm sorry that you don't believe in ghosts, Inspector,' he said, 'because I've had cast-iron proof of their existence.'

'I'd be interested to hear what it was,' said Colbeck.

'I'd rather not distress the ladies.'

'Nonsense!' said Lady Culverhouse. 'Your wife and I are not shrinking violets. Besides, I daresay that Emma has already heard the story.'

'I have,' confirmed Emma, 'and, disagreeable as it is, I believe every word.'

'And so must the rest of you,' warned her husband. 'The bishop's word is akin to Holy Writ.'

'To which diocese are you referring?' asked Colbeck.

'Gloucester – my dear old friend, Simon Overton, has been bishop there for several years. He's a remarkable man and an experienced exorcist. When I last saw him, he told me about a house in one of the villages nearby that was so frightening to live in that the people who bought it never stayed more than a few months. It was too upsetting.'

'What form did the disturbance take?'

'Inhabitants complained of weird noises, Inspector, as if people were in great pain and pleading for help. Every so often, a strange smell permeated the house.'

'Was the cellar examined?'

'Everyone who lived there did that, but they found nothing to explain either the voices or the stench. The tragedy was that the house was eventually abandoned and would have become derelict if someone hadn't had the sense to call in the bishop.'

'What did he do?' wondered Culverhouse.

'Well, first of all, Simon spoke to people who'd slept under that roof. Once he'd taken their testimony, he spent a night there himself.'

'That was brave of him,' said Colbeck. 'What happened?'

'He heard none of the strange noises,' explained the archdeacon, 'but the stink was almost overpowering. Search hard as he did, he could find no source for it. Next morning, miraculously, it had gone.'

'How peculiar!' said Lady Culverhouse. 'Did the bishop ever find out the cause of the unpleasant smell?'

'Yes, he did. He searched through the cathedral archives and discovered that Gloucester had been afflicted by the plague on more than one occasion. Rather than have the victims rotting in the city,' said Piper, 'they were taken out to a huge pit and thrown in.'

'So the house was built on top of it, was it?' said Colbeck.

'That's what Simon established. Once he'd identified the problem, he was able to perform a ceremony of exorcism and drive away the troubled spirits from the house. Since then, there's never been a hint of trouble at the property.' He looked at Colbeck. 'What do you make of that, Inspector?'

'I can't challenge the bishop's account because I wasn't there at the time, but I recall a scholarly article I once read. When the plague struck, people were so desperate to avoid infection that they had the bodies of the victims collected as soon as possible and tipped into pits before being covered by quick lime. In this article,' Colbeck went on, 'the author claimed that they didn't always wait until a plague victim was actually dead.'

Emma was horrified. 'They were still *alive*?'

'It was felt that they were so close to death that it made no difference. They were tossed uncaringly onto the carts with the real corpses.'

'That's inhuman!'

'It explains what happened in the case I told you about,' contended Piper. 'Those piteous cries in the night must have come from poor wretches who were buried alive.'

'Could we please talk about something else?' said Lady Culverhouse with a shudder.

'I'm sorry. I thought that the bishop's experience was instructive. It might even have made the inspector think again.'

Colbeck smiled. 'It's an interesting story,' he said, 'but it has no bearing on what happened here at Hallowe'en. I'm convinced that no ghosts, apparitions or plague victims were responsible for your son's disappearance.'

'That brings me to the wall of flame,' said the archdeacon.

'Yes,' said Culverhouse, 'Rodney has this wild idea that it was symbolic of hell and that Alex has descended into the nether regions. I thought the notion ridiculous.'

'I'm slowly coming to believe it,' said Emma.

'It's what you were *meant* to believe,' said Colbeck. 'What really happened that night, I would suggest, was an example of careful stage management devised to spread confusion.'

'Have you any idea who is behind it all?'

'I'm building up a very clear picture of him in my mind. As to his confederates, I feel I'm getting closer to them all the time. I'm well aware of your desire for an early resolution but I ask you to be patient.'

'Someone must have *despised* our son,' said Piper, 'and that troubles us. We know that he could be impetuous at times, but did he really provoke someone into killing him?'

'It appears so.'

'Find him, Inspector. Make him pay the ultimate price for his crime. Before they hang him, however, I'd value a word with him alone. I want to look into his eyes and ask him why he *dared* to take our son's life. When I know the bitter truth,' he went on, 'I'll pray for the salvation of the killer's soul.'

As soon as he heard of the latest arrest, the superintendent went in search of Alan Hinton. The latter was seated at a desk as he wrote out his report. When Tallis walked into the room, the detective constable jumped up to his feet.

'I didn't mean to startle you, Hinton.'

'You took me by surprise, sir.'

'I just came to congratulate you on the latest arrest.'

'It wasn't me who actually put the handcuffs on him. We knew that the robbers had help from someone who worked at the bank and the man in question almost gave himself away.'

'You were part of a successful team,' said Tallis, 'and I wanted to acknowledge that. You'd only just finished with that case of attempted arson, so you've had two triumphs in a short period of time.'

'I only did what I've been trained to do, sir.'

'Colbeck would be proud of you.'

'The inspector is my idol.'

'I rather disapprove of idolatry but at least you've chosen the ideal detective on whom to pattern your own career.'

'My ambition is to work alongside him one day.'

'That day may have to wait,' cautioned Tallis, 'but you are taking steps in the right direction. Well done, Hinton.'

'Thank you, Superintendent,' said the other, glowing. 'Is there any news of the inspector?'

'I had a full report from him in this morning's mail. It's a complex investigation but Colbeck loves a daunting challenge.' He chuckled. 'There was a time when working for me might be viewed in that light.'

'That's how we all thought of it, sir,' said Hinton.

'Did you, indeed?' growled Tallis.

'Well, no, not really, sir.' The grin froze on his face. 'What I mean is that—'

'I know only too well what you mean and I resent it

strongly. Things have obviously become far too lax in my absence and I'm serving notice that we're going to have some real discipline here again. Do you hear that, Hinton?'

'Yes, Superintendent, I do.'

'Then spread the word,' said Tallis, tapping his own chest. 'I'm back and I'll brook no mockery.'

Leeming sat in the room at the rear of the shop and pored over the poems that the barber had given him. Garside, meanwhile, was busy cutting the hair of his latest customer. There was a problem. Careful and precise with a pair of scissors in his hand, the barber was far less competent with a pen between his fingers. His handwriting was so wayward that Leeming had to guess at some of the words. Ink blots were another hazard. They were sprinkled liberally over the pages.

The first poem that the sergeant tried to read had been written by Garside himself. Its title was 'Beneath the Water' and the barber had transformed himself into a creature that lurked in the depths of Lake Windermere and surfaced from time to time to bask in the sun and admire the beautiful landscape on all sides. The kindest thing that could be said of the halting verse and the thudding rhymes was that the poem was a worthy effort by a writer with a lot to learn. After a couple of verses, Leeming gave up in despair.

When he turned to the work of Norman Tiller, the contrast was striking. 'Railway of Ruination' was a devastating attack on the Kendal and Windermere Railway for its destruction of the countryside. What fascinated Leeming was the passion that inspired Tiller to write it. Where the barber's language had been trite and woolly, the honeyed words of a real poet soared to heights that Garside could never reach. The sergeant was also sympathetic to the claim that railways defaced the British countryside. He could imagine Tiller declaiming his poem from a stage and being cheered to the echo by those who protested against the building of the railway.

Leeming searched for the poem about the disappearance of Gregor Hayes. When he read the opening verse, he realised that it was a very different piece of work. It was dark, mysterious and troubling.

Geoffrey Hedley was in his office, trying to work his way through the backlog of letters and tasks that had built up while he'd been otherwise engaged. It was not long before he was interrupted by the arrival of a visitor. Colbeck was shown into the office. Hedley was on his feet at once.

'Do come in, Inspector, and please take a seat.'

'Thank you, Mr Hedley,' replied the other, sitting next to a small table. 'I heard from Sergeant Ainsley that you were looking for me.'

'That's true. You're proving hard to track down.'

'I've been here and there, following my instincts.'

'Have they led you in the right directions?'

'I believe so,' said Colbeck. 'The first person I tackled was Dr Dymock. I'm grateful that he's not in charge of my health. He was altogether too spiky for my taste.'

'What did you learn from him?'

'I learnt that he had a very good motive for locking his antlers with Alexander Piper. Apart from the boundary dispute, he had to put up with the rumpus from the frequent parties held next door. I daresay you attended some of them.'

'I always tried to make Alex keep the noise down.'

'What about the boundary dispute?'

'In my role as his legal advisor, I told him that he would never win the case, but he insisted on pressing ahead with it. Once he got a bee in his bonnet, he was out of control.'

'I gather that Walter Vine came to the parties.'

'That was in the early days, when Alex had just moved in. Having so much in common, they were on good terms then.'

'What about Miss Treadgold? Was she invited as well?'

'No,' said the lawyer. 'They were almost exclusively celebrations with his male friends. Besides, Alex was trying to distance himself from Miss Treadgold. Once he'd met Melissa Haslam, he wanted to spend as much time as he could with her.'

'Incidentally,' said Colbeck, 'I spoke to Miss Haslam earlier on. She was rather put out that you've made no attempt to visit or write to her.'

'I felt it was unwise.'

'I would have thought it was obligatory.'

'Miss Haslam is well aware that I put the idea of the excursion into Alex's head. She is bound to blame me. I didn't wish to make things worse by turning up in person.'

'A letter or a card would have been welcome.'

'I felt too embarrassed to send either. As for those parties,' he went on, hurriedly, 'they quickly tailed off and Miss

Treadgold was gradually eased out of his life.'

'It didn't sound very gradual to me,' said Colbeck. 'Her version is that she was dropped abruptly like a red-hot brick. She is still wounded by the way that he treated her.'

'And yet she was eager to join in the search party.'

'What emotion prompted that, do you think?'

'I believe that it was love.'

'Are you sure it wasn't guilt?'

'I'm certain, Inspector. I saw Alex and Miss Treadgold together. They were very happy in each other's company. It's just that he never saw her as . . . well, the sort of person he'd choose to marry.'

'Most women in her position would feel that he'd been trifling with their affections. Was that your opinion as well?'

Hedley looked uncomfortable. 'It was to some degree,' he said. 'I felt that Miss Treadgold merited more than brusque dismissal. On the other hand, she was worldly enough to know full well what she was letting herself in for when she befriended Alex. The relationship would never have achieved longevity.'

'That's a polite way of saying that it was doomed.'

'Sadly, that was the case.'

'Miss Treadgold was cast off and became the first victim,' noted Colbeck, 'then it was Mr Piper's turn to suffer. That gave immense satisfaction to the three men you named as potential suspects – Cecil Dymock, Walter Vine and Norman Tiller. Which one of that trio is the likeliest to seek revenge?'

'I'd have to say that it would be Walter.'

'You must have been present at that duel he fought.'

Hedley gulped. 'I don't know what you're talking about,' he said, eyes darting. 'Duelling is illegal.'

'That wouldn't have stopped Mr Piper. He flouted the law at every turn. And if he did – as is quite likely – inflict that nasty wound on Vine's arm, you would certainly have been there to see it happen.'

'I deny that wholeheartedly.'

'To whom else would Mr Piper turn in such a situation?' asked Colbeck, pointedly. 'You supported him in every way. I fancy that you're the only person in his life that he could trust.'

'I was his friend.'

'Friendship means standing by during a duel.'

'It never took place, Inspector.'

'Then why did Sergeant Leeming and I reach the same conclusion about Mr Vine?'

'Did Walter admit there'd been a duel?'

'He did what you did, sir, and lied.'

'Couldn't you accept his word?'

'Since I've been in Kendal,' said Colbeck, rising to his feet, 'I've found it increasingly difficult to accept *anyone's* word. Simple, unvarnished truth seems to be in short supply here. We'll have to solve by other means the mysteries that have tormented this town.' He reached for his hat. 'Do excuse me, Mr Hedley. I won't keep you from you work.'

As Colbeck let himself out, he heard a loud thud as if Hedley had just brought his fist down hard on the desk.

CHAPTER SIXTEEN

Victor Leeming had been so startled by the poem about the missing blacksmith that he read it through three times. He then copied the final verse into his notebook so that Colbeck could read it. Going back into the shop, he waited patiently until the barber had run out of customers. When another gap appeared, Garside apologised for keeping him waiting.

'No need to say sorry,' Leeming assured him. 'It gave me time to think. I've been reading about the disappearance of Gregor Hayes. That poem really interested me.'

'As I told you, Norm has a gift.'

'I didn't know much about the blacksmith when I came in here, but I do now. Was he really such a ladies' man?'

'So they say.'

'But he spent his life covered in dirt, sweat and the stink of horses. Most women would run a mile from someone like that.'

'There's no accounting for taste, Sergeant,' said the barber with a chortle. 'I've heard of women going out of their way so they could pass the forge and stare at Gregor's muscles. His arms were always bare, you see, and they were massive. He made the rest of us look puny.'

'Was the blacksmith married?'

'Yes, he had a wife and children.'

'Norm's poem says he had a way of talking to women that made them feel . . . special.'

'I wish I knew how to do that,' said the other, gloomily. 'When I get anywhere near a woman, I always say the wrong thing. My wife says I'm better off keeping my mouth shut.'

'Was the blacksmith a nuisance?'

'I never heard of women complaining.'

'What about their husbands?'

Garside laughed. 'Oh, they watched Gregor like hawks.'

'Tell me about this phantom who appears in the poem. Is he real or was he just someone that Norm invented?'

'I think he's real.'

'You *think* or you know for certain?'

'Norm made me believe in him.'

'Has anyone ever seen the phantom?'

'They only ever get glimpses.'

'Where does he live?'

'Nobody knows,' said the barber, 'but Norm once saw him for a second or two. He was running among the fells.'

'What does he eat? Where does he sleep? How does he stay alive?'

'He's a phantom, Sergeant. They're different to us.'

Leeming wanted to press for more detail but a customer stepped into the shop. He thanked Garside for his help and turned to go. The barber spoke in a whisper.

'If you want to know more about Gregor, you must ask Sergeant Ainsley. He was his closest friend.'

Geoffrey Hedley was unable to concentrate on his work. After his conversation with Colbeck, he felt bruised and uneasy. He therefore left his office and walked briskly in the cold air to clear his head. His footsteps took him towards Walter Vine's house and, although he'd never liked the man, he felt impelled to pay him a visit. Vine kept him talking in the hall.

'What's brought you here, Hedley?'

'I came to warn you.'

'I don't need any advice from you.'

'It's in your best interests to listen to me.' Vine snorted. 'I know what you think of me and, more importantly, what you thought of Alex. But it's important that we put our differences aside for a moment.'

'Why?'

'Inspector Colbeck has just been to see me.'

'He came here as well. I think he's floundering.'

'Don't underestimate him,' said Hedley. 'He's clever and he's dedicated. Colbeck won't leave this town until he's found out the truth.'

'He'll never do that.'

'He *knows* about the duel.'

'How can he?' asked Vine, disdainfully. 'He wasn't there and has no proof that it ever took place. As it happens, the inspector challenged me about it and I simply denied it.'

'That's not enough. Colbeck is the sort of man who'll go to every doctor in the town until he finds out which one of them dealt with that wound of yours.'

'Then he'll be wasting his time. I had the sense to summon a doctor from Carlisle and he took care of me.'

'Can he be trusted?'

'Of course he can. I paid him a lot of money to keep his mouth shut. Besides, Colbeck would never find him. He's just groping in the dark.'

'That's not my impression.'

'What's wrong with you, man?' asked Vine, studying him closely. 'You're almost dithering. You were never like this when your life consisted of doing whatever Alex Piper told you to do. You were happy to be his lapdog.'

Hedley reddened. 'Don't you dare say that!'

'How could you let anyone *enslave* you in that way? What possible reward could you get out of it?'

'I've no intention of talking about Alex with you,' said Hedley, frostily. 'You'd only sneer.'

'I'm curious, that's all. You're a lawyer and they always expect to profit from any transaction. What did you get in return for all you did for him? Was it money? Was it the satisfaction of serving someone you worshipped? Or was it something else?'

'I'm leaving.'

'Not until I get an answer,' said Vine, stepping between him and the front door. 'I want you to confirm my suspicion. There's only one reason you allowed him to lead you by the nose. You picked up his cast-offs, didn't you? When he'd had his fun with a woman, you were standing by in the hope of taking her off his hands.' Vine smirked. 'It was the only way you'd get to enjoy the gorgeous feel of female flesh.'

'Be quiet!'

'How are you going to manage now that he's dead? Your days of fondling pretty women are well and truly over.'

Hedley could take no more. Lashing out, he caught Vine on his wounded arm and produced a howl of pain from him that was followed by an outburst of foul language. He then pulled open the front door and ran away in undignified haste.

When he called into the police station, a pleasant surprise awaited Colbeck. Bernard Ainsley handed him a copy of the diagram of Hither Wood that was kept with his records of the Gregor Hayes case.

'Sergeant Leeming will have put most of what you need to know in his notebook,' he said, 'but he couldn't draw this diagram on such a small scale. I thought it would show you just how carefully we searched.'

'I'm very grateful to you,' said Colbeck, studying the map. 'You're something of an artist.'

'I'm not, but Constable Ewens is. He was heavily involved in the search for Gregor. I got him to draw the original diagram. All I've done is to copy it.'

'Well, it's very useful.'

'Don't waste too much time in the wood.'

'Why not?'

'Gregor isn't there.'

'The answer to his disappearance might be.'

'Is that why you went there at midnight?' Colbeck was taken aback. 'There's not much that happens around here that we don't get to know about, Inspector.'

'So it seems.'

'Why didn't you tell me about your visit?'

'I chose not to,' said Colbeck. 'Are you aware of what happened when we actually got to Hither Wood?'

'Unfortunately, I'm not. I just know that you went there.'

'You obviously disapprove.'

'Not at all,' said Ainsley. 'I think it was very brave of you and the sergeant. Nobody else would have dared to go there at that time of night. Your interest was aroused and, like any good detective, you wanted to satisfy it. I'm only sorry you didn't take me with you.'

'With respect,' said Colbeck, indicating the map, '*this* would have been more use to us than you, though it would've have been difficult to see it by the light of a lamp.'

'If you must go back, do it in daylight. Oh, and if you need any digging done, I can let you have a couple of men.'

'That's a kind offer but I won't need anyone else. The digging that we're engaged in is metaphorical.'

Ainsley was puzzled. 'I don't follow.'

'We let our heads do all the work, Sergeant.'

'Ah, yes . . .'

'Thinking ahead saves a lot of wasted time.'

'True.'

Looking over the sergeant's shoulder, Colbeck saw the poster that Lord Culverhouse had had printed. In bold, black lettering, a large reward was offered to anyone who could provide information that would lead to the arrest and conviction of those involved in the disappearance of Alexander Piper.

'Have you had much response to that?' he asked.

'Oh, yes,' said Ainsley, wearily. 'Copies have been put up all over the place. I've had three or four people in here already with cock and bull stories. They were kicked straight out with a warning that they'd be arrested if they wasted my time again.'

'It's always the same when money is on offer.'

'We found that out when Gregor Hayes vanished and we papered the town with posters. The reward was much smaller than what His Lordship is putting up, but we nevertheless had half a dozen people in here, claiming they knew what happened. They didn't provide a scrap of useful information between them. Anyway,' he went on, 'you're not here to listen to my woes.'

'I came to tell you what I've been up to today,' said Colbeck, 'but, since you're able to track my movements, you may already know.'

'Nobody's tracking you, Inspector.'

'Then how did you know we'd been to Hither Wood?'

'I bumped into Wilf Chesney at the King's Arms. We often

have a drink together. Wilf told me that you'd hired the horse and dog cart from him and that you wanted to pick it up from the stables late in the evening.'

'But I didn't tell Mr Chesney where we were going.'

'Where else would you go at that time of night?' Ainsley tapped his skull with a finger. 'I did some of that metaphorical digging you talked about.'

'It was a good guess.'

'So what *have* you been doing today?'

'I've been talking to people who interest me.'

'Then I daresay Mr Vine was one of them. There was no love lost between him and Piper.'

'I wanted to know exactly why they fell out.'

'Who else have you seen?'

'I paid a visit to Dr Dymock.'

'Then I daresay he criticised me for not being able to stop the hullabaloo from the parties held by his next-door neighbour. I did exactly what I promised to do,' said Ainsley, defensively, 'and had a quiet word with Piper, but I might as well have been spitting in the wind.'

'Are the two houses so close together?'

'Not really – they must be thirty yards or more apart. That tells you how loud the noise was when those drunken idiots started carousing. The doctor and his wife could hear them clearly.'

'What about this boundary dispute?' asked Colbeck.

'Oh, that was about a paddock at the rear of the two properties. It belonged to Dr Dymock but Piper wanted it for his horses so he got Mr Hedley to search for a means of making a claim to the land. Also,' added Ainsley, 'he wanted to punish the doctor for daring to complain about those parties of his. Piper told me to my face that he'd do whatever he wanted in his own house – only he put it much cruder than that.'

'So he had no intention of being a good neighbour?'

'He was establishing his territory, Inspector.'

'What made him so selfish?'

'When your uncle is Lord Culverhouse, you've got a free hand to be as unpleasant as you like to people you consider as your inferiors – such as Dymock.'

'And the police,' said Colbeck.

Ainsley sucked his teeth. 'We've learnt to live with it.'

'It's possible that marriage to Miss Haslam might have civilised him a little but it's by no means certain. When I called on her earlier,' said Colbeck, 'her view of Piper was unchanged. He is still a paragon to her.'

'I hope she never learns the truth. However,' said Ainsley, 'Miss Haslam is certainly not a suspect. I can see that Vine and the doctor might be. Did you speak to anyone else?'

'Yes, I did, as a matter of fact.'

Colbeck paused to consider the wisdom of confiding in the sergeant. Ainsley still had residual resentment at being pushed aside so that Scotland Yard detectives could take over the case. To his credit, however, was the fact that he'd been helpful with regard to the disappearance of Gregor Hayes, and had even taken the trouble to drive Colbeck out to Hither Wood. The diagram of the area that he'd copied for them would be invaluable. On balance, Colbeck decided, the man deserved to be kept abreast of every development.

'I also called on Mr Hedley at his office,' said Colbeck.

'Why? He's not a suspect.'

'I believe that he might be.'

Ainsley was shocked. '*Hedley?*' he exclaimed. 'No, I don't believe it. He loved Piper as much as Miss Haslam did. In any case, Geoffrey Hedley is harmless.'

'I disagree. When his friend was simply a pleasure-seeker, Hedley had a role to play. If Piper married, the lawyer would be largely redundant. I think Hedley felt rejected. Piper was about to squeeze him out of his life.'

'Why did you bother to go there, Inspector?'

'I wanted to rattle his cage.'

'But he's completely innocent.'

'He didn't behave as if he was.'

'Hedley is the *last* person I'd suspect.'

'That calm and businesslike exterior is just a shield,' said Colbeck. 'Underneath it is a very manipulative man.'

'That's not how *I* see him.'

'Then we must agree to differ.'

'Hedley's whole life revolved around Piper. They were nearly always together. What possible reason could he have to get rid of his friend?'

'Think hard, Sergeant.'

Ainsley shook his head. 'Not Miss Haslam, surely?'

'That would be out of the question.'

'Then who do you mean?'

'Miss Caroline Treadgold.'

'That's a ridiculous suggestion,' said Ainsley. 'Miss Treadgold wouldn't have given Hedley a second look. She was besotted with Alex Piper.'

'I know – but he's not here any more, is he?'

His first thought was that it would be unwise to approach Tiller again because it would alert him to the fact that he was definitely under suspicion. On reflection, however, Leeming realised that the barber was bound to mention the fact that the sergeant had called on him in order to read some of Tiller's poetry. It was better to be honest about what he'd done. He therefore made his way back to the bookshop once more. Leeming was in time to see Tiller about to close it for the day.

'Am I too late?' he asked.

'No, of course not,' said the other. 'Step inside and I'll lock up. Friends are always welcome, whether it's during business hours or outside them.'

Leeming went into the shop and removed his hat while Tiller locked the door. He turned round with a smile.

'I can't believe that anyone would steal a book, but you can't take any chances.' He waved Leeming to a seat then sat on a stool opposite him. 'To what do I owe this honour of yet another visit from you?'

'I went to Mr Garside's shop.'

'Why – you don't look as if you need a haircut.'

'I wanted to talk to one of the poets from your group.'

'Reg has some way to go before he has the right to be called a real poet,' said Tiller, smiling, 'but he's ready to learn and that's always encouraging.'

'I wasn't interested in *his* work – only in yours.'

'You could have bought a copy of my anthology.'

'The poem I wanted to read wasn't in that,' explained Leeming. 'You told me that you'd torn it up because you didn't think it was good enough.'

'Well, yes . . .'

'Yet according to Mr Garside, you were very pleased with it. You read it to your group and warned them to look out for certain things.'

'I'd experimented with different rhyme schemes and with a variety of metres. You must have noticed that?'

'All I noticed was that the lines got much shorter in some verses, though I didn't understand why.'

'There was a double narrative.'

Leeming blinked. 'Was there?'

'I thought I'd made that clear. The story of Gregor's disappearance was told in third-person narrative but what you heard in the verses with shorter lines was the voice of the phantom.'

'Ah, I see what you mean now.'

'You obviously don't believe such a thing exists.'

'Having dipped into that book you loaned me, I think this whole county is alive with phantoms, ghosts, goblins, evil spirits and things that terrify me.'

'The phantom was no invention of mine. He's real.'

'Mr Garside said that you've actually seen him.'

'I did. He flashed before my eyes and was gone.'

'It could've been a trick of the light.'

Tiller was deadly serious. 'I know what I saw.'

Geoffrey Hedley was so chastened by what Colbeck had told him that he took a cab out to the house. Having deliberately kept away from Melissa Haslam, he could understand how she must be feeling. During the time she'd been betrothed to his friend, Hedley had seen her on several occasions and believed that a bond had developed between them. In the wake of Piper's disappearance, however, he'd been so preoccupied with the search that he'd pushed her to the back of his mind. It was shameful.

When he got to the Haslam residence, he was invited into the drawing room by Melissa's mother. She took the opportunity to question him about the progress of the investigation and he did his best to sound optimistic. Bridget Haslam then sent a servant to fetch her daughter. Several minutes passed. Hedley feared that Melissa simply didn't wish to see him. He was relieved, therefore, when she finally came into the room, but saddened by her appearance. The once beautiful face had been shadowed by bereavement in a way that made her look positively ill. Melissa was hunched, subdued and hesitant.

'It was . . . kind of you to come,' she said.

'Had it not been for the constant searches,' he told her, 'I'd have been here much earlier, but I felt that my first duty was to find Alex.'

'You're here now and I'm grateful.'

221

'I gather that Inspector Colbeck called earlier.'

'Yes, he did,' replied Bridget, 'and we found his visit very soothing. We know that he will somehow be able to solve this perplexing mystery.'

'Did he warn you not to expect instant results?'

'Yes, he did, Mr Hedley.'

'Lord Culverhouse has complete faith in him.'

'I hope that *you* do as well,' said Melissa.

'Yes, yes, of course . . .'

There was a long, awkward silence. Each one of them waited for someone else to initiate conversation. Eventually, it was Hedley who plunged in, asking if there was anything that he could do for Melissa while wondering how soon he could take his leave without seeming rude.

'May I ask you a question?' she asked.

'Please do.'

'What drove Alex to go on that excursion? He told me that he thought it would be amusing for himself and his friends to have a midnight picnic at Hallowe'en, but I've learnt a bit more about Hither Wood since then. Apparently, it's haunted by the ghost of the man who was killed there ten years ago.'

'That's only supposition. Alex wanted to disprove the claim.'

'There was *danger* in going there.'

'But we never got that far.'

'Do you think that Alex was being punished for daring to say that there was nobody haunting that wood?'

'I don't believe that's what happened.'

'Melissa and I are of one mind here,' said Bridget. 'On that night of all nights, it was foolhardy of him to tempt any ghosts. I know that Inspector Colbeck believes that the explanation for his death is in no way connected to the supernatural, but we are bound to have doubts. We've read about the weird incidents that have happened there.'

'Most of them can be dismissed as sheer nonsense,' said Hedley. 'Your fears are groundless.'

'Then why won't they go away?' asked Melissa.

'You must listen to reason, Miss Haslam. Just because someone is killed, it doesn't mean that he or she will come back to cast a spell over the scene of the crime. If that were the case, there'd be reports of haunting all over this country. Gregor Hayes, the man who vanished in Hither Wood, is dead and buried. Those who believe that a restless spirit returns there at Hallowe'en are deceived. It simply doesn't exist.'

Leeming began to wish that he'd never dared to raise the subject of the disappearance of the blacksmith. Tiller started using words that the sergeant had never heard before as he talked about the structure, theme and evolution of his poem. It was bewildering. While he'd not actually liked them, he could understand what was going on in the barber's poems. Albeit dull and written in a spidery hand, they were blissfully simple. Reginald Garside's work had none of the technical variations of which the bookseller was talking. Leeming got to his feet and headed for the door.

'You haven't told me the truth yet,' complained Tiller.

'*Why* am I under suspicion? What evidence do you have that I was lurking beside a railway line at Hallowe'en in the middle of the night?'

'We have none at all,' admitted Leeming.

'There you are, then. Let's leave it at that, shall we? If you're interested in my books, come here as often as you wish, but if you're just trying to catch me out, I'd rather be left alone.'

'I'm only doing my job.'

'How would you like it if someone went behind your back and asked your barber about *you*?'

'I wouldn't like it one bit.'

'Then spare a thought for my feelings.'

'I'm sorry.'

'As for my poem,' insisted the other, 'there is absolutely no link between what happened ten years ago in Hither Wood and the incident at Hallowe'en.'

'I'll take your word for it.'

'Please pass it on to the inspector.'

'I will.'

'And put yourself in my position for a moment. If you'd sneaked off to commit a crime at Hallowe'en, don't you think your wife would have noticed you'd gone?'

'Estelle would have noticed at once.'

'It's the same with Ruth.'

'But that's not true,' said Leeming.

'I know my wife, Sergeant.'

'Then why did you tell me she was a heavy sleeper?'

Tiller gaped. 'I don't remember doing that.'

'You told me that an idea for a poem could strike at any time – even in the middle of the night. It made you get up at once because you needed to start putting words on paper. Your wife never woke up, you said.'

The bookseller glared at him and retreated into silence.

Caleb Andrews made a point of crossing the road to speak to his friend. He thanked Kingston for keeping an eye on his house and told him that he was sleeping at home now.

'It was very good of you, Alf,' he said.

'It's what neighbours do. We look out for each other.'

'I'd still like to know who called when I wasn't here.'

'Well, he hasn't been back, I can tell you that. In any case,' said Kingston, 'there's no need to thank me. I enjoyed it, acting as your sentry. It gave me something to do.'

'How is the leg?'

'It's a damn nuisance, Caleb.'

'Are you still in pain?'

'Yes, it keeps throbbing like mad. Don't let's talk about me. I want to hear about your stolen medal. Is there any chance of getting it back?'

'I hope so. I've got a detective constable helping me.'

Kingston's eyebrows twitched. 'That's good news.'

'Ideally,' said Andrews, 'I'd prefer to have my son-in-law in charge of the case, but he's up in the Lake District.'

'What's he doing up there?'

'Someone disappeared at Hallowe'en and nobody knows what happened to him. Robert's job is to find out.'

'He usually gets what he's after.'

'This case will really test him.'

'Why is that?'

'Maddy had a letter from him to say that it was going to be hard work. He warned her that it might be some time before he was home again. It'd be a lot sooner if he let *me* help him,' boasted Andrews. 'I've got instincts when it comes to solving crimes on the railway. He ought to send for me.'

'D'you really want to go all that way in this cold weather?'

'No, I don't. I'm not going anywhere until we catch the thief who stole my medal. I want to see him behind bars.'

'What if the medal just went astray?'

'It was *taken*, Alf.'

'I'm always putting things down and forgetting where they are. It happens to people like us. Our brains are as tired as our bodies.'

'I've still got plenty of life left in me,' said Andrews, thrusting out a defiant chin. 'And my brain hasn't seized up with fatigue yet. A thief stole something that was very precious to me and I won't rest until I get it back.'

When he listened to Leeming's garbled description of the poem about the mysterious disappearance of the blacksmith, Colbeck had to make allowances for the fact that the sergeant had clearly not understood it fully. What interested him was the pivotal role played in the poem by a phantom.

'Norm Tiller has *seen* him,' said Leeming.

'How much beer had he drunk beforehand?'

226

'He was probably stone-cold sober.'

'Then he has a vivid imagination,' said Colbeck. 'It's a necessary precondition for any poet. He or she must be able to let the mind roam freely.'

'But he didn't make the story up, sir. It's all true. The blacksmith really did disappear.'

'That might have been his starting point but, from what you've told me, he used a great deal of poetic licence. You've certainly aroused my curiosity, Victor,' he continued. 'I may have to find time to visit the barber himself.'

'I liked the idea of the phantom.'

'That's all it is – an idea.'

'Norm saw him running among the fells.'

Colbeck was jolted. He remembered the train journey from Birthwaite to Kendal when he'd caught a fleeting glimpse of a figure up on the hill. No sooner had he seen him than the man disappeared as if by magic. But was it really a man he'd seen? Was the figure a human being? Doubts began to form.

Had he been looking at the phantom?

CHAPTER SEVENTEEN

Caroline Treadgold had remarkable self-control. When she was in company with others, she was poised, alert and resolute. Nobody would have guessed that her true feelings had been suppressed and that, once she was alone, she fell prey to an intense remorse that blocked out everything else. The times she'd spent alone with Alexander Piper had been the happiest in her life and she'd hoped that their friendship would one day be translated into marriage. It was not to be. When he announced that he'd met someone else, Caroline flew into a rage and accused him of betrayal. Piper coped with the situation by simply disappearing from view and rejecting all her demands for a meeting. It had been cruel.

Yet she was unable to give him up. Somewhere at the back of her mind was the lingering hope that he might one day recall the wonderful times they'd spent together and realise that no other woman could provide the excitement and devotion that Caroline had offered so unconditionally. Since he was avoiding her, she used Geoffrey Hedley as a kind of intelligencer, feeding off the snippets of information he gave her about Piper's movements. It enabled her to turn up at certain social events and to watch him unseen.

The last time she'd managed to do that, he'd been with Melissa Haslam and her family. Caroline had a close look at the woman who'd dislodged her. What hurt her most was not the fact that her rival was undeniably beautiful. It was the look of contentment on Piper's face. He was basking in his new life, the one from which Caroline had been so ruthlessly excluded.

Alone in her bedroom, she was still thinking about the way that her world had changed for the worst when a maidservant came to tell her that she had a visitor.

'I don't want to see anyone,' she said.

'The gentleman is most insistent.'

'I don't care.'

'He said he'll wait until you feel ready to come down.'

'You heard me,' said Caroline. 'Send him on his way. I know that it must be Mr Hedley but I'm in no mood to see him or anyone else. Apologise to him and say that I'm not available.'

'But it's not Mr Hedley.'

'Then who is it?'

'Lord Culverhouse.'

In order to learn more about the ill-fated blacksmith, Leeming took the barber's advice and went to see Sergeant Ainsley. The latter was surprised and irritated by his request.

'Why do you and the inspector keep harping on about a case that happened ten years ago when you were sent here to solve a mystery that happened at Hallowe'en?'

'We think there's a link between the two.'

'How many times must I tell you?' said Ainsley. 'The events are unrelated. Alex Piper and Gregor Hayes lived in different worlds. They never even met. They had nothing whatsoever in common.'

'Yes, they did,' said Leeming.

'What is it?'

'They both interest us.'

'Gregor's case is a distraction. Ignore it.'

'I can't – and you're to blame.'

'Why? What am I supposed to have done?'

'You were the one who told me that Norm Tiller had written a poem about the case,' recalled Leeming, 'so I went to the bookshop and asked to see it.'

'What did Norm say?'

'He told me that the poem wasn't up to scratch so he'd destroyed it. I didn't believe him.'

'You should have – he's as honest as they come.'

'I had a word with Mr Penrose at the King's Arms. He gave me the names of the other poets in that little group that Norm brought together. One of them was a barber.'

'That's right – Reg Garside.'

'He had a copy of the poem and let me read it.'

'That was clever of you, Sergeant,' said Ainsley with grudging praise. 'I'd never have thought of doing that.'

'I was determined to see it.'

'And what did it tell you?'

'Well, the shock for me was that Mr Hayes was so popular with women. All the blacksmiths I've met have been hairy monsters with ugly faces.'

Ainsley grinned. 'That's a fair description of Gregor,' he admitted. 'What made him so interesting to women was his personality. He could make you feel special just being with him and – this is what I loved about Gregor Hayes – he had a wicked sense of humour.'

'The barber said you were his best friend.'

'I was proud to be so.'

'Policemen usually spend all their time with each other,' observed Leeming. 'It's the kind of job that brings us together because a lot of people don't trust us.'

'Gregor trusted me.'

'I know that the pair of you often went to the King's Arms because the landlord told me.'

'We were always a part of the crowd there, Sergeant. The real treat for me was to go fishing with Gregor. I usually went home empty-handed, but he always caught lots of fish. It was uncanny. He could charm them out of the water.'

Ainsley went on to describe some of the outings he'd had with the blacksmith. They were clearly times that he cherished. It explained why he'd put so much effort into the search for Gregor Hayes when the latter unaccountably disappeared in Hither Wood. Evidently, the blacksmith's friendship meant a great deal to him.

'As for women,' he concluded, 'Gregor was very fond of them but, deep down, he was always a man's man.'

'Thank you for telling me so much about him.'

'Do you have any more questions?'

'Yes,' said Leeming. 'However did you find the time to go fishing? If you were a serving policeman in London, you wouldn't have had a minute to call your own. When you'd finished your shift, you'd be so exhausted that you'd be fast asleep when your head hit the pillow. Things are obviously different up here.'

'I'm glad you recognise that at last,' said Ainsley with an edge to his voice. 'I'd be the first to concede that I'd be lost in a huge city like London – just as you and the inspector are completely lost in a place like Kendal.'

Having spent so much time with his nephew, Caroline had heard a lot about Lord Culverhouse yet had never actually met him. When she did so now, she was instantly aware of his status. Her visitor seemed to embody all the features of the aristocracy. Power, prosperity, condescension and other constituent elements of the titled elite were there. After introducing himself, he sat down opposite her and held her gaze. The smile never left his mouth.

'I came here to thank you, Miss Treadgold,' he said.

She was startled. 'Why?'

'You took part in the search for my nephew.'

'So did lots of other people.'

'Yes, but the vast majority were men and none of them had

had such a close relationship with Alex as you did. He never talked about you, but it was obvious that someone in his life was making him very happy. That, I discovered, was you.'

'Those days are gone for ever, I'm afraid.'

'While they lasted, they invigorated Alex. Until . . .'

'Until he met Miss Haslam.'

'It's not a mistake I would have made,' he said, running a covetous eye over her. 'When I measure you against her, I see a full-grown woman beside a child – albeit a very pretty child.'

'Alex made his choice. That was that.'

'It must have been very painful for you, Miss Treadgold.'

'I'd rather not talk about it.'

'Bottling it up will only lead to a life of misery. A shared trouble is easier to bear and who better to confide in than Alex's uncle?' He gave her a moment to absorb the implications of what he was suggesting. 'Before he bought a house of his own, he lived under my roof. His room is full of souvenirs of his stay with us. I wondered if you might like some of them by way of mementoes to bring back memories of happier times.'

'I already have plenty of mementoes, my lord.'

'There must be some way that I can help you.'

'I don't think so.'

'Come now, let's be sensible about this. At the moment, we are both in mourning over someone we loved – me, as an uncle and you as a . . . close friend. That gives us something in common, Miss Treadgold,' he said in a whisper. 'Why don't we let a decent interval elapse so that we can both recover from the shock, and then, perhaps, we can talk again

233

about how we might help each other through the despair that follows an untimely death?'

'I just want to know what happened to Alex.'

'So do I, dear lady, so do I. It's the reason I retained the services of the man most likely to uncover the truth about Alex's death.'

'Geoffrey Hedley is starting to have doubts about him. At least, that's what I'm beginning to suspect.'

'Then his doubts are misplaced. Colbeck will vindicate his reputation, mark my words.' He rose to his feet. 'I'm sorry to intrude on you at such a time, but I wanted you to know that you're in my thoughts. I understand how you must feel, and I sympathise.' He took a step towards her. 'There is one last thing I need to ask you.'

'What is it?'

'Well, for a period of time, you were closer to Alex than anybody.'

'That's what I believed,' she said, ruefully.

'He must have confided in you.'

'Well, yes, I suppose that he did.'

'Was there any mention of people he thought of as his sworn enemies?'

'Yes – there were rather a lot of them.'

He smiled tolerantly. 'Alex did love to cause trouble.'

'I thought he went too far sometimes,' she confessed. 'Once he disliked someone, his mockery of them was quite relentless. He baited them.'

'Did he never fear retribution?'

'He shrugged off the very idea. Alex thought that people were too afraid of him to strike back.' A memory surfaced. 'Except for one man, that is . . .'

'Oh? Who was that?'

'It was Norman Tiller.'

When he went to the house that evening, Colbeck apologised for calling unannounced. Expecting to be invited into the cottage, he was instead taken into the bookshop and, even though it was very cold, he was glad to be able to see the place. Tiller lit the lamps then offered him a seat. Colbeck's eyes roved the shelves.

'You have a very eclectic stock,' he said, approvingly.

'I have to cater for all tastes, Inspector.'

'It was kind of you to lend that book to Sergeant Leeming. I think it's come as a revelation to him.'

'He wanted to know more about the Lake District,' said the bookseller. 'I was happy to educate him.'

'You are also a talented poet, it seems.'

'That's my true calling.'

'The sergeant was struck by your poem about the way that a blacksmith went into a wood and was never seen alive again.'

'I wanted to find out what happened to him.'

'Why did you leave it so long?' asked Colbeck. 'Gregor Hayes vanished ten years ago, yet your poem wasn't written until five or six years later.'

'I brooded on the mystery until I felt I'd taken everything into account. There was a lot of research involved.'

'I could see that.'

Tiller was shaken. 'You've *read* the poem?'

'After what I was told about it, I felt that I had to. Like the sergeant, I paid a visit to your friend, the barber, and he was kind enough to let me see all the examples of your work that he had in his possession. He's a great admirer of yours.'

'Reg Garside is rather over-enthusiastic about my poetry.'

'I, too, was impressed by it.'

'Thank you, Inspector.'

As they talked, Colbeck was trying to weigh him up. At first sight, Tiller was everything that Leeming had said about him – pleasant, soft-voiced, educated and seemingly contented with his lot. Colbeck sensed a muted resentment absent when the sergeant had called, and there was also a new watchfulness about him. The bookseller had done his best to befriend the sergeant. With Colbeck, however, he was circumspect, like a nervous cat in the presence of a stranger. Tiller didn't yet know whether to purr or to show his claws.

'I was intrigued by the way you shifted between third-person narrative,' said Colbeck, 'and the voice of the phantom. Yet even though he has a central role in the story, you never give us a description of him.'

'Who can describe a phantom, Inspector? You refer to him as "he" but he could equally well be "she" or "it". Apparitions change shape all the time. You can't define them in words.'

'Yet you told the sergeant you'd *seen* the phantom.'

'I believe that I did.'

'What form did it take?'

'It was a human being in miniature.'

'How close were you?'

'It must have been . . . thirty yards or so.'

'Then you had a much clearer view than I did. When I came back from Birthwaite on the train, I glimpsed a figure in black high up on a mountain. At that distance,' remembered Colbeck, 'he was almost tiny and stayed for only a few seconds before flitting away like a bird. Could that have been your phantom?'

'No, Inspector,' replied the other, 'I'm sure that it wasn't. It was probably a climber. They abound in this part of the country. If you visit Scafell Pike, the highest peak in England, you'll see climbers swarming over it like bees.'

'This person was not climbing. He ran off.'

'Then he's one of our many fell runners. Go out among the fells and you're bound to see them running up and down for the sheer joy of it. It's a common sight in the Lakes.'

'You've disappointed me,' said Colbeck.

'Why is that?'

'I was rather hoping I'd caught sight of a phantom – even, perhaps, the one who appears in your wonderful poem. You made him sound so real.'

'He *is* real, Inspector. I'd swear that he is. You must have seen somebody else entirely. And since you were looking out of a moving train, your view would've been slightly impaired. If you'd really seen what I saw,' affirmed Tiller, 'you'd *know* that it was a phantom.'

* * *

Because he'd been told that she'd be there, Alan Hinton hurried along to the Colbeck residence that evening. He was soon talking to Madeleine while relishing the proximity of Lydia Quayle. The two women made him feel very welcome.

'It's so good of you to take an interest,' said Madeleine. 'We know how busy you must be.'

'I can always find time for friends.'

'Let me add my thanks, Alan,' said Lydia. 'Knowing that you're involved has helped to calm Madeleine's father down.'

'Let's go through the facts,' he suggested.

Madeleine gave him the details once again. Her account was supplemented by comments from Lydia. Hinton was attentive. Since the information he gleaned could not be transferred to his notebook, he committed it to memory. He could see how seriously both women regarded what seemed to him like a petty crime. Anxious to help Madeleine and her father, he was even more concerned about winning Lydia's approval.

'I just hope that the superintendent doesn't get to hear about this,' he joked, 'or he'll roast me alive.'

'I thought he was more subdued since his return,' said Madeleine. 'Robert's word for him was "serene".'

'It didn't last. When I said something out of place, he slapped me down at once. It was just like old times.'

'But you've done so well,' said Lydia. 'Superintendent Tallis should be grateful to you. Has he forgotten that you helped to save his life?'

'It was my own fault for provoking him. I went too far. He

238

was right to yell at me. Well,' he went on, 'this crime won't solve itself. I'd better get over to Mr Andrews' house.'

'I'll come with you,' volunteered Lydia, getting up. 'It's time for me to leave, anyway. We can share a cab, Alan. I'll drop you off at the house.'

'Thank you very much.'

Madeleine ushered the pair of them into the hall. 'Don't pay any attention to my father's demands,' she said. 'He thinks that the entire resources of Scotland Yard should be put at his disposal.'

Hinton chuckled. 'All he's getting is me.'

'That will be enough,' said Lydia, fondly.

'I'm glad you have such faith in me.'

'You once came to my aid, Alan, and solved a problem that was causing me a lot of distress. I'm sure that you'll do the same for Mr Andrews.'

Taking pity on his neighbour for being stuck at home all the time, Caleb Andrews was playing cribbage with him. They were seated either side of a card table near the downstairs front window in Kingston's house. Regular cups of tea were supplied by Kingston's wife, Nan, a quiet, shuffling, careworn woman. Wrapped up in their game, the men hardly noticed her. She came and went in silence.

When he lost the fifth game in a row, Andrews was annoyed. He slapped his thigh hard.

'You're having all the luck, Alf,' he said.

'There's skill involved as well.'

'What use is skill if the cards let me down?'

'That's the way it happens sometimes.'

'It's so unfair on me.'

'You had a run of bad luck, that's all. It was good of you to come over. Thanks, Caleb.'

'Shall we have another game?'

'To be honest,' said Kingston, 'I'm getting tired.'

'You've got to give me the chance to win *one* game at least,' insisted Andrews. 'I'm not leaving until I do that.'

'All right – it's your turn to deal.'

'I'll give the cards a good shuffle first.'

As soon as he picked them up, however, he was diverted by the sound of an approaching cab. When it came to a halt, it seemed to be directly outside. Andrews drew back the curtain and saw that it was parked beside his house.

'I'm sorry, Alf,' he said, getting up and dropping the cards, 'I've got to go. Unless I'm mistaken, my detective has finally arrived. Alan Hinton is going to catch the villain who stole my medal and make sure that I get it back at last.'

Rodney Piper had never even seen his son's house, let alone gone into it. Since their estrangement, he and his wife had been isolated from him in every way. They had to rely on letters from Emma's brother for information about Alexander's movements. After lengthy discussion, Lord Culverhouse had finally managed to persuade Piper to visit the house in order to see how his son had been living. Emma went with them. The carriage took them on the relatively short drive to the property. It suddenly rose up in front of them out of the gloom.

Piper and his wife still had reservations about going into it. Given the kind of wayward life they believed that Alexander had been living, they were afraid of what they might find inside. Led by Culverhouse, they approached the house with foreboding. Would there be garish colours everywhere and indecent paintings on the walls? If their son had led a defiantly heathen existence, there would surely be evidence of it. Melissa Haslam might have given him some stability and normality but even she couldn't transform his character so completely in so short a time. It was even possible, they thought, that they'd find clear signs of their son's immorality.

Their qualms were eased when they were admitted to the house by a servant and saw Geoffrey Hedley in the hall. He gave them a polite welcome and offered to act as their guide. Profoundly grateful to him, they followed Hedley from room to room and were pleasantly surprised by the tastefulness of the decoration. There was nothing at all to offend them. Their fears gradually ebbed away.

Culverhouse was curious. 'What exactly are *you* doing here, Hedley?' he asked.

'It's my second home,' replied the other. 'Because I spent so much time here, Alex kindly gave me the use of one of the bedrooms.'

'You obviously know your way around.'

'I helped him to choose some of the furniture.'

'Miss Haslam would have lived here after they'd married. What was her opinion of the house?'

'She was very pleased with it, my lord.'

'I daresay she'd have wanted some changes in time,' said Culverhouse, gently nudging his sister. 'Women always do.'

'You're such a cynic,' she scolded.

'It's exactly what my dear wife did.'

When they'd seen the rooms on the ground floor, Hedley asked his visitors what else they'd like to view. Relieved by what she'd already found, Emma was happy to end the tour, but her husband was keen to go upstairs.

'I'd like to see Alex's bedroom,' he announced.

'Then I'll take you there at once,' said Hedley, dutifully.

While the two men set off, Culverhouse and his sister adjourned to the spacious drawing room and sat down. Emma was bound to compare its relative luxury with the more restrained ethos of their home in Ambleside. Rodney Piper, meanwhile, was being led along the landing by Hedley. When they stopped outside a door, the lawyer indicated that his companion should go in. Piper hesitated. If there was any sign of his son's decadence, he believed it would be in his bedroom and he was glad that his wife was not there to witness it.

'Go on in,' encouraged Hedley.

'I'm just composing myself.'

'It's exactly as Alex left it. I told the servants to keep a lamp burning in there at all times.'

'That was kind of you, Mr Hedley.'

'He'd have expected it of me.'

Overcoming his reluctance, Piper opened the door and strode into the room. It was large, comfortable and well appointed, but the visitor was quite unaware of that. His gaze was fixed on something that lay on the bedside table.

It was his son's Bible.

Caleb Andrews was delighted to see that help had finally arrived. After inviting Hinton into the house, he bombarded the young detective with facts that the latter already knew.

'How many years will he spend in prison?'

'We have to catch the thief first, Mr Andrews.'

'It ought to be a life sentence.'

'That's out of the question.'

'But the loss of that medal has caused me grief.'

'I understand that.'

'Do you know what it's like when somebody invades your house? It's terrible. You don't feel safe any more. You can't sleep properly. Every time a floorboard creaks, you think that you're in danger.'

'That's a common reaction, I'm afraid,' said Hinton. 'I've investigated a lot of burglaries and the victims always say the same. Their sense of security has been shattered. You are one of the lucky ones, Mr Andrews.'

'Lucky!' howled the other.

'Only one item was stolen from you.'

'It was the most valuable thing I own.'

'I would have thought that there's something much more valuable here,' said Hinton, looking at the painting above the mantelpiece with admiration. 'Miss Quayle told me what a wonderful piece of work it was. I'm so glad that I had the chance to see it. Your daughter is a real artist.'

'Forget about Maddy. I want you to concentrate on me. How soon do you think you'll recover the medal?'

'That's anybody's guess, Mr Andrews.'

'What's your first step?'

'Well, I'd like to see where the medal was kept.'

'It was in there,' said the other, pointing to the cupboard.

'Is it kept locked at all times?'

'Of course it is.'

'And where's the key?'

'It's in its hiding place.'

'Could you find it for me, please?'

Andrews went straight to the vase on top of the little sideboard and thrust a hand into it. He pulled out the key and held it up for inspection.

'That's what I mean when I said you were lucky,' Hinton told him. 'Most thieves ransack a house in search of valuables. They leave the place in a complete mess. Sometimes,' he added, 'they leave something else as well and it really disgusts me.'

Andrews was appalled. 'Do you mean . . . ?'

'Be grateful that you didn't find *that* in the middle of the carpet. The first time I saw what a thief had done out of sheer spite in someone's house, my stomach turned.'

'You're right,' said Andrews, sobered. 'I was lucky.'

'Open the cupboard, please.'

'What's the point? There's nothing in there.'

'I was told the medal was kept in a box.'

'Yes, it is.'

'Then I'd like to see it.'

'Heaven knows why,' grumbled the other. 'Who wants to look at an empty box? Maddy and I searched every inch of this house together. The medal is simply not here.'

'I'd still like to look at that box.'

'I want you out there looking for the thief instead.'

Still grumbling, Andrews unlocked the cupboard door and took out the wooden box before handing it to Hinton. The tiny key to the box was still in the lock. After turning it gently, the detective lifted the lid of the box and saw the pouch inside. The moment he touched it, he could feel something. Holding out a hand, he shook the pouch and the medal dropped into his palm.

Andrews was astounded. Hinton turned to him.

'Is *this* what you thought was lost, sir?'

CHAPTER EIGHTEEN

It was the best part of a minute before Caleb Andrews could find his voice. Until then, all he could do was to gurgle, splutter and stare at his medal in wonderment. It was only when Hinton gave it to him that he was able to speak.

'I don't believe it,' he gulped.

'It looks as if you don't need me any more,' said Hinton. 'The case is closed.'

'But it's not. We haven't caught the thief.'

'Are you sure that there *was* one, Mr Andrews?'

'Of course there was. You ask Maddy. When she was here, that box was empty and the medal was nowhere to be found. Someone put it back.'

'Thieves are not in the habit of doing that.'

'This one is, and I want him caught.'

'But your property has been restored.'

'Why was it stolen in the first place?'

'I don't know,' said Hinton. 'Perhaps someone wanted a closer look at it. A more likely explanation is that it was taken just to give you a fright.'

'It certainly did that,' said Andrews with feeling.

'In your place, I'd just be happy that it has been restored to its proper place. The thief – if that's what he was – must have been having fun at your expense.'

'Well, he's not going to get away with it. Find him.'

'That's a task that you could do more easily than me. What's clear is that it was stolen by someone you invited into this house and who saw you take the key to that cupboard out of the vase. Now, who did you show that medal to?'

Andrews pondered. 'I showed it to lots of people,' he said at length. 'In fact, I had eight or nine engine drivers here to celebrate the award when I first got it. They all knew where it was kept. Then there were friends and relatives, of course. I even invited the postman in to show it off to him.'

'What about your neighbours?'

'Half the street has seen it. When word got around, people knocked on the door out of curiosity.' He became shamefaced. 'I suppose that I bragged about it far too much.'

'You were entitled to, Mr Andrews.'

'What happens now?'

'To start with, you must make a list of all the people you've so far mentioned. I reckon there'll be twenty or thirty names at least. Add any others that come to mind.'

'Well, there's Maddy and Lydia Quayle, of course . . .'

Hinton smiled. 'I think we can eliminate them.'

'They're going to be amazed when they know what happened. I can't tell you how relieved I am – but that doesn't mean I'm letting the thief get off scot-free.'

'You'll catch him by a process of elimination.'

'Can't you help me?'

'I don't know anyone on your list. You do. That's why you're best placed to solve the crime. There is, however, one piece of advice I'd like to pass on.'

'What is it?'

'Don't put the medal back in that cupboard. Too many people know where it's kept and how to get at it. Take it to your daughter's house,' said Hinton. 'I know that Inspector Colbeck has a safe and that you'd be very welcome to leave anything in it. *That's* where your award belongs.'

Colbeck and Leeming decided to combine business with pleasure, discussing the new evidence they'd garnered at the same time as they were eating a meal at the Riverside Hotel. In a quiet corner of the dining room, they put their suspects under the microscope.

'Let's take Mr Hedley first,' suggested Colbeck.

'I wouldn't take him at all, sir.'

'Why not?'

'Because I can't see what he'd stand to gain.'

'Then you've forgotten Miss Treadgold. You were the first to spot that he was fond of her, and I noticed the way his tone softens whenever he talks about her.'

'Your argument doesn't hold water,' said Leeming. 'He

248

didn't need to get rid of Piper in order to move closer to Miss Treadgold. Since she'd been cast aside, she was already available.'

'No, Victor. As long as Piper was alive, she wouldn't look at another man. Even when he married, she'd still have tried to get him back. She loved him.'

'But she had every reason to hate him.'

'Those emotions are not mutually exclusive. In her case, I fancy, they were intermingled. It made her volatile. Having met the lady, I can see what attracted him to her.'

'Then why didn't they marry?'

'He met someone he felt would be more . . . acceptable as a wife. When that happened, Hedley saw his chance.'

'I'm sorry, sir,' said Leeming, shaking his head and reaching for a bread roll. 'I usually admire your reasoning but not this time. Hedley was dog-loyal to his friend. Piper only had to whistle and the lawyer would come running.'

'That was until Miss Treadgold came on the scene.'

'I'd put him at the bottom of our list.'

'What we're looking for,' argued Colbeck, 'is someone who knows Piper well, is aware of how he'd react in certain situations and has the intelligence to devise a scheme that ends with his complete disappearance. Hedley stands out most obviously as the person I've just described.'

'But there's no blazing anger inside him. That's what Dymock and Vine have – an inner furnace. You can see the flames dancing in their eyes. Both of them detested Piper.'

'Yet neither of them went on the Phantom Special.'

'What difference does that make?'

'That excursion was crucial. Someone who plotted Piper's death would surely have been on that train to see that everything went as planned.'

'Dymock could have paid someone else to do that in order to escape attention, and so could Walter Vine. Each of them had a real reason for revenge. Hedley didn't.'

'I disagree.'

Leeming was plaintive. 'Do you mind if we actually eat some food now, sir?'

Colbeck laughed. Abandoning their discussion, they attacked their meal with relish.

Madeline was staggered when her father turned up at the house unexpectedly with his beloved medal in his hand. While she shared his delight in seeing his award returned, she had the same underlying unease as Andrews. It meant that somebody could apparently enter the house at will. Only the medal had been taken in the first instance. At a future visit, the thief might steal far more. Her painting of a locomotive was at risk and so were the savings that her father had hidden under a loose floorboard in his bedroom.

As soon as she'd locked the medal away in the safe, she sat her father down and talked seriously to him.

'This man must be caught,' she demanded.

'That's what I told Alan Hinton.'

'What did he say?'

'He told me that *I* had a much better chance of success than him. It has to be someone I know. I have to work very carefully through a list of everyone who's been in the house and seen me take the medal out of the cupboard.'

'I can't believe any of your friends would do such a thing.'

'Neither could I at first. Then I began to wonder . . .'

'Don't start pointing a finger just yet, Father,' she warned. 'You've got to follow Robert's pattern. You gather evidence slowly until you have enough of it – then you can pounce.'

'I'll do more than pounce, Maddy. I'll knock his teeth out.'

'Then you'd be charged with assault.'

'It would be worth it,' he said, malevolently. 'I just wish that I still had Alan Hinton to help me.'

'He's given you good advice, Father. Besides, it's not as if he's left you in the lurch. Alan has told you exactly what to do and it's not as if you're on your own.'

'What do you mean, Maddy?'

'Well, you don't think that I'm going to miss out on the fun, do you? And I'm sure that Lydia will say exactly the same. There'll be three of us in this investigation,' she went on. 'We'll find the culprit in no time at all.'

By the time they reached the main course, they had shifted their interest to Walter Vine. Since the man was still suffering from the wound inflicted on him by Alexander Piper, his desire for revenge was fed by his constant pain and by the humiliation of being vanquished in a duel. Leeming was slowly coming to the view that Vine should be their prime suspect.

'After sending me packing from his house,' he said, 'Vine came to see me here. Why? There was no real need. It was not as if he came to apologise. Men like him never do that. They think that an apology is a sign of weakness.'

'When I met him,' recalled Colbeck, 'he gave me the impression that he expected the apology to come from *me*. Vine thinks that he can dismiss police officers with a lordly wave of his hand. I let him know that he was subject to the law of the land just as everyone else is.'

'Ainsley told me he's had trouble with Vine in the past. You have to feel sorry for the sergeant.'

'Why is that?'

'He's had arrogant snobs like Walter Vine, Piper and Lord Culverhouse to deal with. Then there's Hedley,' said Leeming. 'He's not a snob, maybe, but he knew how to help Piper wriggle out of any charge of criminal activity. By rights, Piper should have been locked up in prison with Vine and Hedley. They all broke the law.'

'What about Lord Culverhouse?'

'He's probably worse than the others.' Colbeck grinned. 'He *is*, sir. Look at the way he indulged his nephew. He let Piper get away with the most dreadful behaviour. My uncle wouldn't have let me do that. If I did so much as speak out of turn, he used to clip my ear.'

'And as a result,' said Colbeck, 'you've grown up to be an honest, hard-working, law-abiding citizen. Lord Culverhouse is a very different sort of uncle to the one you had, Victor. He approved of Piper's disorderly private life because he envied it. At his nephew's age, I daresay he enjoyed the same excesses.'

'We're going astray a bit, sir,' warned Leeming. 'We were

talking about Walter Vine and I think he's a far more likely culprit than Hedley.'

'Suppose that we're *both* wrong.'

'Then it has to be Dymock or Norm Tiller.'

'Not necessarily,' said Colbeck. 'It could be someone else entirely, someone who doesn't even live in Kendal. Then there's another option, of course. We've been looking at four male suspects. What if the person who contrived the disappearance of Alexander Piper was a woman?'

'I thought we decided that Miss Treadgold was innocent.'

'Perhaps we were too hasty in doing so.'

'What was her motive?'

'It could be fury at Piper for casting her roughly aside.'

'Yet she joined the search for him.'

'That might have been an attempt to escape suspicion.'

'Earlier on, you said that she still loved him.'

'I did,' agreed Colbeck, 'but love takes many forms. Miss Treadgold might have been so infatuated with Piper that she refused to let anyone else steal him away from her. I think, on reflection, that we might do well to bear the lady in mind.'

As the vehicle rattled along in the darkness, the driver was wrapped up warm against a persistent wind. The horse kept up a steady trot, its harness jingling and its hooves maintaining a constant drumbeat. There was no sense of hurry. The driver used the journey as a time of reflection, thinking back to the events that occurred at Hallowe'en with mixed feelings. When they finally reached the point where the fire had raged in order to stop the train, the horse was pulled to a halt and the driver got down to the ground.

Caroline Treadgold knelt beside the railway line and looked around. It was a place that had determined her destiny. She found it hard to pull herself away from it.

The visit to their son's house had opened the eyes of Rodney and Emma Piper. Anticipating some rude shocks, they left the building with a degree of reassurance. Alexander had not been the unprincipled rake they thought him, after all. They put it down to the curative effect that Melissa Haslam had had on him. Back at Culverhouse Court, they discussed what they'd found.

'We misjudged him, Emma,' said her husband.

'I know that now.'

'We should have had more faith in our son.'

'Alex was to blame as much as we were.'

'That's true. I thought we'd lost him completely and we hadn't. That Bible proved that he was still ours. I looked inside it. All the places I'd marked when I'd first presented it to him were still there. Though we'd been split asunder,' he said, 'I still controlled his Bible study.'

'Mr Hedley held him in such high esteem.'

'I was glad we met him there. With a friend like that, Alex could never be as promiscuous as we feared.'

'What will happen to that house now, Rodney?'

'Nothing can happen to any of his possessions until he's been found. That may take a considerable time. We're all powerless until then. But there was consolation to be drawn from our visit this evening. I was touched.'

'Yes, I found it very comforting.'

'It will certainly help us to sleep better tonight.'

'Nothing will ever do that,' she said, wistfully. 'Alex went before his time. That's unnatural. Even asleep, I'll be troubled by that thought. We failed him, Rodney. I see that now. We must pray for forgiveness.'

Once started, the names surged out of him like a waterfall. Madeleine had a job to write them down fast enough. They were in the drawing room and Andrews was remembering all the people who'd been invited in to see his medal and – in some cases – to be allowed to hold it. When he finally came to a halt, his daughter thought that it was all over, then five more people popped up in his mind and they had to be added to the list. In the end, he finally ran out of breath and flopped back in the chair.

'That's all I can remember, Maddy.'

She was alarmed. 'You think that there were *more*?'

'I hope not but I can't be sure.'

'Let me add these up.'

Using the pencil to tick off each name, she counted the names and gasped when she realised what the total was.

'Well?' he prompted her.

'It comes to forty-two.'

'I don't have that many friends.'

'That's what worries me, Father. Some of these people are not friends at all. They're strangers. You hardly know them, yet you let them walk into the house.'

'It was a mistake. I realise that now.'

'Let's take a closer look at them,' she said. 'I'm sure that we can cross out some of these names straight away. Vernon Passmore, for instance, and Dirk Sowerby.'

'They wouldn't dare steal anything from me.'

'Neither would most of these people. Mr Kingston is another one who's in the clear. With those crutches of his, he'd have had a job to cross the road. As for the postman, we've known and trusted him for years. Here,' she went on, handing him the list and the pencil, 'you know them better than I do.'

'What am I supposed to do, Maddy?'

'Cross off the ones we don't need to bother with. We can then concentrate on the ones that are left.'

'One way or another, we'll find him,' he said, grimly.

After their dinner, they went up to Colbeck's room to study the diagram of Hither Wood. It was spread out on a small table and they pored over it in silence for some time. Since he'd only been there at night, Leeming was unable to recognise any significant features of the wood. Colbeck, however, pointed out several that he'd noted.

'Somewhere in there is the vital clue that we need,' he said. 'Reading that poem by Tiller has made me more certain than ever that the explanation of Piper's fate is locked away in Hither Wood.'

'But the poem is about Gregor Hayes.'

'I know that, Victor.'

'Alexander Piper isn't even mentioned in it.'

'How could he be? At the time when the poem was written five years ago, Tiller had never even met him.'

'So how are the two disappearances linked?'

'To be honest, I'm not sure. Perhaps one person was involved in both.'

'We've no proof of that, sir.'

'Then we'll have to find it.'

'Wait a minute,' said Leeming, confused. 'In Norm's poem, the victim was killed by a phantom.'

'That could well be what happened in Piper's case.'

'How did you work that out?'

'I started from a different place than the poet. Tiller believes in phantoms. He's lived here for long enough to absorb the folklore of the Lake District and to accept it as proven fact.' Colbeck sat up. 'I'm a committed sceptic.'

'I'm not. When we went to the wood, something made me feel scared. I believe it was a ghost.'

'You won't have that problem when we go back there.'

Leeming blenched. 'I'd rather keep away from that place at midnight, sir. Look what happened last time.'

'We'll be going in broad daylight,' said Colbeck, folding up the diagram, 'and we won't be taking the same route.'

'Why not?'

'It's because I don't want anyone to know where we are. Last time, the man from whom we hired the horse and dog cart happened to be a drinking companion of Ainsley's. That's how the sergeant found out where we'd been.'

'How will we get there, then?'

'We'll take a train to Birthwaite and hire a cab. Nobody in Kendal will be any the wiser.'

'What's the reason for secrecy?' asked Leeming. 'If we took Ainsley with us, he could save us a lot of time. He knows that wood inside out.'

'I appreciate that. He proved it when he took me there. Ainsley is a good policeman, but he has a besetting fault.'

'What's that?'

'He's spent ten long years trying to solve the mystery of Gregor Hayes's disappearance. During that time, his mind has been clogged with theories he's been unable to prove. His brain has ossified,' said Colbeck. 'It just won't accept new ideas. If we go to that wood with Ainsley, he'll recite the same tale that I heard, word for word. We need the freedom to think afresh.'

'I know what I'll be thinking about tomorrow, sir.'

'Do you?'

'It will be November 5th.'

'Ah, yes – you'll be remembering your children.'

'No,' said Leeming, 'I'll be remembering the time we were sent off to Exeter because of what happened there.'

It had been one of their most gruesome cases. The local stationmaster had vanished and nobody could find him. On Guy Fawkes Day, a massive bonfire had been lit close to the cathedral and the whole city turned out for the event. When the blaze finally died out, the charred remains of the missing man were found among the embers.

'I still shudder when I think of it,' said Leeming.

'You ought to be heartened.'

'Why?'

'To begin with,' said Colbeck, 'we solved what had all the hallmarks of an insoluble murder.'

'I never thought that we would, sir.'

'You probably feel the same with this case.'

'I do.'

'Then look at the similarity.'

'There isn't any,' said Leeming.

'I think there is. The stationmaster was burnt to a cinder and Alexander Piper disappeared into a wall of flame. In both cases, they were consumed by fire.'

'I suppose that's true.'

'Let's go back ten years, shall we?' suggested Colbeck. 'Gregor Hayes was a blacksmith. What was the most constant feature of his working life?'

'I suppose it would be the fire he kept going.'

'Precisely – that's the common element here. All three victims are associated with fire. Let that be a warning to us, Victor.'

'Warning?' echoed the other.

'We must ensure that we don't get our fingers burnt.'

Lord Culverhouse had an early breakfast so that he would be ready to receive his visitor. Determined to keep well informed about the investigation, he'd been using Geoffrey Hedley as his go-between. As usual, the lawyer arrived at the house on time. He was shown into the study where Culverhouse awaited him.

'What do you have to report?'

'Very little, I'm afraid,' said Hedley. 'I went to their hotel and discovered that Inspector Colbeck and the sergeant had already left.'

'Where have they gone?'

'I've no idea, my lord.'

'It could be a good sign, of course. Maybe they've picked up a scent and rushed off to follow it.'

'Maybe . . .'

'You seem doubtful.'

'I'm sure that they know what they're doing,' said Hedley, 'but I would like at least a hint of progress. It's not there at the moment, I'm afraid. That's not to disparage their efforts,' he added. 'Both of them have been very assiduous. They can't be faulted on that score but . . . what have they actually found out?'

'Have you spoken to Ainsley?'

'Yes, I saw him yesterday evening.'

'What's his opinion?'

'Well, he didn't criticise them in so many words, but he's clearly worried that they have nothing to show for their efforts so far. And while he was very grateful that you were offering such a large reward,' said Hedley, 'the posters you had printed have only brought in a succession of barefaced liars who have no real evidence to offer.'

'That's disappointing.'

'There's something else that disturbs Ainsley.'

'What is it?'

'Inspector Colbeck has become quite obsessed with what happened to Gregor Hayes, the blacksmith.'

'That must have been a decade ago, at least.'

'It was, my lord. The inspector seems to think that he may be able to find out what happened to the man.'

'Why the devil is he wasting his time on the blacksmith? My nephew's case must take priority. That's what I brought him here to solve,' said Culverhouse, angrily. 'I can see that I need to speak to Colbeck myself. He has to do what he's told. I'll make that abundantly clear to him.'

Though he missed having it in the house, Caleb Andrews knew that his treasured medal was locked away securely in a safe. As he looked at the list of suspects, he saw that he'd whittled it down to nine names. Close friends had all been crossed off the list. Those remaining were mere acquaintances. One of them, he believed, had stolen and then returned his award.

Retirement had brought duties as well as leisure. When she lived with him, Madeleine had done all the shopping, but it now fell to him to keep the larder full. Putting on his coat and hat, he let himself out of the house and locked the door after him. Then he shivered in the cold and trudged off up the street. On his way to the market, he bumped into Nan Kingston, who was carrying a large basket filled with a variety of items. As usual, she looked weary and miserable. They exchanged greetings.

'What are you feeding Alf on these days?' Seeing that she was nonplussed, he explained. 'Your husband had the cheek to trounce me at cribbage. He's never done that before, Nan. You must have fed him with a magic potion.'

'Alf gets what he likes to eat,' she said, dully.

'Well, you can tell him I want my revenge.'

She clicked her tongue. 'It's only a game of cards.'

'Oh, no, it isn't. It's a lot more.'

'I'll pass on the message. Anyway, thank you for coming over, Caleb. It took Alf's mind off the pain in his leg. He hates having to use crutches.'

'*That's* why I lost all those games last night,' he said, seizing on the excuse. 'I realise it now. I took pity on him and let him win. Well, it won't happen again. Next time, I'll beat him hollow.'

The cab driver took them to Hither Wood then waited outside it so that he could take them back to Birthwaite in due course. The detectives plunged into the trees. Light was diminished under the canopy, so they picked their way carefully through the thickets. Colbeck paused beside a tree with some long, low, thin branches sprouting out of it. He took a knife from his pocket and took hold of a branch.

'What are you doing?' asked Leeming.

'We each need a stick to poke around.'

'I'll use mine to fight off any ghosts.'

'There aren't any, Victor. Take my word.'

When they had a stick apiece, they were able to brush their way through the undergrowth, soon emerging into the clearing at the centre of the wood. Handing his stick to the sergeant, Colbeck took out the diagram of the area and consulted it. He pointed to the path that had just brought them there.

'That was the route taken by Ainsley when he came in search of the blacksmith. Each of the other ways into this clearing is marked on this drawing. Somebody was guarding every possible exit.'

'They were obviously keen to make sure that Hayes played to the rules. He had to *earn* that money.' Leeming looked around. 'I wouldn't stay alone in this creepy place in the daytime. As for being here late at night, you'd need wild horses to drag me here at Hallowe'en.'

'What if you stood to win a sizeable wager?'

'Even that wouldn't tempt me.'

'It's not like you to be afraid of anything, Victor.'

'We're dealing with the supernatural, sir.'

'Are we? Let's find out, shall we?'

Colbeck showed him the diagram and pointed to areas that hadn't been thoroughly investigated at the time because the trees and thickets were so densely packed together. Most of the wood had been subjected to a search and Ainsley had marked the places where his men had been. What was left was about ten per cent of the total area.

When he saw Colbeck taking off his hat and coat before placing them carefully on a tree stump, Leeming was astonished.

'You'll freeze to death, sir.'

'It will be in a good cause.'

'I'm not taking off anything.'

'Then your coat may get caught on something and your hat will certainly be knocked off. We need to prod and poke our way in dark corners. The effort will keep us warm.'

'What are you expecting to find?'

'Evidence.'

'Evidence of what?' asked Leeming.

'I'll tell you when we find it.'

'Don't forget Norm Tiller's poem. He thinks that the phantom guards this place and that Gregor Hayes had the misfortune to upset him. I don't want to do that. It might have been better if we'd brought Norm with us,' he suggested. 'He knows how to deal with such . . . strange creatures.'

'Mr Tiller is a suspect. We don't want him or any of the others here. I won't even tell Sergeant Ainsley about this visit. It's our secret. Now use that stick of yours and hack a way through the thickets at the far end.'

'It could be a terrible waste of time, sir.'

'Most detective work is like that.'

'It's ten years since Hayes disappeared in here. Everything will have been overgrown in that time.'

'That's why we need a stick to prod as deep as we can.'

'We may end up finding nothing at all.'

'I'm afraid that you're wrong,' said Colbeck. 'We've already found something that's of interest to us.'

'What is it?'

'Don't you *feel* it, Victor?'

'All that I can feel is this cold wind.'

'Remain quite still and don't react to what I'm about to tell you. If you do that, you'll only frighten him off.'

Leeming blinked. 'What do you mean?'

'We're being watched again.'

CHAPTER NINETEEN

Lydia Quayle was at once amazed and amused. When she heard what had happened to the missing medal, she burst into laughter.

'Don't do that in front of my father,' warned Madeleine.

'But it's so comical, really.'

'He won't see it that way.'

'I'm sorry,' said Lydia, controlling her mirth. 'It must be such a relief to have that medal back again. And it was very sensible of Mr Andrews to lock it away in your safe.'

'That was Alan Hinton's idea.'

'Is he going to join the search for the thief?'

'Unfortunately, he isn't – but *you* are.'

Lydia was startled. 'Me? What can I do?'

'You can do what I'll do and lend moral support to my father. If he goes charging off on his own, he might well offend someone by accusing him of a crime he didn't commit. Part of our job is to stop him doing that.'

'He can be rather fiery at times, Madeleine.'

'That's why he needs some cooler heads around him.'

'Alan Hinton would have provided coolness, but I can see why he's handed the case over to us. He's very busy at Scotland Yard.'

'Oh,' said Madeleine with a smile, 'I fancy that he'll find time to drop in to see how we're getting on.'

'When do we start?'

'We'll have our first discussion with Father this afternoon.'

'Thank you for including me.'

'If I hadn't, you'd never have forgiven me.'

'That's true.'

'Besides, we've both played detective before and had some success.'

'Does Mr Andrews have any idea who the man might be?'

'We've thinned out the list of possibilities. He's convinced that the thief is among the handful whose names are still left.'

'But he may not *be* a thief, Madeleine. What if it turns out be a practical joke?'

'Father will still demand a stiff sentence in a court of law.'

'I can see how upsetting it is to know that someone has broken into your house. On the other hand, that may not be what actually happened.'

'There's no other explanation.'

'Yes, there is, Madeleine. Suppose that your father invited someone into the house and left the room for a few minutes. If the friend was in a mischievous mood, he could have taken the key out of the vase, used it to open the cupboard then pocketed the medal.'

'I suppose that it's possible, but there's a flaw in your theory, Lydia.'

'Is there?'

'How did the friend get back into the house to replace it? He could hardly rely on my father to ask him back and disappear obligingly from the room so that he had time to put the medal back. No,' decided Madeleine, 'I think somebody did break into the house at some point and – prank or not – that's a criminal act.'

Now that he'd been alerted to the fact that they were under surveillance, Leeming's immediate reaction was to find the person as soon as he could. Colbeck advised against any precipitate move, arguing that they ought to carry on with their search as if they were unaware that they had company. Accordingly, the pair of them poked away in the undergrowth with their sticks and tried to work out exactly where the person was. Once they thought they'd established the position, they moved slowly in that direction.

Colbeck remained patient but Leeming was increasingly annoyed at the fact that someone was watching them from a hiding place. When he'd edged several yards closer to where he felt the person was, he suddenly turned round and sprinted towards the trees with his stick held high. There was a rustling sound in the thickets as someone took to his heels. Leeming went after him, sacrificing his hat in the process and getting his sleeve snagged on a bush.

Whoever was ahead of him, however, was faster and fitter

than he was. He also had the advantage of seeing his attacker coming. Leeming went blundering wildly through the wood. When he finally emerged out of the gloom of the trees, he realised that he was too late. There was no sign whatsoever of anyone. What he did hear was the sound of a horse galloping away. Running across to the cab, he saw that the driver had disappeared as well, leaving the horse tethered to a bush. After a moment, the driver came out of the trees, self-consciously adjusting his trousers.

'Did you see him?' demanded Leeming.

'Who?'

'Someone was spying on us.'

'I didn't see anyone,' said the driver. 'I went off to—'

'You must have heard the horse galloping away?'

'I did, but I've no idea who was riding it.'

'Keep your eyes peeled next time.'

'Yes, sir, I will.'

Cursing himself for his impatience, Leeming examined the slight tear in his coat and wondered where his hat was. He picked his way gingerly back through the trees, using his stick as he did so. When he recovered the hat, he saw that it had acquired a nasty scratch. All in all, his rashness had paid no dividends at all.

Colbeck was waiting for him in the clearing. He noticed the torn sleeve at once and shook his head.

'You should have taken your coat off, Victor.'

'I know that now.'

'What happened?'

'I was too slow. He escaped on his horse.'

'The cab driver must have seen him.'

'He didn't, sir. He had to answer a call of nature.'

'That was inconvenient.'

'It was maddening,' said Leeming. 'I'm sorry, Inspector. It was stupid of me to go off like that, but I just hate being under observation.'

'Console yourself with the fact that you gave him a fright.'

'I gave *myself* a fright as well.'

He broke off to take a close look at the torn sleeve and the scratch on his hat. The chase through the wood had had one benefit. It had warmed him up. He followed Colbeck's example and hung both the hat and coat on a branch.

'Do you think it could be the same man?' he asked.

'To whom do you refer?'

'I mean the one who stole our horse and dog cart.'

'I daresay that it's more than likely.'

'Who set him on to us?'

'I don't know,' admitted Colbeck, 'but I expect he'll get a report on us very soon. Last time, we only had a warning. We must be ready for something a little more dramatic this time.'

'How did that man come to follow us here?'

'I hope that we get the chance to put that question to him.'

'He must have been on the same train.'

'That's more than likely,' said Colbeck. 'If he'd got close enough, he'd have heard me giving directions to the cab driver. All he had to do was to hire a horse from that livery stable near the station. I'll make a point of speaking to the man who owns it.'

'What do we do in the meantime, sir?'

'We carry on searching. There's nobody watching us now. We have a free hand. Let's get on with what we came here to do, shall we?'

Bernard Ainsley was not pleased to see Lord Culverhouse at the best of times. When the latter was patently in a foul mood, the sergeant knew that he was about to bear the brunt of it. Without bothering to knock, Culverhouse flung open the door of the office and barged in. Ainsley stood up behind his desk.

'Good day to you, Lord Culverhouse.'

'Where is Colbeck?'

'I don't know.'

'Well, you damn well ought to. I need someone to keep track of him. And while we're on the subject,' he went on, 'I've been talking to Hedley. He got the impression that you had reservations about the inspector.'

'His methods are very different from mine. That's all I meant.'

'And have they yielded any results?'

'He's still feeling his way into the investigation.'

'I'm told that he's actually ignoring it.'

'I can't believe that.'

'According to Hedley, the inspector has got interested in the case involving the blacksmith. That's closed, as far as I'm concerned.'

'It will never be closed until it's solved,' said Ainsley, stoutly. 'I knew Gregor Hayes as well as if he was my brother. I owe it to him and to his family to find out what happened.'

'He got his just deserts, I'd say. Good riddance to him!'

'That's very harsh.'

'I have good reason to say it.'

'With respect, Lord Culverhouse, you were mistaken.'

Culverhouse bridled. 'Do you dare to contradict *me*?'

'It wasn't Gregor who was responsible. I'd swear that and so did he, by the way. It was somebody else who led your servant astray.'

'Then why did she mention the blacksmith's name? He had a reputation for it, Ainsley. You know that. Hayes just couldn't keep his hands to himself. As a result, I lost a good servant and her life was ruined.'

'There was no paternity summons.'

'That's irrelevant.'

'It means that he was innocent.'

'Don't argue with me, man,' said Culverhouse, testily. 'Tell me what I came here to find out. Why is Colbeck paying any attention to a lecherous blacksmith when we're all desperate to know what happened to my dear nephew?'

'You'll have to ask him.'

Because of the way he simply let his hair and beard grow wild, Norman Tiller only ever saw the barber at meetings of the poetry group. He made an exception that morning. Going to Garside's shop, he submitted to a light trim in order to have a conversation with his friend.

'What else did Sergeant Leeming ask you?' he said.

'He wanted to know more about *you*, Norm.'

271

'What did you tell him?'

'I said that you were the best poet in the county and made the rest of us look like the raw beginners we really are.'

'Don't be so modest, Reg. All of you have got talent. It's something you can build on. You've worked hard to get better. Whenever I read a new poem of yours, I can see clear signs of improvement.'

'Thank you,' said Garside, snipping away. 'It means such a lot to me to hear you say that.'

'Tell me more about the sergeant.'

'He was so keen to read your poems – especially that one about Gregor Hayes. He even copied out some of it.'

'Why did he do that?' asked Tiller, warily.

'He liked it.'

'Did he say anything about me that wasn't to do with poetry? For instance, did he mention my family?'

'He said he was touched by the way you cared for your brother because David can't look after himself.'

'What else did he say?' Garside looked blank. 'Can't you remember?'

'I must have spoken to twenty or more customers since the sergeant was here. Everybody loves to have a chat when they're in my chair. You can't expect me to remember what this one or that one said to me.'

'Maybe not, but Sergeant Leeming wasn't a customer. He came here to get information about me.'

'That's right. He asked about our meeting at the King's Arms – the one when Mr Piper interrupted us.'

'I don't need reminding of that, Reg.'

'He had no right to say those things about you.'

'Forget Piper,' said Tiller, face hardening. 'He won't be able to do that again.'

'Whatever happened to him, he deserved it.'

'How long did the sergeant stay?'

'Oh, he was here for quite a time. While I was seeing to customers, he was reading your poems. The one about Gregor Hayes interested him. What puzzled him was the way you sort of became the phantom so that you could tell the story from a different angle.' He paused to admire his handiwork. 'How does that look?'

Tiller stared at himself in the mirror for a few seconds.

'Keep talking about Sergeant Leeming,' he said.

Returning to his office, Geoffrey Hedley simply wanted to relax and reflect on the progress of the investigation but his sense of duty compelled him to work instead. Since he was known for his efficiency, he didn't wish to give any of his clients cause for complaint. Concentration was vital. To that end, he'd told his clerk that he was not available to random visitors. He was therefore irked when the man came into the office and told him that someone was anxious to speak to him.

'I want no interruptions,' said Hedley, peevishly. 'Ask the client to make an appointment. Tell him that I'm indisposed.'

'It's a lady, sir.'

'Then give the same message to her.'

'Miss Treadgold said that she'd be prepared to wait indefinitely until you could find time for her.'

'Miss Treadgold?' repeated Hedley, his manner changing instantly. 'That's different. Show her in at once.'

When Caroline was escorted to the room, the lawyer was on his feet to welcome her. He held the back of the chair as she settled into it, then returned to his own seat behind the desk.

'I wasn't expecting you,' he said. 'Is it a legal matter?'

'No, it's a personal one.'

'Then I'm all ears.'

She was hesitant. 'It's . . . rather embarrassing.'

'We're friends, aren't we? There's no need for any embarrassment between us. You can speak freely, Caroline. I'm very discreet.'

'Yes, I know that.'

'Is it something to do with Alex?' She nodded. 'I'll be happy to help you in any way.'

'Have you been able to go through any letters of his?'

'Of course I have. It was one of the first things I did after the excursion. I thought that I might find evidence of threats against him that could lead us to the person behind Alex's strange disappearance.'

'Did you find that evidence?'

'Unfortunately, I didn't.'

'What about his . . . private correspondence?'

'There was a bundle of letters but, since they had no connection with what happened on the Phantom Special, I didn't bother to read them.'

'Were any of them sent from me?'

'No, they weren't.'

'Are you quite sure?'

'I'd know your handwriting anywhere, Caroline.'

She was at once relieved and hurt, glad that her billets-doux had not been read by a third person yet wounded by the realisation that Piper must have destroyed them. For her part, she'd kept every scrap of correspondence from him, even though it was full of what had turned out to be false promises.

'Can I offer you refreshment?' asked Hedley.

'No, thank you.'

'It may be that your letters *are* still there but not with the bulk of his correspondence. Since I have a key to the house, you're welcome to institute a search of your own.'

'Well . . .'

'I'll come with you, if you wish.'

'That won't be necessary. Alex didn't keep my letters.'

It was not the only consideration. Caroline was fearful of stumbling on the letters sent to him by Melissa Haslam. He'd certainly have treasured those.

'Thank you for putting my mind at rest,' she said, rising to her feet. 'I'm sorry to have disturbed you.'

'It was a pleasure to see you, Caroline.'

'Goodbye.'

He got to the door first so that he could open it for her then savoured the brush of her shoulder against him. Once she'd left, Hedley locked the door behind her and went across to the safe hidden behind a bookcase that hinged outwards when he pulled it. After opening the safe, he took out some letters held together by a blue ribbon and went back to his seat. Undoing the ribbon, he read one of Caroline's letters. The combination of elegant calligraphy and surging passion was almost giddying.

Hedley wished that she had written to him.

Time was against them. In the ten years since the blacksmith had vanished from Hither Wood, it had changed. Trees and vegetation had died and been supplanted by new growth. Areas that had been easily accessible were now hidden by bushes or carpeted by thick ground cover. The detectives searched as thoroughly as they could, but it was to no avail. Leeming was perspiring freely.

'How much longer must we do this, sir?' he protested.

'I thought that you always enjoyed physical exercise.'

'I do if it has a point.'

'The point is to find evidence.'

'Then we should have brought a spade or a fork.'

'There was no need for that,' said Colbeck. 'Once I'd sharpened them, these sticks have been able to go six inches or more into the ground. What I'm looking for will not be much deeper than that.'

'I'm afraid that the cab driver will get bored and drive off. We'll be stranded here yet again.'

'No, we won't. We could easily manage a walk to the railway station. However, I don't think it will be needed. Our driver knows that he'll be well paid for the time he's spent with us. If you're worried about him, why don't you go and tell him that we'll be finished very soon?'

'I'll go at once,' said Leeming, using a handkerchief to mop his face. 'Shall I take my coat and hat?'

'Yes, Victor. I'll join you in five or ten minutes.'

'I'll hold you to that.'

As Leeming walked away, Colbeck took out the diagram once again and consulted it. He looked around in every direction, then came to a decision. His stick was soon being jabbed hard into the ground once more.

Lost in thought, Rodney and Emma Piper sat on the sofa beside each other in the drawing room. It was minutes before he came out of his reverie to break the silence.

'I do apologise, my dear,' he said. 'It was very rude of me to drift off like that.'

'I did exactly the same, Rodney. We both have so much on our minds.'

'I was thinking about Alex.'

'So was I.'

'Where did we go wrong, Emma? How did we transform a well-behaved young man like our son into a rebel?'

'It was just a phase. And he didn't turn away from God.'

'That's the one crumb of comfort.'

'I'm sure that he'd have grown up to be a caring husband to Melissa and a good father. He was on the brink of a new life.'

'Death always strikes at inconvenient times.'

She bit her lip. 'Why is Inspector Colbeck taking so long?'

'It's because he's very thorough.'

'He must have *some* idea by now of what happened.'

'I'm sure that he does,' said her husband, 'but he's wise enough to keep his thoughts to himself until he has absolute proof.'

'I get the feeling that my brother is starting to lose faith in him. That's very worrying.'

'Does he say *why* he's having doubts?'

'I daren't ask him.'

'Patience was never one of his virtues. When your brother cracks the whip, he expects immediate results. In a situation like this, it's an impossible demand.'

'So what must we do, Rodney?'

'Watch and pray, my dear.'

Taking her hand in his own, he squeezed it gently.

Though his wound was slowly healing, Walter Vine still found it too painful to ride his horse. Bouncing up and down in the saddle set off shafts of agony in his arm. When he went out that morning, therefore, he travelled in a curricle and controlled the horse with one hand on the reins. To avoid being jostled, he maintained a moderate speed. For a keen horseman like him, the pace felt almost funereal.

Following the instructions he'd been given, he kept going until the road ran parallel with the railway line. As he maintained the same comfortable speed, he was soon overtaken by a train that shot past him so close and so fast that it frightened his horse and forced him to pull the animal to a halt. Once it had calmed down, he pushed on until he reached his destination. Vine took a long, satisfied look around.

'So *this* is where you disappeared, is it, Alex?' he said with a grin. 'I ought to mark the spot with a statue.'

When he finally returned to the cab, he found Leeming waiting for him with his arms folded and his face masked by a scowl. Colbeck made a gesture of apology.

'You said you'd be five or ten minutes,' complained Leeming.

'I got carried away, Victor.'

'You've been over half an hour.'

'Have I?' asked Colbeck in surprise. 'I can't believe that.'

'What kept you so long?'

'It was the feeling that, sooner or later, my luck would change and I'd find something.'

'There was nothing to find.'

'That's where you're wrong.'

'What do you mean, sir?'

'Blind faith kept me going,' said Colbeck. 'When I looked at the diagram again, I shifted my interest to a different area.'

'And what did you actually find?'

'It was this.'

Colbeck held up an object and flicked the remaining specks of dirt off it. Leeming's jaw dropped in surprise.

'There now,' said Colbeck with a smile. 'Wasn't it worth the effort to find this?'

* * *

When he'd finished shopping at the market, Caleb Andrews walked back home with a full basket. He was still smarting over his defeat on the cribbage board. As soon as he'd delivered his groceries to the house, therefore, he went straight across the road and demanded a game against his rival. Initially reluctant, Kingston changed his mind when a small wager was mentioned. He and Andrews sat down at the table beside the window and prepared to do battle on the cribbage board.

'I know where I went wrong yesterday,' said Andrews.

'Yes – you played against *me*.'

'I felt sorry for you, Alf. It wasn't *you* that won those games. It was that broken leg of yours.'

'Well, I've still got it.'

'It won't work twice. I've got no pity left for you.'

'How many games are we going to play?'

'I can only stay an hour or so because I need to have my lunch before Maddy arrives. We're going to hunt for that thief.'

'What about your detective from Scotland Yard?'

'We don't need him,' said Andrews, airily. 'It's something we can handle ourselves. And by the way, I know who called at my house the other day when you were acting as my sentry. It wasn't a thief. It was an old friend of mine who happened to be passing and thought he'd call in. I met him at the market so that's one little mystery solved.' He picked up the cards. 'Shall I deal?'

'If you want to, go ahead. It doesn't matter which of us deals the cards, Caleb. I'll end up winning again.'

'Don't be so sure. My brain is buzzing this morning.'

Andrews shuffled and dealt the cards.

Back in Birthwaite, they first went to the livery stable to ask if anyone had hired a horse that morning. The owner told them that he'd had no customers so far that day. Mystified, they went off to catch the train. On the journey back to Kendal, they were able to discuss the significance of the horseshoe Colbeck had found. While he was optimistic, his companion was no longer as excited as he had been when he'd first seen it.

'It may have no connection at all with the blacksmith,' Leeming said. 'Lots of horses must have been ridden into that clearing in the course of the last ten years. One of them could have lost a shoe there and the grass grew over it.'

'It's highly unlikely.'

'Why?'

'I found it in a place where horses were unlikely to go, Victor. It was a few inches below ground and close to a tree.'

'How do you think it got there?'

'I believe it was a marker.'

'What sort of marker?'

'I won't know until we can do some digging.'

'There's no need for us to get hot and dirty,' said Leeming. 'Sergeant Ainsley offered us the use of a couple of men. Let them get busy with their spades.'

'No, Victor, I don't want anyone else to know what I found. If Ainsley and his men are told, word will quickly spread and might reach the ears of the person we're after. That will put him on the defensive,' said Colbeck, 'or even frighten him into making a run for it.'

'Do we simply keep quiet about the horseshoe?'

'Yes – and we hope that it brings us luck.'

Arriving back in Kendal, they went straight to the police station and gave a plausible excuse for their absence. Ainsley warned them that Lord Culverhouse had become restive and was enraged by the news that they appeared to be giving the search for Gregor Hayes priority over the hunt for Alexander Piper.

'That's His Lordship's criticism,' said Ainsley, 'and not mine. If you can find out what happened to Gregor, I'd be very grateful. Doing that is far more important in my book than tracking down a despicable hothead like Piper.'

Colbeck decided that, before anything else, he had to calm Lord Culverhouse down. They had, after all, been summoned to Kendal by him. Leeming was dispatched to make another call at the bookshop so that he could question Tiller once more. After the physical effort he'd put in that morning, Leeming found it a restful assignment. The two detectives went off in opposite directions.

Lord Culverhouse was in his study when the sound of an approaching cab made him look out of the window. As soon as he saw Colbeck, he went striding off to open the front door himself. He glowered at his visitor.

'Ah, so you've remembered us at last,' he said, tartly.

'You are never out of my thoughts, my lord.'

'Neither, I'm told, is a long-dead blacksmith.'

'I can explain that,' said Colbeck. 'Might I suggest that I can do it best from the comfort of a chair?'

'Very well,' grunted the other.

Colbeck followed him into the house and along the passageway to the study. When the inspector sat down, Lord Culverhouse remained on his feet to hover over him like a menacing black cloud.

'What's all this nonsense about Hayes?' he demanded.

'I believe that his fate is relevant to our investigation.'

'That's patently ridiculous.'

'Is it, my lord?'

'Gregor Hayes was an excrescence,' said Culverhouse. 'I know that to my cost.'

'Do you?'

'Yes, I do.'

'May I ask why?'

'He dallied with one of my maidservants and left her with child. I had to get rid of the poor girl, but I did provide for her. If it had been left to me,' he growled, 'the blacksmith would have been strung up from the nearest tree.'

'For a Lord Lieutenant,' observed Colbeck, 'you have a somewhat primitive attitude to the rule of law.'

'Hayes had no compunction even though the girl must have been fifteen or twenty years younger than him.'

'Did he confess his guilt?'

'No – he denied it hotly.'

'What about the girl?'

'She mentioned his name at first then withdrew it and swore that it had been someone else.'

'Then you're condemning the blacksmith on dubious evidence, Lord Culverhouse.'

'It *had* to be him, Inspector.'

'Why was that?'

'Where women are concerned, Hayes had a reputation.'

'Reputations are often based on unproven rumours.'

'They were more than mere rumours. My doctor will tell you that. Dymock was infuriated. Had he not intervened at an early stage, his wife might have become another victim.'

'Really?'

'I'm not at liberty to disclose the details but I can tell you this. Hayes was a danger to women. More to the point, the man was married. He was betraying his wife.'

'Sergeant Ainsley seemed to think that Hayes had been wrongly accused.'

'Ignore what Ainsley says. He was the blacksmith's friend. He only saw the good side of the man.'

'From what you're telling me, my lord, there wasn't one.'

'He was skilled at his trade, I'll give him that. I just wish that he'd stuck to it instead of going on the rampage among the female population.'

'I'm disinclined to pay attention to gossip.'

'What I've told you is the simple truth – or do you think that the doctor and I are mere rumour-mongers?'

'I accept what you told me, but I've chosen to disregard the gossip that I heard about your nephew.'

Culverhouse glared. 'Has somebody had the gall to disparage Alex?'

'It's not worth repeating.'

'Come, come, I want to know what's being said.'

'I've no wish to speak ill of someone I've never met.'

'If there's evil gossip abroad, I insist on hearing it.'

'As you wish, my lord,' said Colbeck. 'The general view is that he exploited his charm among the ladies. I met one of them, as it happens – Miss Caroline Treadgold.'

'I, too, have met her. She was merely an acquaintance of Alex's.'

'There were other female friends, I've heard.'

'He's a handsome young man with blood in his veins,' said Culverhouse with a chuckle. 'Of course there were others. When he was released from the restrictions that his parents imposed on him, Alex went on a voyage of discovery. Most of us did that at his age, surely?'

'Are you condoning his interest in young women?'

'My nephew was looking for a partner in life. To do that, he spent a lot of time in female company. Ultimately, he found Miss Haslam and became . . . more settled.'

'It's a tragedy that the couple have been ripped apart.'

'And it's one that you should be investigating, Inspector. Nothing will help Miss Haslam to get over the shock of losing her future husband,' said Culverhouse, 'but one thing may ease her pain, and that's to know exactly what happened to him. Your job is to find out the truth. That's why I sent for you. So, let's have no more diversions like the case of Gregor Hayes. All of your time and effort must be directed at my nephew. Is that understood?' Colbeck nodded. 'If you don't follow my orders,' he went on, 'I'll send you back to Scotland Yard with your tail between your legs and I'll complain bitterly about you to the commissioner.'

CHAPTER TWENTY

There was something different about the bookseller, but it took Victor Leeming a little while to work out what it was. In the interim, he handed back the book he'd borrowed and thanked Tiller profusely for loaning it to him.

'How much of it did you read, Sergeant?'

'I read enough to realise that I couldn't possibly live here.'

'Why is that?'

'There are too many ghosts and ghouls.'

'They enhance the place, in my view.'

'Well, they put the wind up me.' He slapped his thigh. 'I can see it now,' he declared. 'You've had your hair cut. I knew something about you had changed.'

'I got Reg Garside to thin it out for me.'

'Did he ask for any tips about writing poetry?'

'He always does that.'

Even though the bookseller knew that he was under

suspicion, he had given Leeming a friendly welcome and offered him a cup of tea. The two of them were now seated in the shop and sipping away. Leeming was content.

'It's lovely to have a rest at last.'

'Why?' asked Tiller. 'What have you been doing?'

Leeming was evasive. 'Oh, we've been here and there,' he said. 'We didn't come across anything supernatural, though.'

'What about my haircut?' They laughed. 'My wife didn't recognise me when I got back. She thought I was an impostor.'

'I was interested in what she told me about your campaign against the building of railways.'

'They disfigure the landscape.'

'The people who build them argue that they're a boon to holidaymakers and a great help to industries that want to move their produce in bulk.'

'I thought you hated railways as much as we did.'

'I do,' said Leeming, 'but I'd never try to cause them damage. That would be flouting the law.'

'Sometimes the law needs to be flouted.'

'I'll pretend I never heard that.'

'You have to stand up for what you believe in, Sergeant.'

'What did you think when you first heard about the Phantom Special?'

'I thought that it was a big mistake.'

'Oh?'

'It was an act of provocation. You read the book I let you borrow. When you live in a county notorious for its haunted places, you have to negotiate with spirits from the past.'

'Piper didn't do that.'

'He refused to believe such things existed.'

'Are you saying that he was punished for his mockery?'

'Something like that probably happened.'

'Then why was he the only victim?' asked Leeming. 'There were lots of other people on the excursion who laughed at the idea of ghosts. Look at Mr Hedley. It was his idea to go to Hither Wood. Why wasn't *he* punished as well?'

'I think he was.'

'How?'

'He lost his best friend,' said Tiller. 'Everyone on that excursion liked Piper so they suffered badly when he vanished. It often happens to people who thumb their noses at the idea of unquiet spirits – they're forced to repent of their folly.'

Leeming was torn between guilt and apprehension.

Though he was pleased to see them both, Caleb Andrews was embarrassed that his daughter had brought Lydia Quayle to the house. It was a small, draughty, terraced dwelling that would have looked derisory beside Lydia's much larger house in a more affluent area of the city.

'I was going to come to you, Maddy,' he said.

'This is where the crime occurred,' said his daughter, 'so it's the obvious meeting place.'

'Have you had any more thoughts about it, Mr Andrews?' asked Lydia.

'Oh, yes. I was awake for hours last night, going through those names again and again.'

'Did you single anyone out?'

'I didn't, but Alf Kingston did.'

'Who was it?'

'It was someone I'd never even thought of, to be honest. I played cribbage with Alf earlier today,' he said, beaming. 'As a matter of fact, I won every game and earned myself a little money.'

'Don't boast, Father,' chided Madeleine.

'I'm entitled to. Anyway, there's a name I forgot to put on the list. Alf reminded me that I had some slates blown off my roof in a high wind. I got someone to replace them. He came in for a cup of tea at one point and saw me polishing my medal.'

'Did he see you locking it away?' asked Lydia.

'It's more than possible.'

'What sort of man is he?'

'Well,' said Andrews, 'until today, I'd have said that Percy Hopway was very trustworthy. He's done lots of work for me over the years. Percy is slow but reliable.'

'Did you leave the house at any point while he was there?'

'Yes, I did. I walked to the shop to get some baccy.'

'Was the house locked?' asked Madeleine.

'There was no point. I was only away for a few minutes and Percy was guarding the place for me.'

'So he could have popped in while you were gone?'

Andrews was uncertain. 'It's unlikely that he did but . . . it was possible, I suppose.'

'I think you should add him to the list, Father,' she said.

'Then we can work our way through the names one by one. I remember Percy Hopway. He always looked rather sly to me. Put his name at the top of the list.'

After listening to Colbeck's explanation of how much information he and Leeming had so far gathered, Culverhouse realised that he'd been too quick to condemn the detectives. While the effort of rising to an apology was beyond him, he was mollified and, as a result, adopted a less hectoring tone. Hearing that Colbeck was in the house again, Rodney Piper joined them in the study and asked how the investigation was proceeding.

'It's more advanced than I thought,' said Culverhouse. 'I'll give you the gist of it later. There's no point in asking the inspector to go through it all again.'

'I explained to His Lordship that I can't go into too much detail,' said Colbeck. 'I made a point of visiting the place where the fire had been lit to stop the train that night. Sergeant Ainsley took me there.'

'What was the point?' asked Piper.

'I wanted to see the location as the passengers on that excursion would have seen it. In their case, darkness would have contributed to their confusion.'

'What did you learn?'

Colbeck told them about his sprint over the approximate distance that Alexander Piper had run. The two of them were astounded. The idea that the immaculately attired inspector would discard his coat and hat on a cold evening to race beside a railway line made them gape. Neither of the two men could trot, let alone run at full speed. When Colbeck explained why he'd done it, they were intrigued.

'I admire your commitment,' said Piper. 'You certainly don't spare yourself.'

'I felt that the effort was necessary.'

'And you *ran* all that way?' asked Culverhouse. 'You must have been exhausted.'

'It's important to keep fit in my profession, my lord. When you confront them, most criminals will make a run for it. We have to be fast enough to catch them.'

'When do you expect to catch whoever was responsible for our son's disappearance?' said Piper.

'We are working tirelessly to ensure that we do that as soon as possible.'

'Are you talking in terms of days or weeks?'

'We will press on for as long as it takes,' said Colbeck. 'I can't divulge names, but I can tell you that we have a number of suspects in mind. Sergeant Leeming is questioning one of them at this very moment.'

Conversation at the bookshop was interrupted by the arrival of an old man who wanted to browse among the shelves and talk to Tiller as he did so. It was obvious from the newcomer's voice that he had great respect for the owner's knowledge of books. All that Leeming could do was to wait until Tiller was free again. The customer eventually bought three second-hand books and left.

'I'm sorry about that,' said Tiller.

'You have a business to run, Norm. I don't want to interfere with that.'

'He comes in regularly. Since he retired as headmaster of one of our schools, he has time on his hands. I tend to make a fuss over him because he bought my anthology.'

'Did he enjoy the poems?'

'Yes, he did, and so did his wife. She's bedridden, alas, and he reads some of my poems to her every evening.'

'I bet he doesn't read the one about Gregor Hayes.'

'It's not in the anthology.'

'I think it's just as well,' said Leeming. 'It's about a nasty phantom that torments the blacksmith to death. I don't believe that it's suitable for a sick old woman. Parts of it upset *me*, so it'd be bound to unsettle her.'

'That poem has been discarded,' said Tiller, bluntly.

'When I called on Mr Garside, I read some of your other ones as well. You return to the same thing time and again. The barber noticed it as well. You write about nature and the importance of keeping it unsullied. Is that why you objected to the arrival of railways?'

'Yes, it is.'

'Is that *all* you did, Norm?' asked Leeming. 'Did you simply carry banners and shout out slogans?'

'No, I spoke at meetings as well.'

'What were you trying to do – lift their spirits?'

'I wanted to make them fully aware of the dangers to our beautiful, God-given scenery. Once allowed in, railways could go on to turn the whole county into an eyesore. We had a duty to stop that happening.'

'And how would you do that, Norm?'

'We'd hamper any development that was planned.'

'Would that involve vandalism and theft?'

'We'll take appropriate steps,' said Tiller with sudden passion. 'It's a pity that you won't be here for long or you'd see an example of people ready to defend the glorious landscape all around us from those who wish to deface it even more.'

It took Andrews some time to find him. When he called at the man's house, his wife told him that Hopway was repairing a wall that had collapsed days before. Andrews got there to find that the wall had been rebuilt and that Percy Hopway had moved on to another job half a mile away. Not one to give up easily, Andrews began the long walk. He was glad that the women were not with him. At Madeleine's suggestion, they were going to visit another suspect, leaving her father to tackle Hopway on his own.

Andrews eventually found him at the top of a ladder, installing glass in a bedroom window of a public house. He called up to him.

'Is there anything you *can't* do, Percy?'

'That sounds like Caleb Andrews,' said the other without looking down. 'Excuse me if I don't turn round. I have to fix this pane in.'

'You mend roofs, you rebuild walls and you're a skilled glazier. I even spotted you doing some plumbing once.'

'I do whatever needs doing, Caleb.'

'It obviously keeps you busy. Your wife says you never stop. Anyway,' said Andrews, 'I wanted a word. You carry on, Percy. I can wait.'

In fact, it was only a few minutes before Hopway descended the ladder. He was a thickset man of middle height with an ugly face whose defining feature was the half-closed eye set lower in his face than its partner. It gave him the sinister look of which Madeleine had spoken. After wiping his hands on an old rag, Hopway put his hands on his hips.

'What do you want, Caleb?'

'Do you remember replacing some slates off my roof?'

'Yes, I do.' Hopway's voice sharpened. 'They haven't fallen off again, have they?'

'Oh, no, you did a good job.'

'What's the problem, then?'

'While you were on my roof,' said Andrews, 'I went off to the shop to get some baccy.'

'That's right. You did. You asked me to keep an eye on the house – my *good* eye, that is.'

'Did anyone come while I was away?'

'No, they didn't.'

'Are you certain of that, Percy?'

'I'm not blind.'

'If you were lying flat on the roof, you might have missed them.'

'Oh, no, I wouldn't,' said the other. 'Why are you asking, anyway?'

'Something was stolen from my house.'

'When?'

'That's the trouble, Percy. I can't be sure.'

'What was it?'

'It was that medal I showed you, the one they gave me for outstanding service on the LNWR.'

Hopway was roused. 'You think it was *me*, don't you?'

'Of course I don't.'

'Then why are you bothering me? Just because the house was left unlocked for two or three minutes, you think that I must have shinned down the ladder, slipped into the house to grab your stupid little medal, then climbed quickly back up the ladder before you got back.'

'I didn't think that at all, Percy.'

'Then why the hell are you here?' shouted Hopway.

'Keep your voice down.'

'I don't like being accused of something I didn't do.'

'I just thought—'

'I know what you damn well thought, Caleb, and it's an insult. People employ me because they trust me.'

'*I* trust you.'

'Well, I'll tell you one thing. Don't ever ask me to mend your roof or do any other kind of work for you again.' He waved a threatening fist. 'Now, get out of my sight.'

Climbing the ladder, he broke wind by way of farewell.

Madeleine and Lydia took a more cautious approach. When they checked up on another of their suspects, they gave no hint of their true motives in speaking to him. Henry Blacker was a locksmith whose shop was only two blocks away from Andrews' house. Since she had met him once before, Madeleine did all the talking. Pretending to be in search of a small safe, she asked him to show her his selection. She'd even brought a pencil and a notebook with her so that she could write down the dimensions.

Blacker, a dour, laconic man, was inquisitive.

'This for Caleb?' he muttered.

'It might be.'

'Why isn't he here?'

'He doesn't think he needs a safe,' said Madeleine, 'but he does have valuables in the house. I've been trying to persuade him to protect them properly.'

'Important.'

'Is there much theft around here, Mr Blacker?'

'Too much.'

'So you're always in demand.'

'People only come to me *after* a burglary. Too late.'

'We want to improve the security *before* anything happens. My father has a few souvenirs that he'd hate to lose. It would break his heart if they were stolen.'

'Show you what I've got.'

Taking them into the back room, Blacker pointed to three small safes in a row, listing the advantages of each and picking out the one he thought most suitable for Andrews. Madeleine wrote down the dimensions of each one along with their prices. After thanking him, they left the shop.

'Cross his name off the list,' said Lydia.

'Do you think that we should?'

'I'm sure of it, Madeleine. I did what Alan always does when he's questioning a suspect. He watches their eyes and their hands. If they look away, it's because they're nervous and unable to meet his gaze.'

'What about the hands?'

'Guilty men often fidget. Mr Blacker didn't do that. He looked you full in the eye and spoke honestly. Besides, he has a job that's devoted to fighting crime,' said Lydia, 'so he's clearly innocent. In fact, the only criminal in the shop was you.'

'*Me?*'

'You told him a pack of lies. That makes you a confidence trickster. Actually, you were very convincing.'

'I'm so glad that I asked you to help us,' said Madeleine, laughing. 'When I've got *you* beside me, I don't need Alan Hinton.'

Hinton was disappointed. After being involved in two major investigations, he now found himself reduced to office work. It made him feel unappreciated and he made a mental note to mention the fact to Colbeck. There was one bonus awaiting him at the end of the day. In asking Madeleine about progress in the search for the thief who stole the medal, he'd be able to see Lydia Quayle once more. That thought restored his morale.

As he walked down a corridor, he realised that he'd be passing Colbeck's office and couldn't resist taking a look inside. Like the inspector, it was supremely well organised. Since he was untidy by nature, Hinton marvelled at the way that everything was in its place, somehow making the room look much larger than it really was. It was an office that inspired confidence.

He was still admiring it when a firm hand fell on his shoulder. Hinton turned to see the unforgiving face of Edward Tallis behind him. He quailed inwardly.

'Have you nothing better to do?' asked the superintendent.

'I just happened to be passing, sir.'

'Then why didn't you continue on your way?'

'I was curious.'

'That's an asset in a detective whereas the sheer nosiness that you display is not. I can see that I'll have to get this office locked until Colbeck returns.'

'Do you have any idea when that may be, sir?'

'Unfortunately, I don't,' said Tallis. 'This case is proving more challenging by the day. A report from the inspector arrived in the post this morning. Its tone was sanguine, but I know how to read between the lines of his reports. Please don't mention a word of this to his wife, but my feeling is that, on this occasion, Colbeck may have bitten off more than even *he* can chew.'

Back at the Riverside Hotel, the inspector was, in fact, tucking into some delicious steak while Leeming was addressing himself with equal enthusiasm to his own meal. It was a long time before either of them spoke. When they did, they exchanged information about what they'd learnt. Colbeck talked about the hostile reception he'd received at Culverhouse Court and how it had taken him some time to convince Lord

Culverhouse that, as a priority, they were committed to solving the case that brought them there.

Leeming was fascinated by the news about Dymock.

'The doctor had a reason to *hate* the blacksmith?' he said, incredulously. 'What exactly happened to Mrs Dymock?'

'I don't know the full details.'

'I can't see how the doctor's wife would ever come into contact with Hayes. And, even if she did, Mrs Dymock would surely treat him with disdain.'

'There are all sorts of ways in which they might have met, Victor. She might have taken a horse to be shod or needed to have the wheel of a trap replaced. Hayes might even have come to the house for some reason.'

'And her husband would not have been there,' said Leeming. 'He had the look of a man who worked all hours, so Mrs Dymock might have felt lonely.'

'Lord Culverhouse did mention two things that might be significant. Mrs Dymock was years younger than her husband and the couple had no children. In other words, she had nothing to occupy her.'

'Maybe she was bored, sir.'

'We don't know that,' said Colbeck. 'What we can be certain of is the fact that Dymock was very upset about the friendship that sprang up between Hayes and his wife. At last, we have a connection between the two cases.'

'Dymock might have hated the blacksmith enough to have him killed, and done exactly the same in Piper's case.'

'He'd have needed help.'

'I'm sure he could afford to pay for it.'

'Right,' said Colbeck, 'you've heard what *I've* been doing. How did you get on at the bookshop?'

'Oh, I had a surprise as well, sir . . .'

At his suggestion, the women met Caleb Andrews at the house in John Islip Street because he didn't wish to feel embarrassed about his home when Lydia was there. He admitted that he'd bungled his interview with Percy Hopway and lost heart when he did the same thing with another man whose name was on the list. Like him, Madeleine and Lydia had spoken to two of the suspects, but they had done so more tactfully. Since all of the people so far approached had been patently innocent, most of the names could now be removed from the list. Attention was focused on the survivors.

The three of them were still deep in discussion when they had a visitor. Having reached the end of his shift, Alan Hinton had called in to see how the self-appointed detectives were faring. When Andrews described his efforts, Hinton struggled to keep a straight face. He was much more impressed by the approach taken by the two women.

'May I offer some advice?' he said.

'Please do, Alan,' said Lydia.

'Well, perhaps you're asking the wrong question.'

'There's only one question that matters,' said Andrews, hotly. 'Who stole my medal? What black-hearted thief crept into my home when I wasn't there and took something that was very precious to me?'

'Listen to Alan,' advised Madeleine.

'Then get him to talk sense.'

'I do apologise for my father,' she said, turning to Hinton. 'He doesn't mean to criticise you. Losing his medal upset him so much that he spoke in anger.' When Andrews tried to say something, she quelled him with a look. 'Now, what's your advice, Alan?'

'Look at it the other way round,' he replied. 'Instead of wondering who took the medal, ask why the thief would then return it? Did he feel guilty? Was he soft-hearted? Had it been his plan all along to give Mr Andrews a fright before restoring the stolen item? Was it simply the practical joke I suggested it might be when we found the medal safe and sound in its cupboard?'

'If it was a joke,' said Lydia, 'then it's another reason to rule out Mr Blacker, the locksmith. He was so humourless that he should have been an undertaker.'

'Alan's idea is a good one,' said Madeleine.

'Thank you,' he said. 'It's the reason why Mr Andrews is in a better position to solve the crime than I am. Knowing the people who are still on his list, he can get into the minds of each one of them and have some idea of the way that they think.'

'That's sound advice, Father.'

'It is,' conceded Andrews, 'and I'm sorry for what I said earlier. I went about it the wrong way.'

'You did, I'm afraid,' said Hinton. 'You questioned people in a way that made them feel accused. That put their backs up. Next time you speak to a suspect, tell him what happened and ask him if he has an idea who might have done such a thing. If you take someone into your confidence like that, you might just be able to catch him off guard.'

'Oh, I'm so glad you called in, Alan,' said Madeleine.

'So am I,' added Lydia, softly.

'Well, I did have something to pass on,' he explained. 'I assume that you've heard from the inspector?'

Madeleine nodded. 'I had another letter from him today.'

'When you reply to it, you can tell him that the old order has been well and truly restored. Superintendent Tallis is back and he's more of a tyrant than ever.'

Since he had so much work to do, Geoffrey Hedley stayed in his office until well into the evening. He was the only person in the building. When he heard the doorbell, therefore, he had to go downstairs to see who had called on him. Opening the door, he was surprised to find Rodney Piper standing there.

'I'm sorry to disturb you,' said the visitor, 'but, when I went to your home, I was told that you'd be here.'

'The pressure of work kept me at my desk, Archdeacon. Please come in.'

He stood back so that Piper could step into the hall, then he led him upstairs to the office. After trading a few niceties, they sat down. Piper was plainly nervous.

'I hope that you won't disapprove of my request,' he said.

'That's highly unlikely.'

'My wife and I were talking about the way that Alex had

become far more responsible when he'd found the woman with whom he wanted to share his life.'

'That's very true.'

'Instead of taking each day as it came, he must have looked to the future. Caring for a wife entails a major commitment. One has to plan for every eventuality.'

'That was exactly the advice I gave him.'

'Did you suggest that he might make a will?'

'Yes, of course,' said Hedley. 'Alex owned a house and had independent means. A lot of capital was involved.'

'Would it be possible for me to see the will?'

'I'm afraid not, Archdeacon.'

'But Alex was our son.'

'That makes no difference. The last will and testament can only be read in the wake of someone's death and that has so far not been established.'

'We've all accepted that he's no longer alive.'

'The law is the law.'

'I'm not asking on my own behalf,' said Piper. 'Our needs are modest. We neither expect nor need any money to come to us. What would bring us succour at this difficult time is some indication of Alex's state of mind.'

'I can tell you that now. He was leading a blameless life.'

'Is there evidence of that in the will?'

'I'm not sure that I understand you, Archdeacon.'

Piper sat forward. 'I dedicated my life to God,' he said, 'and I've never regretted it for a second. Alex was brought up in my shadow and I'd hoped that he might follow me into the Anglican clergy. Instead, he chose a different and, I'm sad to say, more selfish path.'

'I can see what you're asking me,' said Hedley, 'and I have great sympathy for you. What you're seeking is a sign of repentance from your son.' Piper nodded. 'Then I'm afraid that my answer remains the same. You'll have to wait.'

'Is there a bequest of any sort to the Church?'

'I'm sorry I can't help you, Archdeacon.'

Piper raised both hands in surrender. 'No, no,' he said, 'you're not at fault. I see that. To be candid, I feel rather embarrassed now. I'm asking for something that, as a lawyer, you simply can't give me.'

'I'm glad that you appreciate that.'

After chatting with Hedley for a few minutes, Piper got up and made his way downstairs. At the door, he apologised yet again for taking up the lawyer's time. Hedley bade him farewell then returned to his office. The first thing he did was to unlock the cabinet in which his files were kept. Taking out the one that related to Alexander Piper, he extracted a copy of his friend's will. There was a good reason why he didn't want Rodney Piper to view it. Had he done so, the archdeacon would have noticed that Geoffrey Hedley was a major beneficiary.

Colbeck was interested to hear how quickly Norman Tiller had gone from being a mild-mannered bookseller to a fervent enemy of Cumberland railways. In spite of its many contradictions, the inspector was an admirer of the British railway system. He just wished that it had developed in a much more orderly and coordinated manner instead of being rushed into existence by greedy investors in search of large profits.

'I disagree with Tiller's view,' he said, 'but he has perfect right to hold it.'

'He doesn't have the right to cause wilful damage. And didn't you tell me that Lord Culverhouse had received some poison pen letters when he was trying to arouse interest in the Kendal to Windermere railway?'

'Oh, I don't think that Tiller sent those, Victor. He's a poet, after all, with a love of language. Had he sent a letter to Lord Culverhouse, it would have been in verse.'

'Yes,' agreed Leeming. 'He told me at one point that he wrote in the language of Shakespeare and Milton.'

'I can't imagine Milton being interested in a case like that of Hayes. There's no religious element in it. Shakespeare is a different matter,' said Colbeck. 'Woods and forests crop up in many of his plays and he loved the idea of weird creatures. Think of the witches in *Macbeth*.'

'I didn't know there were any, sir.'

'There are three of them. They make strange predictions.'

'Do *you* have any predictions to make, sir?'

'Only this one, Victor,' replied Colbeck. 'When we finally discover who was responsible for Piper's disappearance, we are going to be in for a big surprise.'

They discussed the case at length once more, without coming to a firm conclusion. Leeming then announced that he was going to the King's Arms.

'I thought you preferred the beer here.'

'I do, sir, but Sergeant Ainsley drinks at the King's Arms and I'd like to have a talk with him. I want to know more about the claim that Gregor Hayes got too close to the doctor's wife. If it's true, it would explain a lot about Dymock.'

'I'll wait here until you get back.'

Leeming took his leave and stepped out of the hotel. He was immediately reminded that it was November 5th. Kendal was ablaze. The crackle of bonfires was augmented by the sound of exploding fireworks and the laughter of children. A dark, cold, cheerless night was warmed and lit up in all directions. Leeming was saddened to be so far away from his family at such a time. Bonfire Night was such an important event for his young sons. He strode off resignedly down the road, promising himself that, whatever happened, he'd spend the whole evening with his family in exactly a year's time. It was in the nature of a sacred duty to him.

Leeming felt no sense of danger. It never occurred to him that someone might be lurking behind a tree and waiting for him.

CHAPTER TWENTY-ONE

It was too good an opportunity to ignore. Having been told simply to watch the detectives, the man had been sitting at a table in the corner and catching the occasional word from their conversation. When he heard that Leeming was about to leave, he rose at once, finished his drink and slipped quietly out of the hotel. He had just enough time to choose a hiding place before the sergeant came into view. Reaching inside his coat, he took out his cosh and waited.

Leeming was in no hurry. At one point, he paused to inhale deeply and look around. He then adjusted his top hat to its customary angle and continued his walk. The man fingered his weapon and thought about the praise he'd get for using his initiative. There'd be financial reward as well. All it would take were some well-directed blows at a man who was completely unaware of his presence. As a result of his attack, the investigation might be stopped dead in its tracks.

Listening to the sound of approaching footsteps, he was poised for action. The moment that Leeming walked past him, the man waited for a split second then leapt out from behind the tree. He knocked Leeming's hat off then got a brawny arm around his throat, intending to beat him senseless with the cosh and leave him in a pool of blood. But the sergeant reacted too quickly, using his elbow to dig hard into the man's stomach and twisting sharply at the same time. When the first blow came, therefore, it missed Leeming's head and hit his shoulder, producing a yell of pain and a sudden explosion of energy.

He threw himself backwards with tremendous force, knocking his assailant off his feet and falling on top of him. Though he still had the cosh, the man was unable to use it effectively. He was also forced to release his hold on his victim's neck. Spinning around, Leeming grabbed the wrist of the hand holding the cosh and dashed it repeatedly against the ground until the man had to let the weapon go.

They were on even terms now and the attacker realised that he'd made a grave mistake. Leeming was much faster and stronger than he'd thought. While the man was getting in some solid punches, he was taking even harder ones. It was only a matter of time before he was overpowered. Escape was vital. Gathering up all his strength, he managed to hurl Leeming off him and scramble to his feet, getting in a last kick before haring off into the darkness. He kept running until he was certain that he was not being followed.

* * *

Victor Leeming, meanwhile, was rubbing the shoulder that had been struck by the cosh. Had it hit his head instead, the force of the blow might have knocked him unconscious. He reproached himself for being caught off guard. It wouldn't have happened in London. Years of walking the beat in uniform had given him a sixth sense for danger. His shoulder was on fire but, when he slipped a hand under his coat to feel it, he didn't think that any bones had been broken. He was still able to move his arm, albeit with a stab of pain.

In the course of the struggle, his coat and trousers had become ruffled and he was conscious of being scruffy. Leeming did his best to smarten himself up then retrieved his top hat. Last of all, he picked up the cosh and felt its weight in the palm of his hand. He was chastened when he realised that it could easily have been used as a murder weapon.

Colbeck was surprised to see him return to the hotel so soon. When he saw the state that Leeming was in, he knew that there'd been trouble. He followed the sergeant upstairs to the latter's room and had a close look at him.

'What happened?' he asked.

'This did,' replied Leeming, holding out the cosh.

'Are you badly hurt?'

'I don't think so, but my pride is smarting.'

'Look at the state of your coat.'

'I'd be grateful if you could help me off with it, sir. He hit me on the shoulder and I can't move it properly.'

'Would you like me to summon a doctor?'

310

'I don't think that's necessary,' said Leeming. 'Besides, Dr Dymock might turn up and I'd hate to let *him* examine me. He'd prefer to kill rather than cure either of us.'

Leeming managed a weary smile. While Colbeck removed the sergeant's coat with great care, he was given a detailed account of what had happened. Probing gently with his fingers, he could find no evidence of any fracture. Though he winced, Leeming did not complain. Colbeck helped him to a chair.

'You did well, Victor,' he said.

'No, I didn't. I made myself an easy target.'

'Your attacker would never call you that because he'll have his own wounds to lick now. You taught him a lesson.'

'I learnt one myself as well.'

'How would you describe him?'

'He was about my height and weight, but he was a bit sluggish so may have been older. I couldn't see his face, but I felt a beard. Also, he had bad breath. At first,' said Leeming, 'I thought that he was after my wallet, but it's clear now that I was set on because someone wants to stop us finding out the truth.'

'That's all the more reason to press on with the investigation.'

'I agree, sir. I might start carrying that cosh with me.'

'If we need weapons, I've brought pistols with me.'

'So what do we do now?'

'I know what *I'm* going to do,' said Colbeck. 'To start with, I'll have a talk with the landlord. The man who ambushed you must have been inside the hotel so that he could keep a watchful eye on us. He'd have had no reason to wait outside in the cold in the hope that you or I would eventually come out alone. When he saw that you were about to leave the hotel, he got out of here before you.'

'What are you going to say to the landlord?'

'Two things,' replied Colbeck. 'The first one concerns your attacker. He's probably a local man and may be a regular visitor to the hotel. At all events, I'm hoping that the landlord may have seen him, if not actually recognised him.'

'You said that you'd ask him two things.'

'That's right, Victor. My second request relates to you. I'll ask him to recommend his best malt whisky. After what you've been through, you deserve a stiff drink.'

Leeming's face glowed like a beacon.

Alan Hinton had given them wise counsel. After he'd left, the three of them reflected on what he'd told them. Instead of levelling an accusation at a suspect, they were instead to pretend to take him into their confidence by asking for his advice. Caleb Andrews felt that he was uniquely qualified for the role.

'I know how to charm people,' he said.

'That's not true at all, Father,' his daughter pointed out. 'You upset Mr Hopway so much that he'll never work for you again. You've no idea how to be tactful.'

'Yes, I have, Maddy.'

'Your talents lie in other directions.'

'I can do anything I want when I turn my mind to it.'

'You're too set in your ways.'

'Why not let *us* deal with the remaining suspects?' said Lydia with an appeasing smile. 'Madeleine can tell them how deeply upset you were by the theft and work on their sympathy. If anyone can find the thief, it will be her.'

'Thank you, Lydia,' said Madeleine.

'You know how to win people's confidence.'

'So do I,' bleated Andrews.

Madeleine exchanged a knowing glance with her friend.

'I *do*,' he insisted. 'I have more experience of life than either of you.'

'It isn't only a question of age, Father,' said Madeleine. 'You're almost thirty years older than Robert but he has far more knowledge of human nature than you do.'

'Then why isn't he here to give us the benefit of it?'

'You know quite well.'

'Write to him, Maddy. Tell him of the crisis I'm in.'

'I've already done that, and he sent his love to you in the letter I received this morning.'

'I don't want his love. I need his advice.'

'He gave it when you first received that medal. Robert told you to leave it in our safe, but you refused because you wanted to be able to enjoy looking at it whenever you wanted.'

'It was *my* medal. I had every right.'

'Of course you did,' said Lydia. 'Ordinarily, there'd have been no problem – until someone saw your award and took a fancy to it.'

'I still think it may have been Percy Hopway.'

'Don't be silly, Father,' said Madeleine. 'We *know* that he's innocent. You admitted it earlier.'

Andrews was bewildered. 'Did I?'

'Yes, you did – after you'd offended him. Lydia and I just want to stop you offending anyone else.'

'But I'm a friendly person by nature.'

'I make no comment,' said Lydia, suppressing a smile.

'That's why I was so popular with the other drivers.'

'They certainly looked up to you, Mr Andrews.'

'And they knew that the award had been richly deserved,' said Madeleine, proudly. 'That's why I don't think any of them would have dared to steal it. The thief *has* to be one of the people still on the list.'

'I'll speak to them one by one tomorrow,' said Andrews.

'No, you won't, Father.'

'*We* will,' said Lydia. 'At least, Madeleine will, because she has a gift. Put your trust in your daughter. Of the three of us, she's by far the best detective.' She indicated her friend. 'Have you forgotten what Alan Hinton told us?'

'Yes, I have,' said Andrews.

'He told us that Madeleine was the perfect substitute.'

When he'd left the hotel, Leeming had planned to walk to the King's Arms to speak to Bernard Ainsley, who routinely drank there of an evening. Colbeck went off in his stead. Ainsley was talking to a group of friends in a crowded bar. It was obviously not the ideal place for a private conversation. Colbeck therefore detached Ainsley from the group. On their way back to the police station, Colbeck informed his companion about the attack on Leeming.

Ainsley was shocked. 'Someone tried to *kill* him?'

'It's more likely that he wanted to disable the sergeant in order to hamper our investigation.'

'How badly is he hurt?'

'He'll be confined to his room for a day or two.'

'What about the attacker?'

'Sergeant Leeming has given me a rough description that I'll pass on to you. Our belief is that he was at our hotel to keep us under surveillance. I spoke to the landlord to see if he'd seen and recognised the man but all he could remember was a bearded stranger.'

'Well,' said the other, adjusting to the information, 'the first thing I must do is to apologise. This is normally a very safe town. I take care of that. Whoever assaulted the sergeant must be tracked down and arrested. I'm not having a thug like that loose in Kendal.'

'As long as he's at liberty, he could strike again.'

'In future, I suggest I assign one of my men to act as your bodyguard.'

'It's a kind offer,' said Colbeck, 'but I must refuse it.'

'You and the sergeant are marked men.'

'We're rather accustomed to that. It's the reason we've learnt to look after ourselves. The attack on Sergeant Leeming was unexpected but he survived it and put his assailant to flight.'

Discussing the implications of the incident took them all the way back to the police station where they adjourned to Ainsley's office. When Colbeck gave him details of the attacker, the sergeant pulled a face.

'I can think of lots of people who fit that description.'

'When you're engaged in a desperate fight, you don't have time to study the person grappling with you. Given the plight he was in, Sergeant Leeming did well to remember any details at all about the man.'

'I'll go through my records,' said Ainsley. 'We do, alas, have criminals in the community. That's inevitable. But the only violence we get here as a rule comes from people who are drunk and disorderly. I can't remember when we last had a case like this.'

Colbeck was pleased by Ainsley's strong reaction to news of the assault but it was not the only thing that had made him seek out the sergeant. He turned to the subject that Leeming had intended to discuss with Ainsley.

'I need to ask you about Gregor Hayes again.'

'Ask away, Inspector.'

'Lord Culverhouse is furious that I've taken an interest in his case, not least because he has a reason to loathe the man. According to him, the blacksmith was responsible for leading one of his maidservants astray.'

'That's arrant nonsense.'

'The girl was forced to leave as a result.'

'Well, I can assure you that Gregor wasn't the father. To start with, how could he get anywhere near her? Culverhouse Court is well protected. Outsiders aren't allowed near the place.'

'Then why was Hayes named as the servant's seducer?'

Ainsley lifted an eyebrow. 'Why do you think?'

'Was the blame shifted to him in order to divert attention from the *real* father?' Ainsley nodded. 'Do you have any idea who the culprit was?'

'Gregor wasn't the only man with a fondness for pretty young women. It's a question of access. Since the girl never left the house, she must have been picked on by someone who lived under the same roof.'

'Was it one of the other servants?'

'She could have said "no" to them. But,' said Ainsley, both eyebrows aloft this time, 'there was someone she was unable to resist.'

'Lord Culverhouse?'

'You can see why he might need to shift the blame.'

'Do you have any evidence that he was the father?'

'No,' admitted Ainsley, 'but I'm told that the female members of staff are always worried when Lady Culverhouse is away for any length of time. That's proof enough for me.'

Geoffrey Hedley arrived at the house and was immediately shown to the study. When the lawyer stepped into the room, Lord Culverhouse rose from his seat.

'Ah, there you are, Hedley.'

'You sent for me, Lord Culverhouse. Does that mean there's news?'

'Yes,' said the other. 'I've ordered Colbeck to forget about that blacksmith he's taken an interest in and address himself solely to Alex's disappearance.'

'That was a sensible move.'

'I need positive results and I want them soon. However, that's not why I summoned you. I'm curious to know a little more about a friend of yours. I suppose that the lady was really Alex's friend until he met someone else, but I daresay that you will have got to know her well. I am speaking about Miss Caroline Treadgold.'

'I gathered that,' said Hedley, quietly alarmed.

'Take a seat and tell me all you know about her.'

Alone in his room, Leeming was starting to feel better. The throbbing pain in his shoulder had eased somewhat, though a dark bruise was starting to emerge as a memento of the attack. Equally pleasing was the fact that his coat and trousers were not as badly stained as he'd feared and could be brushed clean. The main reason for the smile on his face, however, was that he'd been given a whole bottle of malt whisky to aid his recovery. After pouring another glass, he lifted it up in a silent toast then took a long, delicious, invigorating sip.

Bernard Ainsley talked far more freely than he'd felt able to do before. Confident that his comments would not find their way back to Culverhouse Court, he told Colbeck about the foibles of its owner and the many rumours that swirled around him.

'He's one of those Sunday Christians,' he said, bitterly. 'Lord Culverhouse is as devout as Archdeacon Piper on the Sabbath, knowing that he has six days of unlicensed sinfulness ahead of him.'

'Thank you for being so frank,' said Colbeck.

'I know I can trust you to be discreet, Inspector.'

'I'm glad that you finally realise that. Let's put Lord Culverhouse aside for a moment, shall we, and turn our attention to the blacksmith? Another name has been linked to him.'

'And who might that be?'

'Mrs Dymock, the doctor's wife.'

'Ah,' sighed Ainsley, 'there was some truth in that. Gregor told me as much. Mrs Dymock is the sort of person who could turn any man's head. She'd been out riding with friends one day when her horse cast a shoe. Mrs Dymock went straight to the forge and asked for help. That's how it started.'

'Was the attraction mutual?'

'Gregor claimed that it was but that could have been his vanity talking. He swore that nothing actually happened between them – how could it? – but he talked about her all the time. The gap in their ages didn't worry Mrs Dymock. She married the doctor, and she's much younger than him.'

'How did her husband find out about the friendship?'

'I'm not sure.'

'What steps did he take?'

'First of all,' said Ainsley, 'he started yelling at Gregor, but it was a complete waste of breath. Gregor just stood there and grinned at him. That only enraged the doctor. He went off in a temper, vowing to get his revenge.'

'Is he the kind of man who'd keep that vow?'

'I've often wondered that.'

'What happened when the blacksmith vanished?'

'Mrs Dymock was heartbroken, I'm told.'

'That wouldn't have pleased her husband.'

'It serves him right,' said Ainsley, seriously. 'A husband should protect his wife from other men. Gregor was only able to get close to Mrs Dymock because the doctor was too busy to take much notice of her. That's changed, of course. He watches her all the time now.'

'Did you think he was connected in some way with your friend's disappearance?'

'His name was the first that came into my mind.'

'What did you do about it?'

'I went to speak to Dr Dymock. As soon as I began to ask probing questions, he threatened to sue me for slander. I had to back away. The doctor has a lot of power here.'

'I can imagine that he would,' said Colbeck. 'Now then, there is someone else I wanted to ask you about.'

'Who is it?'

'Norman Tiller.'

'Oh, he wasn't involved in what happened to Gregor,' said Ainsley. 'They hardly knew each other. Besides, Norm is as harmless as a newborn baby.'

'Is he? I wonder. Thanks to you, Sergeant Leeming heard about that poem about the blacksmith. He tracked down a copy and read it. Because of its subject, I made a point of reading it as well.'

'Neither of you should have bothered. It's rubbish.'

'The sergeant liked it, though he was very confused about

the phantom that appears. Tiller assured him that there is such a thing in this part of the Lake District.'

'Norm may believe that,' said Ainsley with contempt, 'but I don't. One or two people claim to have seen this so-called spirit running among the fells. They need their eyes testing – and so does Norm Tiller. There's no such thing as a phantom in these parts.'

It was past midnight when the figure descended the hill at a steady lope and came into the town. Keeping to the shadows, he ghosted along the street until he came to the place where he spent each night. He took a key from his pocket and unlocked the door of the bookshop before stepping quickly inside it.

Leeming was not, as it had been reported, staying at the hotel to recuperate. That had been a deliberate lie. When he rose early that morning, he felt as if he was in fine fettle. After a breakfast served in his room, he left the building with his face half-covered by a cap. Having changed into the old clothing he took with him whenever they left London, he looked more like a factory hand than a Scotland Yard detective. On his walk to the railway station, he made sure that nobody was following him. The train then took him off to Birthwaite.

Caution was paramount. On their previous visits to Hither Wood, he and Colbeck had been followed. He was determined that it was not going to happen again. Having chosen an empty compartment, he felt that he was safe. When he arrived at Birthwaite, however, he looked in every direction before he walked to the cab rank. Even then, he was taking no chances. Halfway to his destination, he ordered the driver to pull the cab to a halt behind a stand of trees, staying there for ten minutes before he was absolutely certain that nobody was following him.

When they reached Hither Wood, he took out the diagram of the area that Colbeck had given him and used it to guide his footsteps. In his pocket was the horseshoe that had been found earlier. Leeming made his way to the exact spot where it had been unearthed. Colbeck had marked it in pencil on the diagram. He'd also provided the sergeant with a trowel borrowed from the man who tended the hotel's garden. Taking it out – and hoping that the horseshoe would bring him luck – Leeming began to dig away.

With Lydia Quayle at her side, Madeleine set out to visit the three people who'd been identified as possible suspects. Both felt the thrill of the chase coursing through them. On a drab morning in London, they wore broad smiles.

'How many of them do you already know?' asked Lydia.

'Only one of them – Mr Lawton, the baker.'

'Then the other two are complete strangers.'

'Yes, Lydia. Since I moved away, I haven't met any new friends that Father has made.'

'They're hardly friends if they stole his medal.'

'I fancy that we're only looking for *one* thief.'

Lydia stopped. 'I've just thought of something,' she said, worriedly. 'What if he turns nasty?'

'That's very unlikely to happen.'

'Robert once told me that thieves usually put up a fight and try to get away.'

'But we're not going to arrest anyone,' said Madeleine. 'We're simply trying to find out who got into Father's house.'

'I still think that we should be careful. I know that we're not there to accuse any of them, but they're bound to wonder why we're talking about what happened to that medal. If we do find the thief,' said Lydia, 'he might take offence.'

'There's no reason to do that. After all, the medal was returned intact to the house. As far as he's concerned, the man who took it in the first place is in the clear.'

'Then he doesn't know Mr Andrews.'

'You're right,' said Madeleine with a laugh. 'Father won't rest until he knows the truth. Even if it was a prank, he'll want to find out who was behind it.'

'And then . . . ?'

'He'll demand retribution.'

Having sent Leeming off on his mission, Colbeck had not been idle. He made a point of going to the bookshop. Norman Tiller gave him a guarded welcome.

'You usually send the sergeant to interrogate me.'

'He enjoys talking to you.'

'Then where is he?'

'He's not in the best of health today,' said Colbeck.

'I'm sorry to hear that.'

'As he left the hotel last night, he was attacked.'

'Dear me!' exclaimed Tiller. 'That's terrible news. Was he hurt? Did he have anything stolen? What exactly happened?'

Colbeck gave him an abbreviated account of the incident, exaggerating Leeming's injuries somewhat. As he talked, he watched Tiller carefully, looking for any hint that the bookseller might have been somehow party to the assault on Leeming. If Tiller *had* been involved in some way, however, he didn't give himself away. His face remained a mask of concern.

'Is he going to leave the hotel today?' he asked.

'I've advised him to stay indoors.'

'Then I'll make the time to pop in and see him.'

'That's not a good idea,' said Colbeck, quickly. 'He needs complete rest. I'd rather you let him get better in his own time.'

'At least I can give him a book to read. If he's stuck in a hotel room, he's bound to get bored.'

'It's one of the reasons I came here. I'd like to buy a copy of your anthology.'

'Oh, that's very flattering but there are far better poets on my bookshelves. Compared to giants like them, I'm a pygmy.'

'I'd still like to purchase a copy.'

'Sergeant Leeming can have it as a free gift.'

'Poets must eat and drink,' said Colbeck. 'Take the money and be glad that someone admires your work so much. As you know, the sergeant was very taken with your poem about Gregor Hayes.'

Tiller smiled. 'I'm not sure that he really understood it.'

'It held his attention. That's an achievement.'

Going behind the counter, Tiller reached under it to get

a copy of his anthology. He wrapped it in brown paper and tied up the parcel with string. Colbeck paid and took the book from him.

'Since you don't believe in ghosts,' he said, 'you may find some of my poems far-fetched. In fact, they're quite the opposite. I simply write what I know to be true.'

'Not everyone appreciates that, I'm afraid.'

'Cynics abound everywhere.'

'When I mentioned the phantom fell runner to Sergeant Ainsley, he was rather contemptuous.'

'That's a common reaction of the ignorant.'

'Why do you write poetry, Mr Tiller?'

'Why do you work as a detective?'

'I feel that it's my duty to fight against crime,' said Colbeck. 'It's less of a job than a mission.'

'Then we have something in common. We're driven to follow a particular path in life. In my case, I have a passion for poetry. Ideas bubble inside me all the time and I'm compelled to express them in poetic form.' He studied Colbeck for a few seconds. 'Have you ever read *Samson Agonistes*?'

'Yes, I have. I know most of Milton's poems.'

'He was blind when he wrote that particular one. Most people with that affliction would be forced to narrow their working lives, but he didn't. He kept producing remarkable poems like *Samson Agonistes*.'

'He was one blind man writing about another,' said Colbeck, 'but he was also using a Biblical story as a comment on the world around him. The restoration of the monarchy was anathema to Milton. He was a firm supporter of Oliver Cromwell, a natural rebel.'

'All poets are rebels, Inspector. It's what sets us apart.'

'Who are the enemies *you* fight against?'

'People who desecrate nature are my main targets, but there are several others. Read my poems and you'll see what they are. I mean no disrespect to Sergeant Leeming,' said Tiller, 'but he can never get under the surface of a poem. You have the intelligence to do so. Now that you've bought my anthology,' he went on, 'please be kind enough to tell me the *real* reason that you came here.'

Leeming had never expected it to be easy. When he'd been given his orders, he'd been told to dig in the area of the wood that had, supposedly, already been searched. Colbeck had been confident that the sergeant might unearth something close to the place where the horseshoe had been found. After a couple of hours of systematic digging, however, Leeming had started to lose heart. His hands were dirty, his shoulder hurting and, even on a cold day, he was now sweating. He sat on a fallen log to rest and to review the situation.

During the years they'd been together, Colbeck had asked him to do a number of strange things and, though he usually grumbled, Leeming knew that the inspector's decision was a sound one. That was no longer the case in this instance. To institute a proper search of the area, he needed a spade rather than a trowel and a week instead of a single day. He'd been given a Herculean task with insufficient means of completing it. When first put to him, Colbeck's theory had a definite logic. Now that it had been put to the test, it had disintegrated. Leeming was tempted to abandon his work and make his way back to Kendal. Then he looked down at the horseshoe he'd brought with him. When Colbeck found it, it had been caked with mud. Now that it had been properly cleaned, it was gleaming.

In other words, Leeming realised, it had not fallen from the hoof of a horse. It had never been used. Why had someone left a newly made horseshoe under the ground in Hither Wood? It was a question that sent him back to work on his knees again.

CHAPTER TWENTY-TWO

Calling at her house, Geoffrey Hedley was relieved to hear that Caroline Treadgold was at home. Though she consented to see him, it was apparent that she did so out of politeness rather than any desire for his company. He was there on sufferance. Hedley sat opposite her and searched for the right words to use in what was a delicate situation. She was impatient.

'Don't keep me waiting,' she said, prompting him. 'I can see from your face that you've haven't brought good tidings, so why have you come here this morning?'

'I came out of concern for you, Caroline.'

She shrugged. 'Am I in need of your concern?'

'I believe so.'

'Pray tell me why.'

Hedley cleared his throat. 'I received a summons from Lord Culverhouse this morning,' he said, plunging in. 'Not to beat about the bush, he asked me to tell him all that I knew about you. That worried me.'

'I can't say that it worries me unduly.'

'You don't know him as well as I do, Caroline.'

'I know his type,' she said. 'He's the sort of man I've spent my life avoiding. Alex hinted more than once that his uncle's pleasures were not confined to the marital bed. It was the reason he kept me well away from him.'

'I felt that a warning was in order.'

'That's very touching, Geoffrey, and I'm grateful to you.'

'If he should start to pester you—'

'Then it would be down to me to deal with the problem,' she said, pointedly. 'I don't need your help or anyone else's.'

'I see.'

'Other women might be flattered by the attentions of a member of the aristocracy – no matter how old and grotesque he may be. I am frankly insulted.' She rose to her feet. 'Thank you again for coming here. I won't detain you.'

Hedley was disappointed. Instead of being treated as a friend, he was being kept at arm's length. All he could hope was that things would change in time.

His conversation with the bookseller had left Colbeck with much to ponder. The man's obsession with poetry was an unlikely motive for murder but it could not be ignored. Mocked in public, Norman Tiller had been the victim of Alexander Piper's cruelty. If he'd decided to strike back at his tormentor, where better to wreak his revenge than on a railway, a symbol of all that Tiller hated? He'd see a poetic justice in that. Colbeck knew that the bookseller couldn't act entirely on his own. Who had been recruited to help him? Walter Vine? Dr Dymock? Geoffrey Hedley? Or had one of those men persuaded Tiller to act in concert with *him*?

While speculating on the possibilities, Colbeck had walked in the direction of the railway station. As soon as he arrived there, he went straight to the telegraph office in the conviction that that was where he might find the vital clue he still needed. For the first time since he'd been in the town, he felt an upsurge of optimism.

Pride went before a fall. The two women were so confident in their ability to secure the desired result that they never even contemplated failure. It therefore came with a resounding jolt. Madeleine Colbeck and Lydia Quayle set off to find a thief as if it was a relatively straightforward assignment. They were soon deprived of that illusion. They first visited the shop run by Oswald Lawton, the baker, a pale-faced man of middle years.

Since she'd met him before, Madeleine intended to question him by pretending to ask for his advice with regard to the theft. In the event, she didn't even have the chance to speak. When he saw her entering the shop, Lawton broke off from stacking loaves of bread and turned on her.

'I've heard about you,' he snarled. 'Henry Blacker, the locksmith, warned me that you might try to blame it on me instead. It's about that blooming medal of your father's, isn't it? Well, I wish I'd never seen the damned thing. I certainly had no wish to steal it.' He crossed to the door and opened it wide. 'Good day to you, ladies,' he said, brusquely. 'Don't come back.'

They fared no better with the other two people on their list of suspects. One was an old man who couldn't even remember seeing the medal, and the other quickly realised what Madeleine was trying to do. Instead of berating them, as the baker had done, he simply slammed the front door in their faces. It left them shaken and rueful.

'He didn't have to be *that* rude,' said Lydia.

'We deserved it,' admitted Madeleine, 'or, at least, *I* did. There was I, congratulating myself on how cleverly I'd handled the locksmith, when he wasn't in the least deceived. Alan Hinton overestimated my talents, Lydia.'

'I don't agree. You had the right idea.'

'Then why didn't it work?'

'We were unlucky, that's all.'

'We failed,' said Madeleine, 'and I'll have to admit that to Father. He'll say that we should have let him sort everything out on his own.'

'It looks as if he's run out of suspects.'

'He'll have to cast the net wider. Someone took that medal, and he'll find out who it was even if it takes him the rest of his life. Father is like a dog with a bone.'

'Do we go to the house and confess that we failed?'

'I've got a better idea, Lydia.'

'What is it?'

331

'We take a cab back home and have some tea and biscuits. I'm not facing Father's anger on an empty stomach.'

After an hour of unremitting work, Leeming stopped for another rest. As he mopped his brow with a handkerchief, he realised that this was his third visit to Hither Wood and the only one when he didn't feel uneasy. Even when he'd been there in daylight with Colbeck he'd been troubled, sensing that the place was haunted, after all. On both previous occasions they'd been followed. This time he was aware of being entirely alone. There was no sense of threat. Birds were singing. Sunlight was slanting through the branches.

While working so conscientiously with the trowel, he'd forgotten about the pain in his bruised shoulder. It now returned to remind him that it had not gone away. As he massaged the shoulder gently, he thought about the assault. The intention, he believed, had been to render him incapable of taking part in the investigation. That meant a broken arm or leg or facial injuries so serious that he'd be swathed in bandages. He might even have been blinded. If his attacker had been too forceful with the cosh, Leeming might never have recovered consciousness. He could imagine the destructive effect on his family if he returned home in a coffin or, at the very least, disabled for life. Having faced danger on a daily basis during his time in the police force, he'd come to scorn it. On the previous day, he'd been jerked out of his complacence. He was human, after all. He could be badly hurt. Valour had to be tempered with discretion.

Serious injury was a disturbing possibility and the fear of it banished the ache in his shoulder. The only way that he could confront his attacker was to solve the crime that they'd been hired to investigate. It was the spur he needed to get him back to work. Snatching up the trowel, he got back down on his knees again and began digging away with a new zest.

Robert Colbeck had also received a stimulus that put fresh energy into him. The visit to the telegraph office had been a revelation. It had helped him to answer a question that had been buzzing away incessantly at the back of his mind. In search of additional answers, he walked to Geoffrey Hedley's office and was pleased to find that he was not in consultation with a client. The lawyer pressed for details of the latest developments and was told enough to convince him that progress was being made. He was astonished to hear of the assault on Leeming and hoped that the sergeant would soon recover.

'I'd be grateful if you could pass the information on to Lord Culverhouse,' said Colbeck. 'He hauled me over the coals yesterday, accusing me of getting hopelessly distracted.'

'He's not renowned for his patience, Inspector.'

'How well do you know him?'

'Reasonably well,' said Hedley, 'and I often heard Alex talking about his uncle, of course.'

'I spoke to Sergeant Ainsley earlier on and asked him about a rumour concerning the late blacksmith and one of the maidservants at Culverhouse Court.'

'He'll have denied that Hayes was in any way involved.

Ainsley and the blacksmith were as close as brothers.'

'He pointed the finger at someone else.'

'Who was it?'

'Lord Culverhouse himself.'

'That's an absurd suggestion,' snapped Hedley.

'Ainsley didn't think so. He argued that it had to be someone with easy access to the girl. Hayes didn't have any means of getting close to her. The master of the house did.'

'So did the entire male staff at Culverhouse Court.'

'None of them was sacked as a result of the scandal.'

'Ainsley is just trying to cover for his friend. Everyone knows what Hayes was like. His antics were common gossip in the taverns. No woman was safe when he was nearby.'

'Did that include Ainsley's wife?'

'No, of course it didn't.'

'He must have known her well. If he was the sergeant's closest friend, he'd have been to the house many times.'

'I'm sure that he did but he had the sense not to bother Mrs Ainsley. If he'd done that, he'd have lost the friendship of the one man in the town who really liked him.'

'Hayes obviously had a talent for upsetting husbands,' said Colbeck. 'I'm told that Dr Dymock was one of them.'

Hedley frowned. 'Why are you bothering with irrelevant gossip?'

'It may have a bearing on the case.'

'I thought you were looking for the person who abducted and probably killed Alex Piper.'

'It's not impossible that it was Cecil Dymock. *You* were the person who whispered that name in our ears, Mr Hedley.'

'That's true.'

'Have you ever seen his wife?'

'Yes, I have. Dymock used to be my doctor. When he and Alex fell out, I moved to someone else.'

'What sort of woman is Mrs Dymock?'

'She's lively, intelligent and very attractive.'

'Did your friend never take an interest in her?'

'She was married, Inspector.'

'That didn't deter the blacksmith.'

'When it came to women, Alex had high standards.'

'Yes, I've noticed that,' said Colbeck. 'I've also observed that you acted as an intermediary between him and both Miss Treadgold and Miss Haslam. Why wasn't he able to take care of his private life on his own?'

Hedley blanched. 'You're being very impertinent.'

'It's in the nature of my profession.'

'Then the answer is this,' said Hedley, irritably, 'Alex had no talent whatsoever for organisation. That's why he left everything to me.'

'Yet he organised the excursion at Hallowe'en,' recalled Colbeck. 'Why didn't he delegate that task to you?'

There was a long pause. Though Hedley tried to hide his exasperation, it still showed through. When he asked a question, it came out like a bullet from a gun.

'Why did you come here?' he demanded.

'It was because you said that you'd be available at all times. Evidently, that's not true.'

'My offer was limited to Alex's case. All you want to do is to talk about a blacksmith's sexual peccadilloes.'

'They might yet be relevant.'

'I can't see how.'

'Neither can I,' confessed Colbeck, 'but my instincts have been aroused. Do you know a man named Norman Tiller?'

'Yes, I do. I've bought books from his shop.'

'He thinks that the disappearance of your friend was a supernatural event that has no rational explanation. I disagree. In my opinion, it was the result of ingenious planning.'

'Then please find out who was responsible for it.'

'I will – in time.'

Colbeck met his gaze and held it for a long time. He was pleased when the lawyer eventually turned aside with a gesture of petulance. Colbeck smiled.

'Let's start again, Mr Hedley, shall we?'

After taking refreshment back at the house, they hailed a cab and set off to confess to Caleb Andrews that they'd failed in their attempt to find the thief. Madeleine knew that her father would be furious and – even though he'd sought her help – accuse her of interference. Lydia tried to console her.

'You did your best, Madeleine.'

'It was so embarrassing.'

'That's not your fault.'

'Yes, it is, Lydia. I was overconfident. It's not just my father who'll look askance at me. What about Alan Hinton? And then there's Robert, of course.'

'Alan won't blame you and neither will Robert.'

'I wonder.'

When the cab had deposited them outside the house, it was driven away, allowing the two passengers to be visible. Before she could knock on the door, Madeleine heard a sound behind her. She turned to see that Kingston, in the house opposite, was rapping on the window. Madeleine went across the road. With some difficulty, Kingston lifted the sash window to speak to her.

'Caleb is not there at the moment,' he said.

'That's all right, Mr Kingston. I'll get the key from Mrs Garrity.'

'I'd like to speak to you first, please. Why don't you and your friend come in for a few minutes? I won't keep you long.'

'Oh,' said Madeleine. 'As you wish . . .'

Leeming had been at it for hours now. His back was aching, his shoulder in agony and his mouth dry. Because there'd been rain during the night, the ground had been softened, making his task marginally easier, but there was a disadvantage. The knees of his trousers were now covered in mud and his hands were filthy. He was grateful that he wasn't wearing his usual apparel. It would have been highly unsuitable for the task in hand.

Tempted once again to give up, he looked down at the horseshoe for inspiration. Colbeck had found it a mere six inches below the ground and had instructed Leeming to go no deeper than twice that amount. After rubbing his shoulder again, the sergeant returned to his work, but he was no longer as hopeful as he had been. He was now digging in a half-hearted manner, turning the soil over and seeing another array of worms wriggling beneath it. It was so demoralising that Leeming was on the point of losing faith in the enterprise.

Then the trowel clinked against something.

Putting pressure on Geoffrey Hedley had paid dividends. He told Colbeck far more about Alexander Piper's life than he'd hitherto been prepared to do, and it was clear that his hero worship of his friend was shot through with envy. Though he denied it, the lawyer had patently tired of being exploited by his friend. Something else irked him. Caroline Treadgold had been put aside in favour of Piper's new love, but she'd still remained out of reach of Hedley.

'When we first arrived here,' said Colbeck, 'you named four possible suspects.'

'I never believed that Miss Treadgold could be involved.'

'It was conceivable that other people would. Like you, I've exempted her from blame. That leaves three people. Have you had time to consider each of them more carefully?'

'Yes, I have,' said Hedley.

'Whom would you single out – Walter Vine?'

'I'm not sure that he'd have the courage.'

'What about Dr Dymock?'

'He'd have the motive and the money that'd be needed. However,' said Hedley, 'I think he'd be held back by a consideration that would never occur to Vine.'

'And what's that, Mr Hedley?'

'In arranging Alex's death, he'd be ruining Miss Haslam's

life. Dymock's awareness of consequences might have made him stay his hand.'

'Wouldn't that same thought pass through Mr Tiller's mind?'

'No,' replied Hedley. 'Of the three of them, he's the one who suffered most. I was there when Alex tore his work to shreds in front of Tiller's friends. It was brutal. I recall the look in Tiller's eye. The man was in agony, forced to watch his beloved poems being dismembered.'

It was years since Madeleine had been inside their house and she'd forgotten how it smelt in equal parts of damp, decay and fried food. When Lydia followed her in, she recoiled slightly. Seated in his chair with his leg up on a stool, Kingston gave them a muted welcome. He seemed embarrassed.

'My wife has something to tell you,' he said.

Head down, Nan Kingston shuffled out of the kitchen.

On the train journey back, Leeming was divided between elation and fatigue. Certain that he'd made a significant find, he was too weary to understand fully what it might portend. It was not long before he surrendered to exhaustion and fell asleep. He was awakened by the clamour and discomfort as the train juddered to a halt in Kendal Station. Eager to find Colbeck as quickly as possible, he was amazed to see the inspector striding towards him along the platform.

'Get back into the train, Victor,' said Colbeck. 'I've bought two tickets to Birthwaite.'

'But I've just come back from there, sir.'

'I've been waiting for you to do so. Let's find a seat and you can tell me how you got on.'

He ushered Leeming into an empty compartment and they sat opposite each other. Colbeck could sense the other's excitement and soon saw what had caused it. Taking out a handkerchief, Leeming opened it with the effulgent pride of a prospector revealing a cache of gold nuggets.

Colbeck stared at the remains of a human hand.

When she heard what the woman had to say, Madeleine took pity on her. She could see the effort that it had taken Nan Kingston to make her confession and how uncomfortable her husband had been when she did so.

'I didn't know about it until today,' he explained. 'What my wife did was wrong. She realised that in the end. Caleb has every right to call the police.'

'It may not come to that,' said Madeleine.

'Your father has just returned,' said Lydia, looking through the window. 'He needs to hear what we've just been told.'

Nan Kingston quailed. 'I can't face him.'

'You won't have to,' said Madeleine, soothingly. 'I'll handle this. I'm just glad that we now know the truth.'

Excusing themselves, the visitors went across the road. They were soon let into the house by Caleb Andrews. He was thrilled to see them.

'You found out who did it, didn't you?' he asked.

'Yes,' said Madeleine, 'we did.'

'Give me his name.'

'Father—'

'Come on. I want to go straight to the police station to demand that he's arrested. Losing that medal had caused me no end of misery. Now who is he?'

'Nan Kingston.'

His jaw dropped. 'Are you sure?'

'She's just admitted it to us,' said Lydia.

'And before you start threatening her with prison,' added Madeleine, 'let me tell you why she did it and how much she's suffered as a result. It was your fault, Father. In her eyes, you have everything whereas her husband has nothing to be proud of. He was just an ordinary ticket collector while you were an engine driver who'd won an award. You kept boasting about it time and again.'

'Well,' he said, 'wouldn't you have done the same?'

'No, I wouldn't, Father.'

'And you boasted about Madeleine as well,' said Lydia. 'You never stopped telling them that your wonderful daughter was married to a famous detective. It made them feel that they'd failed. Your daughter has been successful while their son can barely scrape a living.'

'Nan Kingston was upset on her husband's behalf,' said Madeleine. 'It was as if you were crowing over him all the time. With that broken leg of his, he has enough on his plate without being forced to listen to you telling him how successful you were. It was cruel of you, Father.'

'It wasn't meant to be.'

'That's how it felt to Nan Kingston, so she wanted to give

you a shock. Once she took the medal, she said it was like having a red-hot stone in her hand. She felt so guilty and she was terrified that her husband would find out.'

'In the end,' said Lydia, taking up the story, 'she slipped back when your cleaner was here and waited for a chance to put the medal in the cupboard. Since then, she's been tortured by guilt.'

'And it was all because of you,' said Madeleine.

Andrews was humbled. 'Was I really that bad?'

'Yes, you were.'

'Nan Kingston? I can't believe it. I'd trust her completely. She's such an honest woman.'

'Yet she was driven to steal something from you. She'd have to be pushed to the limit to do that.'

'Mrs Kingston wanted to come here to apologise,' said Lydia, 'but Madeleine stopped her from doing that.'

'Maddy was quite right,' decided Andrews. 'I should be apologising to her and to Alf Kingston. I must have talked their ears off. I feel so ashamed.'

'Tell *them*,' suggested Madeleine.

'I'll be surprised if they let me into their house.'

'Speak to them right now, Father. The longer you wait, the more difficult it will be. The matter has to be resolved or you'll lose two good friends.'

Andrews nodded. Accepting that the fault lay on his side, he let himself out of the house and walked across the road. His daughter watched through the window and saw him being invited into their neighbours' house. It was a start.

* * *

By the time the train set off again, they'd talked at length about the hand that Leeming had found in Hither Wood. Since the compartment had no other occupants, they were able to converse freely.

'You still haven't told me why we're going back to Birthwaite,' said Leeming.

'It's for *your* benefit, Victor. I thought you'd like to meet the man who attacked you last night.'

'You know who he is?'

'Not exactly,' said Colbeck, 'but I've discovered how to find him. I've been vexed by the fact that we were followed to Hither Wood when we last went there. How could someone possibly know that we were heading there?'

'We weren't followed. No horse had been hired from the livery stables at Birthwaite.'

'It didn't need to be. The man had his own mount.'

'So how was he able to lie in wait for us?'

'I finally worked out the answer,' said Colbeck. 'There's a telegraph station at Birthwaite. He received a message from someone who saw us getting onto the train.'

'Are you sure of that, sir?'

'I'm absolutely sure. When I went to the telegraph office in Kendal, I noticed that information had been sent to the man on a daily basis. He must have arranged to pick it up every morning so that he knew what his orders were.'

'Who was giving those orders?' asked Leeming.

'Work it out for yourself.'

As the sergeant began to speculate, the train surged on

until it reached the point where Alexander Piper had vanished nights earlier. When he and Leeming had driven there at night, they'd been under observation. It was chilling to realise that they'd been totally unaware of it at the time. Leeming suddenly snapped his fingers. Light had dawned.

'That's the man,' agreed Colbeck. 'Let's go and find his accomplice, shall we?'

'Yes, please – I want to return his cosh.'

Saul Pugsley was working on the jetty, scraping off the hull of an upturned boat. He was a thickset man of medium height in his early forties. Matted dark hair was complemented by a full beard. When he heard footsteps behind him, he broke off and turned to see Colbeck standing there.

'There's no need to introduce myself, Mr Pugsley,' said the inspector. 'You know full well who I am.'

'No, I don't,' grumbled the other.

'You've been following me and Sergeant Leeming. There's no point in denying it. When I went to the telegraph station in Kendal, I saw the messages that you sent. And I've just come from reading the ones you received at Birthwaite. You're well known there, Mr Pugsley. They gave me your address. That's what brought me to Windermere.'

'What do you want?'

'Ideally, I'd like to arrest you but, in the circumstances, I feel that that pleasure should be reserved for someone else.' Leeming stepped into view from behind the boathouse. 'You remember my sergeant, don't you?'

'You've got the wrong man,' said Pugsley, defiantly. 'I've never seen either of you before.'

'Then let's see if you remember this,' said Colbeck, motioning Leeming forward. 'Show him what you found today in Hither Wood, Sergeant.'

Coming closer, Leeming held out the handkerchief in which the bones were nestling. Pugsley shrank back at the sight.

'I found it where you buried it,' said Leeming.

'*He* did that,' whined Pugsley, 'not me. I only cut the body up. *He* was the one who killed Gregor and buried the bits.'

'Then the pair of you will hang side by side.'

Colbeck produced a pair of handcuffs from under his coat and handed them to Leeming. Pugsley had seen enough. He hurled the scraper he'd been using at Colbeck but only managed to dislodge his hat. Jumping off the jetty, Pugsley paddled frantically in the shallow water until he reached dry land. He did not get far. Enraged that the man was trying to escape, Leeming gave the handcuffs to Colbeck before going after the fugitive. After splashing through the water, he ran up a grassy bank and gave chase. Fury put extra speed into his legs.

Pugsley, by contrast, was already puffing and slowing down. There was no way that he could outrun Leeming. Deciding to fight instead, he turned around, only to be knocked flat as Leeming hurled himself with all the force he could muster. Straddled across him, he hit Pugsley with a relay of punches that took all the resistance out of him and left his face covered in blood. Leeming dragged the man to his feet.

'We have a score to settle with you, Pugsley.'

'I only did what I was told.'

'I'm doing exactly what *I* was told,' said Leeming, 'and that's to place you under arrest so that you can answer for the terrible things you did.'

'*He's* the person who should really take the blame.'

'Oh, he will, I promise you.'

After taking a firm grip on the prisoner, Leeming marched him unceremoniously away.

When they'd returned to Kendal by train, they took Pugsley straight to the police station. Though Sergeant Ainsley was not there, Colbeck had a good idea where to find him and headed accordingly for the King's Arms. Ainsley was just coming out of the front door. When he saw the inspector with his hands on his hips, he read the message clearly. Colbeck reinforced it by taking the horseshoe from his pocket and letting it drop to the floor with a clang. Ainsley turned white.

'We've had an illuminating conversation with Pugsley,' said Colbeck. 'He told us how you arranged to murder the blacksmith and why that horseshoe was buried with him.'

'The man was an animal!' hissed Ainsley.

'Then you should have let the law take its course.'

'I wanted justice and I got it.'

'Then you were no better than the man you killed.'

'I used to laugh at those rumours about Gregor chasing various women. I never really believed them. Then I learnt the truth – under my own roof.'

'Pugsley told us about your daughter.'

'She was twelve years old – still only a child. How would *you* feel if you found that horseshoe under your daughter's pillow as a love token? Gregor claimed to be my best friend, yet he did *that* to me. He wasn't fit to stay alive.'

'That's why you tricked him into taking on that wager,' said Colbeck, piecing the bits of evidence together. 'You needed him alone and off guard. Hayes was to spend Hallowe'en in Hither Wood, not realising that you and Pugsley would be there as well. You were waiting to kill, dismember and bury him in the shallow graves you'd already prepared. It was ingenious and you got away with it for ten years, hiding your guilt by pretending to devote your life to the search for Hayes's killer.'

Ainsley scowled. 'How did you find out?'

'The diagram of Hither Wood gave you away. You'd marked all the places that had, allegedly, already been searched. It was a device to keep me away from the area where the remains of Hayes had actually been scattered. I stumbled on the horseshoe first – then Sergeant Leeming found a hand.'

'Well, at least you'll never find Alex Piper,' said the other with a note of triumph. 'The moment he ran through that fire, he was stabbed to death by Pugsley and whisked away into the trees. I had him dumped in the deepest part of Windermere. You'll have to drain the whole lake to get him out. How did I do it?' he added with a taunting laugh. 'It was easy. I preyed on people's fears of the supernatural. That kept them conveniently out of my way while the murders were committed.'

'I know that you hated Piper, but did you have to kill him?'

347

'He's thumbed his nose at the law for far too long.'

'That's a reason for arrest not murder.'

'There was something else,' said Ainsley with a sneer. 'You may find this ironic. That slimy little bastard took an interest in what happened to Gregor Hayes. Can you believe it? After breaking laws left, right and centre, he suddenly wants to play at being a policeman. He was clever, I'll give him that. Piper found out things that were too near the truth for comfort. Luckily, he came to me for advice. I tried to put him off, but he had the bit between his teeth. He was determined to solve the crime to show his future wife and her family what a decent, honest, upstanding young man he was. *That's* why he had to be stopped at all costs. The Phantom Special gave me my chance to get rid of him for good.'

'You certainly did that.'

'Congratulations, Inspector! I thought that my plans were foolproof.'

'A lot of killers make that mistake.'

'Two of the corpses are in a sorry state, I fear. Gregor is buried in several bits in Hither Wood and Piper is being nibbled by fishes in Windermere. The least I can do is to offer you one body in reasonable condition.'

Before Colbeck could stop him, he reached inside his coat for a pistol, brought it out in a flash, pulled back the trigger then thrust the barrel into his mouth and shot himself. Blood spurted everywhere. Ainsley slumped to the ground, inches away from the horseshoe that had brought about his downfall.

* * *

They left Kendal with the plaudits of Lord Culverhouse still ringing in their ears. Colbeck had been delighted that they'd been able to solve two cases at the same time, but Leeming was simply happy to be on his way home again.

'I kept changing my mind,' he admitted. 'I thought at first it was the doctor, then Vine, then Norm Tiller. I even dallied with the name of that lawyer.'

'All four of them merited a close look, Victor.'

'When did you first suspect Ainsley?'

'It was when he drove me beside the railway line. I felt that he was testing me out, wondering how clever I was.'

'I could have warned him about you, sir.'

'Fortunately, you didn't.'

'What will happen to Piper's family?'

'I don't know. We did our duty when we found out how and why he'd been killed. They can mourn him properly now.'

'Oh,' said Leeming, stretching himself, 'I'm so glad that we're going home at last. I can't wait to see Estelle and the boys again. They'll have missed me.'

'So did Superintendent Tallis.'

'I'd forgotten him.'

'According to Hinton, he's the same old black-hearted slave-driver once more. I find that reassuring.'

'I don't.' Leeming fell silent for a while then sat up. 'There's one thing I'm sorry I missed about the Lake District.'

'What is it?'

'Well, Norm Tiller was so certain that there really was a phantom fell runner. He was the hero of that poem about the blacksmith. I just wish that I'd caught a glimpse of him.'

'Forget him, Victor. He doesn't exist.'

As evening shadows lengthened, the black-clad runner glided along without any apparent effort. When he paused on the summit of a hill, he gazed down at Hither Wood and emitted a strange, high-pitched laugh.

EDWARD MARSTON has written well over a hundred books, including some non-fiction. He is best known for his hugely successful Railway Detective series and he also writes the Bow Street Rivals series featuring twin detectives set during the Regency, as well as the Home Front Detective series.

edwardmarston.com